THE GHOSTS OF CULLODEN MOOR

VOLUME II

By L.L. Muir

The Ghosts of Culloden Moor
Volume II

ISBN-13: 978-1973861577

ISBN-10: 1973861577

PUBLISHED BY
Lesli Muir Lytle

www.llmuir.weebly.com

Cover Art © 2017 Kelli Ann Morgan
www.inspirecreativeservices.com

Interior book design by: Bob Houston eBook Formatting

DEDICATION

To all the Muir Witches in my life.

BOOKS IN THE SERIES

(as of July 2017)

The Ghosts of Culloden Moor
by L.L. Muir

***The Ghosts of Culloden Moor**

1. The Gathering
2. Lachlan
3. Jamie
4. Payton
5. Gareth (Diane Darcy)
6. Fraser
7. Rabby
8. Duncan (Jo Jones)
9. Aiden (Diane Darcy)
10. Macbeth
11. Adam (Cathie MacRae)
12. Dougal
13. Kennedy
14. Liam (Diane Darcy)
15. Gerard
16. Malcolm (Cathie MacRae)
18. Watson
19. Iain (Melissa Mayhue)
20. Connor
21. MacLeod (Cathie MacRae)
22. Murdoch (Diane Darcy)
23. Brodrick

24. The Bugler
25. Kenrick (Diane Darcy)
26. Patrick (Cathie MacRae)
27. Finlay
28. Hamish
29. Rory (Jo Jones)
30. MacBean (Diane Darcy)
31. Tristan (coming soon!)

You'll find all of L.L. Muir's current works at the end. The next collection includes DOUGAL, KENNEDY, AND GERARD.

A NOTE ABOUT THE GHOSTS

The names of Culloden's 79 are historically accurate in that we have used only the clan or surnames of those who may have died on that fateful day. The given names have been changed out of respect for those brave men and their descendants. If a ghost happens to share the entire name of a fallen warrior, it is purely accidental.

VOLUME II

FRASER 11
RABBY 141
MACBETH 185
ALSO BY L. L. MUIR 293
ABOUT THE AUTHOR 297

FRASER

CHAPTER ONE

It had been a strange night on Culloden Moor, far more eventful *after* the Solstice revelers had left the grounds. If they had any ken of what was transpiring at the moment, they'd be back in droves—as would the ghost seekers, hoping to see what was never meant for them to see.

Standing before the memorial cairn, Culloden's ragtag collection of 79 Highland spirits had been gathered, enthralled by Soncerae Muir, their wee mortal mascot-turned-witch. With a promise of revenge, the sixteen-year-old had begun luring them, one by one, to step close to her unworldly fire and leave the moor for a brief quest. Only after winning their enthusiasm had she declared that, whether or not they succeeded, they would be moving on to the afterlife.

Number 18, Lachlan McLean had been the first to depart. Jamie Houston, Number 64 had followed soon after with no hesitation. Fitz Payton, Number 48, had just stepped forward and been welcomed with a smile from the lass—which proved the order in which they'd risen from their graves had nothing to do with the order in which they would be sent away. A pity, that, since the youngest laddie's number was 8, his chance would have come soon.

In case there was some reason for the order in which they'd risen, they'd always held tight to their number in line, so to speak. Some had even forgotten they'd had a name to go along with their number. So Alexander had remembered for them.

But if God or the devil were calling them out of order, then perhaps the wee laddie could go straight away! *Camhanaich*, the dusk of morning, wouldn't be long in coming. And if only a few could depart this night, he'd rather young Rabby was part of the first wave.

The concern was whether the boy would be up to the quest he was given.

Alexander glanced to his left, locked eyes with Rabby, and read the same question there. The wee lad's hand gripped his hound's fur and held—a stark variation from petting the animal continually for nearly two hundred seventy years. A mortal dog would have lost its hide a thousand times over from all the comfort this one got.

"Best stay alert, aye?" he told Rabby. "And ye as well, Dauphin," he said to the dog simply because it pleased Rabby when anyone addressed his loyal beast.

The lad nodded solemnly and Dauphin's ears pointed forward as if he'd understood his instruction too.

After a quick nod to the witch, Fitz Payton disappeared into nothing, but not before the rest of them caught sight of an excited grin on his face.

Alexander glanced at the boy again and found the light of hope gleaming in his eyes like heavy tears waiting to fall. "Would ye care to give her a try, Rabby?" For he could think of nothing more satisfying than getting that brave child off the moor and where he belonged. Culloden, with all its horrors and memories of horrors, was no place for one so young. And if there had been someone to whom Alexander could have complained, he'd have done so the first day they'd risen from their graves.

The lad shook his head quickly. "I canna do it, sir. I canna! What if they've gone...to the devil?"

Alexander laughed quietly so as not to draw attention from the others. "Can ye imagine our Soncerae doing such a thing? Suggesting such a thing?" He shook his head with a touch of reproach. "For shame to think it, Rabby. For the lass is as good as one of us, aye?"

Rabby nodded, placated. Then he brightened. "Would ye go first, sir? I believe I could do it, if...if ye go first." He swallowed painfully, then began petting Dauphin again as if it was the animal that needed soothing. "And perhaps, if ye find something...*disagreeable-like*, ye'll find a way to let me know?"

The lass had warned that once a man left the moor, he wouldn't be coming back again. But surely, if God was in his Heaven, he'd allow Alexander to get word to the laddie. It was plain all the boy needed was a nudge and he'd jump at the chance to leave.

As would Alexander.

Thanks to the fictional character named Fraser, in a well-loved Scottish novel, Alexander's existence on the grounds of Culloden had become its own bit of Hell. His common Scottish name had become nigh unto a war cry for romantic minded lasses the world over. And for a man who'd been denied his own true love in life, it was torture to see so much affection wasted on a fellow who had never truly existed in the first place. And it was getting worse by the day thanks to the story being played out on film.

Aye. It was a fine time for making his own escape.

Alexander nodded to Rabby, then motioned for Number 55, to watch over the lad. The other ghost, Kennedy, had a way with Rabby the others did not. And if Alexander couldn't be by the boy's side, 55 was the next best thing.

Only after he got a nod from Kennedy did he start forward, weaving between his comrades as he closed the distance between himself and the wee witch. But he stopped when 26 started kicking up a ruckus. Apparently, the man was trying to jump the line when it was clear his brother had been invited forward at the whim of the witch. But it seemed she didn't wish for Gareth MacGregor to be next.

Alexander waited for the argument to end, and while he waited, he met the gaze of the others who stood at the perimeter of the witch's fiery display. Without a word, he made it clear that he would be the next to step forward, if Soni would allow it—as soon as the troublesome MacGregors worked out their family squabble.

Finally, the hot-headed Gareth MacGregor was allowed to have his way, but instead of disappearing into nothing, as the others had done before him, he darted off, defiant as ye please, ignoring Soni's demands to return. The others watched him go, but Alexander was more interested in the witch. He kept his gaze upon her, waiting for his opportunity to speak up for himself.

Soncerae turned back to her fire and the trace of a smile was quickly wiped from her expression before she faced the rest of Culloden's 79, a number quickly dwindling. The fleeting smile left Alexander wondering if the hot-headed Gareth hadn't been as defiant as he'd supposed. For wherever he'd gone, it seemed Soni was all too pleased about it.

Alexander spoke quickly before he had time to reconsider. "Soncerae!"

"Alexander Fraser," she said. "Ye'd like to go next, would ye?"

"Aye, lass," he said, stepping forward. "I have reason to."

Soni glanced past him in the direction of a certain young lad and his dog. "I see."

She waved him closer for a private word, as she'd done with some of the others. If she'd had any instruction for MacGregor, he'd missed the chance to hear it by running off.

"Alexander," she said, then bit her lip for a moment. The action tightened his belly with worry. "'Tis a noble thing ye do, even now."

He frowned down at her. "Surely ye'd not reward a boon just for my volunteering. As ye can guess, the lad watches me to see that it is safe to go. So ye must send me...somewhere. And if it is possible, in any way, for me to come back and tell Rabby there is nothing to fear, I must do it. The lad trusts ye, no mistake. But he...trusts me more, ye ken?"

Soni nodded with a knowing smile and a wink. "Oh, I'll be sending ye somewhere. Never fear. Only..."

Again, his belly tightened. "What is it, lass?"

She inhaled loudly through her nostrils as if inflating her courage. Then she let the breath go quickly and forced her lips back into a pretty bow. "Only, if ye wish to come back to speak with Rabby, there will be a price to pay."

"Ye mean to tell me that I'll lose my boon? That I'll lose my chance to call out Bonnie Prince Charlie?"

Her lips twisted in regret and she nodded.

"Done."

"Just like that?" The lass was taken aback.

"Just like that. Now, let's get on with it. I dinna wish for Rabby to fret overlong."

Soni shook her head. "The sun will rise soon, and I've a mortal body to care for, aye? Ye'll be the last to leave this night. Rabby and the others may find their rest for a few days while I tend to...business. Do ye understand?"

He nodded his head. "Auch, I understand only one thing, truth be told." He braced his feet apart and held out his hands for balance, unable to imagine what might truly happen to him next. "I only ken that it is high time Rabby left this place."

"Oh?" she said. "And what of ye? Will ye miss the chance to bask in the celebrity of being a Fraser? Even the ghost of one?"

He snorted. "Even as a man, I would not welcome such a thing."

Soni clicked her tongue and shook her head, a look of mischief in her eyes. "'Tis too bad then…"

"What do ye mean?"

She bounced her brows and grinned. "Ye'll see."

With Soni's teasing still ringing in his ears and the sight of her not yet faded from his vision, he felt the ground disappear from beneath him. And though he had no sensation of falling, he had sensations a' plenty. But just as he was beginning to revel in the feel of blood coursing through his veins again, a wave flooded him and washed him out into a deep sea of slumber.

CHAPTER TWO

Chelsea stood before the framed, oval mirror and stared at her reflection because that was what she was supposed to do, right? Once a bride was dressed in her dress and the last touches were touched, she was supposed to stand and stare at herself and concentrate on burning the memory into her brain. Wasn't she?

She wished Austin was there with her. Then the picture would be complete. He always made her calm, happy, relaxed. Like nothing in the world could be wrong as long as they were together. She really was the luckiest girl in the world.

A wedding in Scotland, something she never would have dreamed of, never would have been greedy enough to ask for, but Austin had insisted.

She stood in the bride's room of what was called a *small* chapel. But Scotland's version of small was an American version of *cathedral.* The ancient stone walls were covered with tapestries depicting equally ancient wedding ceremonies. In one, the bride and groom stood with their arms tied together with a cloth, and she was pretty sure the red splotches were supposed to be blood, because some guy standing next to them was holding up a red-tipped knife. She could almost imagine him grinning.

It was like a Scottish version of a blood-brother ceremony only with a couple. But lucky for her, she wasn't marrying a Scot and she was pretty sure they didn't do that anymore anyway.

The closest she and Austin had come was to have a blood test, and only because his mother insisted on it. The woman was almost disappointed when Chelsea's report came back with no dormant family illnesses lurking in her, waiting to spring up and taint the Forbes family name.

Just a few more hours, and she'd be able to latch on to Austin and never let him out of her sight, leaving the wedding party behind while they started their honeymoon trip around the country. But it didn't matter how much she wanted to tour castles and listen to Scottish legends, she would much rather lock herself away in a cottage with her new husband for a few weeks and let the stress of the wedding fade into a memory.

She would never truly be able to relax, though, until the best man left the island. He was scheduled to fly to Paris the next morning, but she wouldn't believe it until she saw it. He was so attached to Austin, she could just imagine waking up after their wedding night to find Rick sitting at the end of the bed, glaring at her whenever Austin's back was turned.

The vivid memory of that glare sent a shiver through her that rippled up her spine and shook the layers of her dress.

A knock on the heavy wood door made her jump, and before she had time to take a step, it opened. She smiled, hoping it was Austin, sneaking in for a quick kiss and a promise it wouldn't be long now. In the mirror, she could see the clear white vee of a tux shirt front glowing in the dim light of the hallway.

"You're not supposed to see me yet," she said as she turned. But she dropped her smile when Rick barged his way into her cold and lonely sanctuary. "What do you want?"

He sneered. "Careful, Cheese. You don't want Austin to hear you use that tone with me."

He called her Cheese when he thought someone might hear. Others assumed it was a form of endearment, telling her she was one of the guys, but when they were alone, he called her Cheesy, and he meant it in the worst way.

She was so close to finally getting between that weasel and Austin, she really should have expected him to attack her one last time. But at least she wasn't stupid enough to rise to the bait. He had to feel desperate at the moment, and there was no guessing how dangerous he could be. His eyes always promised she would pay for rejecting him once. And what better time to make her pay than on her wedding day?

She braced her feet apart a little, hidden by the wide white skirt, just in case he tried something physical.

He closed the door and locked it. The snap of the bolt slipping into place turned her stomach. It also made her regret every chance she'd had to tell Austin his best friend hated her, but it was too late now. Holding her tongue and hoping for the best had been a stupid move. And Rick had promised that Austin would believe his very different version of the truth if she ever tried to come between the two men.

He walked a slow circle around her, and though every instinct screamed not to turn her back on him, she never moved. He looked down his nose at the dress, then brought his gaze slowly up to her face before stopping in front of her again. But he didn't speak. No off-handed compliments. No glaring. Nothing.

She glanced at the clock. Fifteen minutes. Could she hold her tongue that long?

"Not much time left," he said quietly.

Don't say anything. Don't say anything.

He frowned. "If you're going to do it, you'd better hurry."

She had no idea what he was talking about, and she wasn't gullible enough to ask. She knew she should stick her fingers in her ears until someone came to say it was time to head down the aisle, but her pride wouldn't let her do anything Rick might laugh at.

He snorted. "You stupid cow. Don't tell me you haven't at least been considering it."

She raised an eyebrow. She instantly wished she could have taken the move back.

"*Leaving,* you idiot. You should leave, *now.* You know you should. You're not good enough for Austin and you know it. You understand the kind of woman he needs—not a low-class waitress from the wrong side of the tracks. You *know* he wants to do well in politics and you will only be the death of him." He pointed his finger at her. "You see? Even now you don't say anything because you know I'm right."

He'd grown more passionate as he spoke, but still hushed. He knew that someone would be knocking on the door in the next few minutes, and he was always so clever about keeping his revulsion of her a secret.

All she had to do was wait for that knock.

It didn't matter what the hateful pig said, he was just making a last ditch effort to stop the wedding. If he got rid of her, he would be more careful about the women Austin was able to meet. But he'd made a fateful mistake one night when he'd gotten the flu and allowed his friend to go to the Celtics game without him. And Austin, being Austin, hadn't thought twice about stopping at a diner that was so unworthy of someone like him.

She smiled at the memory of a too-charming blond guy with rows of dimples dumping his pie on his own lap just so she would have to come to his rescue.

"I'm so sorry," she'd said, trying to wipe up the mess on the bench beside him with a wet towel.

"I'd do it again in a heartbeat," he'd said quietly. "But I am sorry about the ice cream hitting the floor."

She'd looked at him sideways. "You're not right in the head, are you? You've stolen the doctor's nice clothes and escaped from the facility, right?"

Austin shook his head. "I'd never do that to someone else's pants."

They'd laughed together then. The first of a thousand laughs.

"Maybe this will help convince you, Cheesy." Rick said, holding up a small digital recorder. He pressed a button and sat it on the dressing table, then walked out.

"Too bad you're not marrying Erica Winston." Rick's voice was unmistakable. *"Did you see that her father is running for Congress?"*

"Yeah. I saw that." Austin's voice had a wistful edge that she couldn't miss—not there, alone, with no one to keep a straight face for.

"If I hadn't been sick that night, when you went to the Celtic game without me, we'd be waiting for Erica right now."

Austin laughed. *"Can you imagine? Erica Winston settling for a small wedding in some dusty old chapel in Scotland?"*

Rick laughed too, but Austin probably didn't know a fraction of how pleased his friend was to be recording him at that moment. *Waiting for Erica right now*, he'd said. So the conversation had just taken place? Had they been standing in the chapel? It was their wedding day, and he was still thinking about Erica?

How long had Rick been recording her fiancé, hoping for just the right sound bite? She could only imagine how pleased he was with himself at the moment. In fact, he was probably standing outside her door waiting for her to fall to pieces.

If she was smart, she'd turn it off.

She reached for the recorder, but paused when Austin spoke again. *"Marrying her would have cost me a whole lot more than moving the wedding party to Scotland."*

"Yeah," Rick said, *"but it would have been worth it."*

"You think?"

Well, that was hardly a quick denial. But she could only hear his voice, not see the expression on his face. He'd probably rolled his eyes when he said it. After all, he knew Rick well enough not to argue with him when he didn't have to.

The devil chimed back in. *"Only if you want to be a Congressman someday. Or better. Can't do that if you marry a waitress with drug-addicted parents."*

"Well, too late now, isn't it?"

"No, man. It's not too late."

The recording cut off.

Too late now, isn't it? It wasn't just the words, but the regret in his voice that stung.

Chelsea realized she'd been holding her breath and sucked air deep into her lungs. She only wished it didn't hurt so bad to do it. Her chest seemed determined to empty itself of all oxygen, blood—even her heart. Her ribs felt like clamps squeezing everything together, waiting for something to pop.

Suddenly, having Austin with her didn't seem like such a comforting thought after all. But she needed...something.

Knuckles rapped softly against the door. "Miss Chase? They're ready for you." The vicar's wife. So, true to form, Rick must have taken his place again, smiling like there was nothing wrong. Would he be whispering in Austin's ear while they waited? Trying to convince him he shouldn't go through with the ceremony?

She was so mad at the weasel she wanted to scream, but she couldn't, not without Austin coming to see what the matter was. Then all of the ugly truth between her and Rick would have to come out. Only, Rick would have his own twisted version. Either way, the day would be ruined. No matter how blissful the rest of their wedding day might be, the memory would be half-covered in mud.

Unfortunately, those emotions bottled up inside her still demanded a release and escaped as a river of tears down her cheeks. It only made her madder.

Oh, Austin!

She did need him. But the secret he seemed to be keeping from her—that he regretted the loss of his ambitions—created a chasm she couldn't see across. A chasm created by her enemy.

She took tissues and stomped close to the mirror to dab away the tears. They had burned a trail through her makeup, but brides cried all the time, right? She forced a smile to see if she could pull off the happy-tear look, but it was a stretch.

One deep breath later, and she was looking for her bouquet and headed out the door. *Rick Burrell was not going to win today.* And soon, she would start eliminating him from her and Austin's lives altogether.

The vicar's wife was gone. There was a tall, skinny young man standing at the doors to the chapel, but he was leaning in, watching something. No one was there to notice her. And since she had declined having Austin's dad walk her down the aisle—in favor of walking alone—there was no one waiting for her. No one to signal the wedding march.

She stepped quietly to the door so she didn't startle the young man, then peeked in to see what he was looking at. She kept her body back so no one noticed her.

Austin stood at the front, grinning and hugging a woman in white wearing a wide brimmed hat. Then he turned and introduced her to the vicar. Rick grinned too and glanced at the doorway. His eyes locked on Chelsea's for only a fraction of a second. He winked, then looked back at the woman in white. And Chelsea realized, without seeing her face, it had to be Erica Winston.

Austin was standing at the altar next to the woman he really wished he was marrying.

It didn't matter than it had all been set up by Rick. It didn't matter if Austin was just being polite and greeting his former girlfriend while he waited for the wedding march to start. The chick was probably in on it too, planning just the right time to barge up to him and demand a hug.

If Chelsea had stuck her fingers in her ears and not listened to Rick, she would be waving for someone to start the music and gliding, happy and oblivious, down the aisle. She would have said her vows, held her breath only for a second or two when the clergyman asked if anyone objected, then accepted the ring. She would have been minutes away from kissing the groom and going on her merry way, relieved when she knew for sure that the devil would never be able to get between them again.

So what was stopping her? Why didn't she do just that?

It would gall Rick to see her play the game and win. And the competitor in her wanted just that, to win. But she also loved Austin too much to make him unhappy. Too much to ruin his career, if he still wanted to change the world, like he had when they'd met. And if she loved him too much to give him up? Was that selfish? Or just Rick's brainwashing kicking in?

Her next decision would determine everything. Did she hurt him now? Or later on, after the regrets surfaced? By then, it wouldn't matter if he divorced her. His political future would be tainted. The Worm was at least right about that. But maybe he was wrong about Austin really caring about that future.

The woman in white stepped back a few feet and sat next to Austin's parents like she was one of the family. Austin frowned and looked at his watch, but then leaned toward Rick who was whispering to him—a few choice tidbits, no doubt, about how convenient it was that Erica was wearing white. And since the bride was running late, he could fix his future if he just moved fast enough?

The young man finally took his attention off the diva in white, now that only her wide, obnoxious hat was all that was visible. He noticed Chelsea standing there, gasped, and started to raise a hand—probably to signal the organist.

Chelsea shook her head and he lowered his hand. "Could you do me a favor," she said quietly. "Could you go tell the groom I'd like a word with him? Discreetly?"

"A word?" He rolled the r with his thick brogue. She thought he might sprain his tongue. "Aye, miss."

He walked quickly but calmly to the front of the chapel and bent toward Austin. Rick leaned close to eavesdrop, then he laughed and clapped Austin on the shoulder. But it wasn't Austin that headed back with the young man, it was Rick!

No! She should have just allowed the guy to start the music and gone to him herself. There would be no getting close to him now. Rick had peed a circle around him, staked his territory, and was going to defend it to the death.

He paused and bent down to speak to someone and Chelsea took one last look at Austin.

Look at me, baby. Just one look. That's all I need.

But Austin's attention was on his parents, or rather, on the woman sitting beside them. She waved a long, gloved hand and beckoned him closer. He never so much as glanced Chelsea's way.

Rick stood and started walking again, hiding a pleased grin inside that pleasant smile.

Chelsea grabbed handfuls of her skirt, lifted it…and ran.

CHAPTER THREE

Alexander woke to the feel of someone licking his forehead. For a moment, he marveled at the sensation of being touched, but he quickly brought his arms up to defend himself from an overly friendly dog. The first, besides Dauphin, that had truly seen him in centuries. There had been plenty a creature that could sense the ghosts on Culloden Moor, but none that dared stray near them. It had been an additional pang of loneliness, in truth, to have the animals shy away. And Dauphin's attention had been for Rabby only.

"Ye'll have to forgive Wallace," said an old man hiking up the gravel incline.

It was a road with a trail of grass down the center and soft loam to either side. And it was the loam where Alexander had apparently slept the night away. He jumped to his feet and brushed at the dirt that was no longer clinging to his plaid—after being ever-present for nearly three centuries. Also missing were his weapons.

Soni expected an heroic deed from him without a blade to hand? So be it.

"That dog will lick anyone with a little sweat on 'im. Likes the salt, ye see?" The man leaned on a tall walking stick while he looked Alexander over. "Ye've arrived early, then. I was not to be here until eleven o'clock."

He nodded to hide his confusion and looked about. A large cottage with a fine, smooth roof was tucked into the trees at the top of the rise. A small black car sat at the bottom of the hill where the man had come from.

The man squinted at his boots. "No car? Someone dropped ye?"

Dropped? Lifted and dropped by the witch, he supposed. So he nodded. "Aye."

"Weel, it's a good thing I've brought some things to stock the cold box. It was all part of the arrangement, of course. But at least ye willna have need to hike into town anytime soon."

Alexander followed the man to the building, wary for whatever heroic opportunities might arise. But there was none to molest them but the dog, and he tried to smother them with affection was all.

"Now. I'll unlock the door for ye, but ye'll find another set of keys on the hook in case ye go somewhere and wish the lock up behind ye. When ye depart, in two days' time, ye flip the locks and pull the doors closed, leaving those keys on the hook where ye found them, aye?"

Alexander shrugged. "Aye."

The man unlocked the door as he spoke and pushed it open. "Would ye care to look about, see that everything is in order while I hike back to the car for the foodstuffs?"

"Food?"

The fellow frowned. "Aye. For the cold box."

"Would ye like me to fetch it for ye?" Any good deed would surely work in his favor.

The old man rolled his eyes. "No. What I'd like is for ye to take a look about and see if ye need anything else from me before I go. There's no telephone, and paltry service at best, aye? So ye canna ring me up to complain later. And I would like Mr. Muir to be pleased."

"Mr. Muir arranged for me to stay here, did he?" A relation to Soni Muir, no doubt.

The poor man's face fell. "Will it not suit ye? I can see if there is somewhere fancier for ye, but he specifically asked for this property, mind. But if ye dinna care to be out in the woods, cut off from—"

"The cottage is fine, sir. And glad I am for it. If Mr. Muir said I am to stay here, then here I shall stay."

The disgruntled fellow sighed mightily, then nodded his head and started down the hill. As he picked his way, he poked at the air and mumbled something about actors not knowing their own minds. Alexander looked down at his clothes and realized that in the current day and age, even in Scotland his kilt would be considered a costume. But he didn't care for the notion of being mistaken for an actor.

He remembered his immediate duty was to check inside the large cottage and see if there was aught more he should need, though he had no idea what his heroic deed would require, therefore he could not predict those needs. In any case, he stepped inside as he'd been encouraged to do.

It was a much larger building than he'd first suspected. A great deal of it must have been hidden behind the trees and shrubbery. The ceiling was foolishly high and empty of anything but rafters. In winter, there would never be enough wood to keep the place warm. It was a wonder any trees at all could be found nearby. But then he remembered that heat was acquired another way as well. And a quick look at the hearth suggested that fires indoors were few and far between. The grate appeared clean and fairly new, as did the stones along that wall. Nary a speck of dust could be seen.

Two long couches sat at right angles to each other and were covered in fine soft leather that lent its smell to the place. Above one wall was hung the preserved head of a red stag. On the opposite wall, the head of a smallish boar.

"Take a good look at the bedroom and water closet, now, while I put these things away." The old man carried a large box into the next room after nodding toward a door beyond the stag's wall.

Alexander was more interested in the kitchen, but the fastest way to be rid of the man was to do as he was told, so he walked to the door and pushed it open. And when he did so, his mortal ears heard the faint gasp of a woman. His gaze flew to the bed, but it was piled with so many furs and blankets there was no telling what truly lay beneath. But he was sure—

"The toilet's through here, ye see." The proprietor pushed past him in spite of his movement to block the man, but the fellow was in such a hurry he never glanced at the bed. "Bespoke linens, of course," came his voice from the water closet. Then he poked his head out. "Shower. Large bathing tub. Plenty of towels unless you have some to-doin' in the Jacuzzi." He gave Alexander a glower that suggested he expected nefarious deeds to take place as soon as he drove away.

"I expect no one," Alexander assured him, but the old man just grunted and strode out of the room, again, still not glancing at the bed.

"Ye've plenty of back-bacon, eggs, tomatoes and mushrooms. There is milk and some orange juice, of course. And two roast chickens, as was ordered. I left the bottle of wine on the counter so ye can do as ye please with it. But since yer not expecting guests..." He wagged his head back and forth, again, like he didn't believe the claim.

"Thank ye, kindly."

The man took one more look around. "Well, then, I'll leave ye to yer solitude, shall I?"

Alexander escorted him to the door, shook his hand, then watched through the sheer cloth over the window until the man drove away. He smiled and hoped wherever Soni was, after her long night on the moor, that she knew he was pleased to have been given a place to stay, and apparently, food for his belly. At least he wouldn't need to spend his first mortal evening hunting in unfamiliar woods.

The sound of the automobile was all but gone when he jumped back and hurried to the kitchen to find the food and wine. He tried to discover how to open the ice box, or refrigerator—he knew the name of it from the television he'd watched over the past few decades—but he suddenly remembered that he was not, in fact, alone.

Food. Wine. A private shelter. And a woman in his bed.

He pulled his fingers away from the ice box as if it had burned him, then he backed out of the kitchen while dividing his attention between the bottle of wine and the bedchamber door to his left. A few more steps and he'd be out the door. Then he would run.

For surely, Mr. Muir was the devil himself sent to steal his soul before he could fulfil his quest.

CHAPTER FOUR

Chelsea had no option but to huddle under the blankets and wait to be busted. Deep voices in the next room woke her when she hadn't even realized she'd nodded off. The place had looked deserted enough, and she didn't see any harm in seeking a little refuge while she figured out what she'd do next. After all, it wasn't like she was going to rob the place, and she'd picked the lock without making a mess of the back door. No harm, no foul.

But then she'd decided to take off the wedding dress and lie down for a little while. Two miles was only a warm-up for her usually, but she *usually* wasn't running it in a wedding dress and fancy shoes.

The dress she draped over a large frumpy chair and crawled under the covers looking for comfort more than warmth. Then she'd forced herself to think of a blank white wall. White. White. Nothing...

When the voices worked their way into her dreamless sleep, she'd first thought they belonged to Austin and Rick. But one was too high. The other too deep. And then suddenly, the door opened and she froze.

The higher pitched voice sounded like an old man. She couldn't understand him easily thanks to the blankets over her head combined with his thick accent. But the other voice gave her chills, like some sexy vampire purring over her shoulder from behind. It didn't matter what he said. A word or two. That was all. But she was dying to get a look at him if only to put her imagination to rest.

I expect no one. Brief and cryptic. *Thank ye, kindly.*

Finally, the old man left, but then she was horrified by how excited she was that Deep Throat was still there. It was stupid of her, really, when she should have been putting every ounce of energy into praying the guy would leave, too, so she could get dressed and get the heck out of Dodge.

The minutes ticked by with no sound in the house, only the start of an engine and that sound fading. Finally, a few distant footsteps, then…nothing.

Had the guy gone outside?

The reality of the situation shocked her into action. She was alone with a strange man, in a house she'd broken into, and she was lying in his bed in little more than a slip!

I don't think so.

As quietly as she could, she slipped off the edge of the mattress, stepped over to the chair, and picked up the edge of her skirt. She started climbing up through the dress, intending to have it fall into place without the need for help. After all, she'd chosen that dress because of the long ribbons she could use to zip herself into it. She had no idea that Austin's sister would finally be nice enough to offer a hand at the last minute. It was just too bad she hadn't stayed with Chelsea until it was time to walk down the aisle. If she had, Rick wouldn't have been able to ruin her day…and her life.

Don't think about it now, you idiot! This is no time to cry!

"Beggin' yer pardon, lass?" That deep voice rumbled through the room and seemed to echo in the rafters. Or was it her bones? "I considered leaving the house to ye, but then wondered if perhaps ye're in need of savin', aye? And here I find ye, hoisted on yer own petard, as it were. Do ye need a hand, then?"

The thick seam of the dress' waist caught across her open mouth, but she spoke anyway. "Juss a ittle ivathy, pleathe."

"Privacy?" He chuckled and the vibrations of it nearly shattered her. "If ye're certain…"

"Uh, huh." No way would she try talking again. She wasn't going to move either. For the moment, the huge skirt covered her important parts. And she'd rather stand there with both her arms sticking out the top of the dress like a couple of sock puppets than risk it all falling into a puddle at her feet while he watched.

"As ye wish." The door clicked shut.

She waited for a few seconds, listening for the sound of his breathing.

Who am I kidding? My ears are covered with satin!

She managed to get the rope-like seam out of her mouth and down past her chin, but then the zipper caught on her up-do. *Expensive zippers had no business catching on hair!*

She growled, then pulled the dress back off a bit, turned her head, and tried again. She felt a slight adjustment to her hair that had nothing to do with the movement of the dress and she froze. The guy was still there! Standing close enough to touch her!

Better to face him with a dress on and half bald than to face him in my underwear, right? So she braced herself for pain, pulled her arms and elbows through the holes, then forced the bodice down over her boobs. Miraculously, her hair never caught. She reached behind her skull to see how bad the damage was and turned. But no one was there.

However, a mouse-soft click of the door handle told her she hadn't been imagining it. Either that, or the place was haunted.

CHAPTER FIVE

Alexander paced back and forth along the hearth and wondered which woman would appear first, the lass from the bedchamber or the wee witch. He'd performed some noble deeds already—helping the lass get free of the metal teeth of a hungry zipper, sparing her dignity while doing so, and leaving her untouched when she had obviously meant to waylay him in his own bed. He was only grateful she'd kept her shift on.

It had been a surprise to find her with a modern wedding gown at the ready. He'd thought such machinations to gain a husband had ceased long ago.

He strode to the cottage door and pushed the curtain aside. The empty drive was slowly losing its shade as the sun climbed toward its zenith, but there was no sign of a lass in a black robe, or a green ring of light headed his way. His actions were by no measure heroic, but just the same, it was a noble thing to walk away. However, since Soni did not deign to show herself, the acts of a gentleman apparently didn't qualify.

The floor creaked and he turned to find the lass bedecked in her white gown stepping out from the bedchamber. His fingers tingled at the memory of her soft, rich brown hair. When their gazes met, she stopped moving and swallowed. It was a long moment before she smiled.

The room lit up instantly.

"I'm sorry," she said. "I hope I didn't freak you out."

American then.

"I'm nay the sort to freak out, lass."

From across the room he discerned a shiver pass through her, but he dared not offer her comfort until he knew why she'd come. Other than losing a battle with a zipper, the lass seemed capable enough. She was beautiful, not fragile. And he doubted she was there because she needed a warrior to rescue her.

Thus, if she wasn't in some sort of danger, she must be trying to seduce him into marriage, as he'd first suspected.

"Are ye with child?" He looked to her midsection and gestured with his chin. "Is that why you would attempt to seduce a man before ye've even set eyes on him?"

Her frown of confusion turned to that of displeasure. "Are you kidding me?"

Her mouth opened and closed a few more times while she looked about the room as if searching for the words to continue. Finally, she found them. "You think I broke in here to seduce you?" She grunted and the sound of it was quite charming, he had to admit—like a small animal throwing a tantrum.

It was a pity, truly, that the lass didn't need his aid, for he could clearly imagine her throwing her arms around his neck and bestowing her heart-felt gratitude on his lips. And he was tempted to remind her that he'd not only helped her with the zipper, he'd kept her presence a secret from the proprietor. But at the moment, gratitude was likely the last thing she was feeling toward him after his tactless accusation.

"Forgive me, lass. I should have allowed ye to explain before I made assumptions. Can ye forgive me, then?"

Her indignation subsided and she nodded. It was a fine woman who could forgive easily.

A familiar noise grew in the distance and the woman panicked, her eyes widened, and she appeared to be genuinely frightened.

"I'm not here," she said and waved her hands out in front of her. "Just... Please! I'm not here!" She turned and disappeared back into the bedroom and closed the door with a boom.

Alexander's heart danced a wee jig then, given the renewed hope that the lass might be needing his help after all. At the moment, if someone asked him if he would prefer a kiss from the lovely lass to a few moments to vent his spleen with Bonnie Prince Charlie, he couldn't say which he would prefer!

The only explanation that offered itself was that he was easily charmed after so many years of speaking to no women save young Soncerae. And before Culloden...

Well, he'd best forget all that.

He walked outside to clear his head a bit, for surely his imagination had grown cagey from being indoors so long at a go. And judging from the lass' reaction, she might need protection from whomever was approaching on a utility vehicle.

Alexander had a grand ear for car engines, and whatever was headed down the road in his direction sounded much like the Cushman Utility Buggy driven on Culloden's grounds by the security guards.

The small set of steps off the wee porch were made of a material that resembled wood but felt foreign to his hand. Though the surface was by no means smooth, there were no slivers in his palm after he ran his hand along the railing.

Impressive. But how would it fare against the winter weather of the Highlands? He stomped a foot, and though the steps shook, they were sturdily built. The pleasant surprise came with the realization that Soncerae, bless her, hadn't left him defenseless after all. The weight of his skean dhu shook against his ankle to let him know it was there.

And the handy thing about the wee dagger in his sock was that he could use it to make other weapons. With some unknown calamity due to arrive sometime in the next few minutes, or at least the next two days, he determined there was no time to waste and set about searching the edges of the yard for a sturdy branch. All the while, he watched the drive, of course.

He had just freed a straight limb from a tree when a strange sight appeared at the bottom of the hill. The buggy was expected. The two men riding inside it were not. They were dressed in morning suits instead of guard uniforms.

The vehicle rolled to a stop in the same spot the old man had used. Both men dismounted and headed up the incline on foot. As they neared, Alexander could immediately identify which man was the more likely threat—the one on the left, whose eyes narrowed even as he smiled. The other man was taller, of a size with Alexander, but there was nothing threatening about him.

He sliced off a bit of bark and sent it flying to land at the feet of the dangerous one and both men stopped. Ten feet still separated them.

"Good morning," said the taller one.

"Good morning." He sliced off another slab of bark before giving the man his attention.

"I'm Austin. This is my friend, Rick. We're sorry to bother you, but we're looking for..." He rubbed a hand across his face. He was clearly uncomfortable, and there was a redness to his eyes. "Well, we're trying to find my fiancée. We were supposed to get married this morning, but it looks like she got cold feet." He waved both hands defensively. "Not that there's anything wrong with her getting cold feet, of course. But she ran off. No car. Probably still in her wedding dress. And I just don't want her getting hurt out here in these woods, you know?"

Alexander hid his surprise and disappointment in the woman hiding in the house and played the part of a simple huntsman. "Aye. A lass alone in the woods wouldna fare well for long, I would think."

"So, you haven't seen her?" The other man looked relieved, but his eyes kept darting to the door of the cottage.

"I've only just arrived," Alexander said. "I checked the house a moment ago. I'm afraid ye'll need to continue yer search."

The tall one nodded. "Thanks anyway. Sorry to bother you." His demeanor was clearly dejected as any man's would be after being left at the altar, as he appeared to have been. Alexander would have invited the man in for a drink of wine and some commiseration, but under the circumstances, he still felt compelled to protect the woman in spite of what she'd done.

"Nae bother," Alexander said. "A pity about the lass. I hope she is found safe."

The groom nodded and headed back down the hill. His friend took one last look at the cottage, windows and all, then stepped close, ignoring the end of the branch held between them.

"Look," he said, and reached into his pocket. He pulled out a small card and offered it. "If you do see her, I want you to call me at this number. And I'll make sure you get a nice finder's fee. Got it?"

Alexander took the card only because he expected the man to keep at him until he did. But he said nothing.

"Look," the man said again. "This is the first house in two miles of the castle, so unless she found a ride—on a road that has had no traffic all morning—I'm sure she stopped here. If you've got her in there, fine. Just have her call someone and let them know she's all right so Austin can stop looking for her. He doesn't deserve this."

"No man deserves such betrayal," Alexander said, more to himself than to the troublesome man before him.

"So, you don't deny it?"

"Deny what?"

He looked askance at Alexander. Though they spoke the same language, there always seemed to be a breakdown in communication between Scots and Yanks. And this time, it seemed to work to Alexander's advantage.

"Well, if you see her," the man said, uncertain again, "make sure you call me. Okay? Don't call anyone at the castle. I don't want the Forbes family bothered with her inappropriate behavior ever again."

"Understood," Alexander said, and went back to sharpening his new weapon. It wouldn't surprise him if, when all was said and done, he found the need to use it on the fellow before him.

The fellow assessed the cottage again. "What is this, a hunting lodge?"

Alexander watched a chip fly off to the right. "Today it is."

"And what are you hunting? Wild boar?"

Alexander sent another slice at the man. This one hit him just over his heart. "Nay. Not today."

The small pucker between that one's eyes said he was confused again, though Alexander supposed the man would understand the threat after he took some time to ponder their exchange. And when he did understand, he suspected this Rick to come back. Until then, he would continue to play the innocent.

"Have a fine day," he said casually.

Rick studied his expressionless face for a moment, nodded, and turned away.

But Alexander didn't go back inside the cottage, he continued to prepare his new weapon. Because, although one possible adversary was gone, fading in the distance with the sound of the buggy, there was still another enemy waiting…inside the house.

CHAPTER SIX

Chelsea listened to the whine of the golf cart move up past the cottage and slowly fade into silence. But still she didn't dare move. The glass doors of the shower were frosted, and looking in, her white dress would blend with the white walls, so it wasn't a completely stupid place for her to hide. But one thing was for sure, she wasn't about to hide in that guy's bed again. She could just imagine the snide comments Rick would have if he found her there, not to mention what Austin would think.

Austin.

Her heart twisted like someone was holding it over the sink trying to wring out every drop so they could hang it on the edge of a counter to dry. Every breath hurt. Every thought was a kick in the gut.

What have I done to Austin?

It was too painful to think about. She'd never get out of this guy's house and get back home if she curled up into a ball and wept like she wanted to. So she had to concentrate on something else. She had to think about Rick and how she might ensure Austin knew who had really ruined their wedding.

And no matter what Rick had to say, no matter what lies he told, she held onto the hope that one day his story would have one too many holes. He couldn't keep lucking out like he did. One day, his hatred of her would slip out and Austin would realize his twisted friend would have done anything to keep her away from him.

Sadly, though, Austin never seemed to recognize that Rick protected him like he did, not out of love or loyalty, but out of defense of his own ambition. He wanted Austin to run for Congress one day because he wanted to hitchhike on his coattails. He wanted to share in Austin's glory without the need to do any work for it. Just like he'd done all their lives.

And Rick was too ugly, deep down under his pleasant face, to ever go far himself. And if he did try to run for office, *ever*, Chelsea would make it her personal mission in life to make sure he never won an election.

Way to go, Rick. You've got a bitter enemy for life.

He could have settled for second place, allowed Chelsea to marry Austin and take first, and would have still had Austin's friendship and political connections. Chelsea would have never ruined their friendship if it meant hurting Austin to do it.

But not anymore. Somehow, she'd make sure Austin got a good look at the snake standing next to him, and it would all be over.

Rick probably thought she would run home and lick her wounds, and one day look back at the fairy tale she almost lived. But she couldn't allow someone that ruthless, that hateful, to remain so close to the man she loved. The man she still loved.

Had it only been hours since hope had been a living, breathing thing in her life?

She sucked air into her lungs and reminded herself that *she* was still alive, and she needed to stay that way, even if her heart had taken sick leave. She had to get to the airport, change her ticket, and get home. When she was safely behind her locked door, she would finally be able to deal with the hurt.

Thank goodness she'd taken two seconds to grab her purse with her passport, or she'd have no choice but to tuck her tail between her legs and go back to the castle grounds.

Finally, she couldn't take the chill of the shower tile any longer and summoned the courage to leave the bathroom and face reality again. The Scotsman wasn't in the bedroom, for which she was grateful. That was a vision she didn't need haunting her for the rest of her life—a Highlander in a kilt, with broad shoulders and long dark hair, standing next to a large inviting bed...

He wasn't in the living room or kitchen either. So she carefully peeked out through the sheer curtains over a window and saw movement.

The guy was whittling a giant stick and the little pieces of wood flying from the end of his knife were the only things moving in the yard. No one else. No one she needed to hide from. So she tucked her purse under her arm, pushed the door open, and stepped onto the landing. She was trying to choose her words carefully, but she got distracted by the bulge of his triceps as he gripped the heavy branch under one arm and carved with the other. His shirt sleeves were rolled up high and the muscles he'd been hiding looked like something on the cover of a fitness magazine. Sweat had just begun to dampen the hair at his left temple and drip along his jaw.

Whatever she'd hoped to say was forgotten.

She might have watched him for five minutes straight before he noticed she was there. Or at least, he pretended to just be noticing her. With the noisy swish of tulle and chiffon sliding against satin, she couldn't move quietly. But after getting a look at the scowl on his face, she realized he might have been deep in thought and really hadn't noticed her step outside.

"So..." she began.

"So," he repeated, then ignored her and turned back to his project.

"Did someone come looking for me?"

"Aye," he said. "The man ye promised to marry. Austin, was it? Aye. A man with a broken spirit if ever I've seen one."

Broken spirit! Austin's name, said aloud, brought tears to her eyes. The rest was a punch in the gut. It took a painful swallow before she could reply. "But he wasn't alone, was he?"

"Nay. An unpleasant fellow came along."

"Rick."

"Aye. *Rick* had a message for ye."

Rick? But no message from Austin...

"He prefers ye make a telephone call and let folks ken ye're safe, so they can stop searching for ye."

She finally noticed how violently the brawny man was whittling. If he wasn't careful, he might cut himself. Small chips of wood went flying six feet away, but the pile around his feet proved the violence was a recent development. Obviously, he was angry.

And if he was feeling so sorry for Austin, he had to be angry with her. But she wasn't going to bother explaining herself. She felt stupid enough for falling into Rick's trap, and now she wasn't sure The Worm hadn't been right. If Austin would have come to the back of the chapel, she was pretty sure he would have convinced her that marrying him was the right thing to do, and everything would have been fine. But the question was, for how long would it have been fine?

A broken spirit now, or a broken dream later?

She'd been hoping that nothing would have to break if she just ran fast enough and far enough. But that had been stupid too.

"Um," she began, to get the Scot's attention again. "I'm sorry if all this has ruined your morning. I'll get out of here and hopefully, you can pretend I was never here." She walked down the steps and turned her head to face him as she headed down the drive. "I appreciate you covering for me."

"I did not lie for ye, lass." Even when he raised his voice, it was deep enough to rattle the leaves. Or maybe it was just a stray breeze that gave her another chill.

She stumbled to a stop and faced him. "You didn't?"

"Nay. I only said that they would need to keep searching. What they concluded was their own business. Though that Rick fellow was fairly certain ye were inside."

"But not Austin?"

"Nay. I suppose he's not the suspicious sort."

She laughed lightly because the guy had nailed it on the head. "No. Austin is too trusting."

"Aren't most men, until they are betrayed?" After a pointed look at her dress, he concentrated on his whittling again.

Betrayed? It sounded so horrible to phrase it that way when deep down, she'd been so sure she was saving him from a future he didn't really want. But no, that wasn't the truth. Deep down, she'd been saving herself, hurting Austin before he had a chance to hurt her to her face. Or worse, keep his disappointment to himself for the rest of their lives.

"Well," she said, forcing a smile. "Let's hope he won't be so trusting next time, right?" She turned back to the slope and concentrated on her footing. Her heels made the angle much worse than it was and she couldn't decide between walking on the rocks or the grass down the center. "Thanks again," she said, then scooted to the left, hoping the gravel would give more traction if she slipped. If she fell, she would try to land on the soft grass that ran along the outside edge between her and the wall of high bushes blocking her view of the forest beyond.

Somewhere behind her, a large piece of wood bounced hard against the ground and made a strange ringing sound and she nearly jumped out of her skin. She turned to see an angry Scottish god bearing down on her and she quickly stepped backward. The satin of her slight train was pinned beneath her heel. She lost her balance and landed on her butt.

He reached out to catch her but their hands never connected, and his fleeting concern turned back into a scowl, like it was her fault she'd fallen.

"That's all ye have to say for yerself?" He grunted. "That ye hope he's learned his lesson? That ye have no care that the man will likely never trust another woman again? Ye *hope* for it?" He shook his head, disbelieving. "Have all women become the vixens we've seen on the tellie?"

It wasn't his words that made her tremble, though they made her feel pretty guilty. And it wasn't the fact that he was practically yelling at her when he didn't really know why she'd run away from her own wedding. She already knew what a fool she was.

But the passionate god looming over her was absolutely beautiful. His hair flew out behind him like some wind machine was blowing in his face. His powerful jaw jumped beneath his dark, tanned cheeks, and for a second, she wondered if he was actually going to wring her neck.

And no matter how dangerous the situation seemed, she couldn't help wondering how many thousands of women flocked to Scotland every year for a one in a million chance encounter like this, with a passionate man in a kilt?

But probably none of those women had come to the country intending to marry the knight in shining armor they'd sat next to on the airplane…

Too bad Austin was never that passionate about anything. In fact, their only arguments had been pretty one-sided because Austin never got mad. He was reasonable. He was wise. He was wonderful. And she couldn't imagine anything she could do that would send him into such a rant.

Or loom over her while he lectured.

No. Austin would never be a danger to her. Not like this guy. And she wasn't imagining it out of a sense of her own guilt. He was genuinely pissed.

Where is that knife he was whittling with anyway?

The romantic image, complete with a kilt-wearing hero suddenly dissipated like a morning fog when the sun came up out of the ocean. But it wasn't the sun chasing the haze away, it was a real threat. This angry stranger could drag her inside and chop her up into little pieces without anyone being the wiser. Because the only man on earth who suspected where she was just happened to be her mortal enemy who never wanted to see her again anyway.

She had to get out of there or that airline ticket would never be used—Chelsea Marie Chase from Boston, Mass, would never be heard from again. And as Rick pushed Emily into Austin's arms, he'd whisper in his ear not to worry about Chelsea, she'd probably thrown herself into a loch and drowned, just as mentally unstable as her addict parents had been.

Nope. Not going to happen.

She looked up at the Scot and raised her hand, inviting him to pull her to her feet. It was clear she would never be able to get off her dress and stand with him looming over her like he was.

"Do you mind?" she asked sweetly. "This dress cost more than I can make in three months."

He glanced at her hand, then his face cleared as if he was just realizing what a bully he was being. He wrapped his hand around her thumb and wrist and pulled.

And she pulled.

Only, as she did so, she pressed one bare foot against his rock-hard calf and yanked him off balance. As he fell, she only had to guide him over her head and let him land in the prickly bushes behind her. A surprised grunt was the only sound she heard as she grabbed her shoes and purse and started sprinting down the strip of grass that ran down the center of the drive.

"Never mess with a waitress."

CHAPTER SEVEN

Five feet from the end of the drive, Chelsea had to decide which way to turn. If she went back down the road, she'd end up at the castle where she would have to face the music. But at least she could gather her things and get a ride to the airport. She also wouldn't have to walk past the cottage again and maybe face a guy she'd thrown into the brambles.

If she took the sharp angle to the right and continued up and over the hill, she wouldn't have to face Rick again. And when she did face Austin, it was not going to be with The Worm in the room.

Denial still felt like the right thing to do, so she slowed down to make the drastic turn. The crunch of gravel startled her and she turned to look over her shoulder.

"Never mess with a Highlander," he growled, then reached for her shoulder.

She squealed and spun her shoulder away, which had her running backward into the road and tripping on her skirt again. That time, as she was falling, she gave up any hope of getting money back for the dress.

The Scot reached out to catch her, but he failed again, pulling his hand back and wincing like he'd jammed it into something. She did what was necessary to keep from turning her back on him while she got to her feet and gathered her things, but thankfully, he'd taken a step back.

"Forgive me, lass. I've frightened ye. It was instinct, I suppose, that had me chasing after ye." He spoke gently enough, but his eyebrows where still slammed together. And his eyes moved back and forth like he was searching the trees for something he didn't trust. "I'll not harm ye," he said, then went back to searching the trees.

But the real kicker was when he reached out and touched empty air in front of him, prodding it like some mime, like he was being contained in an invisible box.

She carefully lifted her skirts high enough to get her train off the ground and took a few more steps backward. She'd seen some crazy acts on the streets of Edinburgh a couple of days before, but there was absolutely no doubt in her mind—this guy was *not* acting. His cheese had definitely slipped off his cracker!

He slid one of his boots forward and it stopped abruptly where the drive ended and the road began.

"Just like Culloden," he mumbled, then started prodding the air above the spot where his boot had stopped.

She took another step. His attention shot to her and she jumped and started backing quickly down the road. The castle was going to be the safest place for her after all. No matter how embarrassed she was, she would face Austin that day rather than risk this guy following her up the longer road to town. At least there would be people at the castle.

"What is yer name, lass?"

"Uh." The little voice inside her head warned her to lie. "Chelsea."

He nodded and held up his hands like he was surrendering. "I'll not harm ye, Chelsea. And I've not gone mad. There is a barrier I cannot breach, so I'll come no closer."

She couldn't help snorting. "A barrier? Like a force field? Look, I'm just going to get out of here and leave you alone, okay?"

He sighed. "Aye, lass. Do what ye must. Far be it from me to advise another to fight instinct, aye?" His smile was half-grimace. "It was lovely speaking with a woman again, and being spoken to. I thank ye. And I hope ye can overlook my poor manners. It's been a long while since I've needed any, and I'm afeared I let my thoughts escape through my mouth."

He went back to prodding the air and Chelsea saw it as a sign to move faster. But just as she was about to turn and run, he picked up a handful of dirt, spit on it, then threw it onto the road.

Only it never made it to the road.

She didn't remember making a conscious choice to stop. Or to start walking back. It was just an automatic response, like passing a darling pair of shoes in a shop window and finding yourself staring down at them, wondering if they have your size.

She pointed where the dirt had landed. "Would you mind doing that again?"

He studied her for a minute, bit his lip for another ten seconds, then bent and scooped up a little rock. He turned away to spit on it, but it was always in sight. Then he pulled back his hand and tossed it, underhand, toward the road.

There was no sound when it suddenly stopped and fell straight down to the ground, landing and rolling to a stop right at the edge of the driveway.

She met his gaze. "Why the spit?"

He shrugged, picked up another pebble, and tossed it. This time it landed on the other side of the road and thumped against the low stone wall that might have been built hundreds of years ago.

"A barrier," he said. "*I* am not allowed to leave this place. Nor any part of me, it would seem. Just like...the place I came from."

"You said Culloden. As in, Culloden Moor?"

"Aye," he said softly.

"Is there like a prison there or something? A mental institution..." She realized how rude she was being but it was too late to take the words back.

He snorted then. "I'm nay mental, lass." Then he lifted both his shoulders again, held them, then dropped them. "Or mayhap I am..."

"May *hap*?"

"'Tis a long story, lass. Best ye be on yer way." He shooed her away with his fingers. "Ye're clearly able to save yerself when needed, so it was likely not intended that my destiny and yours intertwine after all. I was never meant to be yer hero, aye? But perhaps ye'll have a pleasant thought for me, now and again, when you remember your time in bonny Scotland." He put fingers to his temple in a mock salute. "Alexander Fraser, miss, at yer service. Like I've said, it's been a pleasure."

The guy gave her a little bow, then gave up tossing rocks and started back up the drive. And though she wasn't really hoping to see anything...inappropriate, she couldn't help but watch the back of his kilt swinging forward and back as he went, tapping lightly against the backs of his thighs.

When he passed from view, she peeked around the edge of the bushes that grew ten feet high between the drive and the road, creating a long hallway with the bushes on the other side. He collected the branch he'd carved into a giant pencil, then took it inside the house. He then turned and lifted it over the door, probably propping it over the curtain rods above the windows to either side. When his gaze lowered, he noticed her and gave her a sad little wave. Then he disappeared.

She turned back toward the road and realized she had to make that decision all over again. And this time, there was no rush to decide.

Which way to go?

And when the little voice in her head suggested she go back, she knew that voice hadn't been referring to the castle.

CHAPTER EIGHT

Alexander had done something he would have never thought himself capable.

After decades of resenting the romance novelists—those who had lured impressionable women to Culloden in hopes of a glimpse of something resembling a certain Fraser character—he'd stooped to using the same tactics to lure the lass back to the cottage.

She didn't seem particularly impressionable, but he was always surprised by which of Culloden's female visitors would produce a tear or two while standing before the Clan Fraser stone. For all he knew, those women had been moved by the Fraser soldiers who had truly perished in the battle, but he had his doubts. After all, it was the Fraser stone that continually had flowers lying on the ground before it, and though other graves were honored regularly, there was no comparison.

It had been pitiful, truly, to be unable to appreciate the place of his own clan in that famous but fictional world. But as he stood there waiting for the lovely fish to take the bait, the bitterness washed away, and he wondered if perhaps he'd been jealous of that Fraser character all those years. And perhaps romance novelists knew something he hadn't—the way to a lass's heart.

A pity he hadn't known, in his own day, how to keep a certain lass's affection...

It seemed this Chelsea, as well as being a capable woman, was also the stubborn sort. He waited nearly half an hour for her to come back up the drive. His senses told him she was still out there deliberating.

Or perhaps she was the proud sort and wouldn't return unless she had a reasonable excuse to do so. Would he have to swallow his own pride and go invite her back?

He couldn't imagine what Soncerae had in mind when she'd placed him there and left a barrier around the place to ensure he stayed put. In any case, he would be unable to drum up any true act of heroism while sitting alone in a cottage, drinking wine and dining on chicken someone else had cooked for him. Clearly, others would need be involved. And the lass had been all but dropped in his lap. He should have kept her inside...

When he'd gone tumbling arse over teakettle into the bushes, he'd only given a heartbeat's notice to the sting of the thorns. He'd panicked when he thought his one chance to prove himself was getting away. And after realizing he wouldn't be able to catch her, contained as he was, he'd had to stoop to whatever means were available to him to bring her back again.

He had to admit that feeling the lass's gaze upon him as he'd made his way up the rise and into the house had lent a bit of puff to his chest. It had been a good long while since anyone had appreciated his form, let alone a beauty like Chelsea.

He sighed, and stood, brushing the dust from the hearth from his backside and preparing his belly for some humble pie. But then he heard the low hum of a weak engine, perhaps the Cushman Utility Buggy returning from over the hill.

And he smiled, realizing he wouldn't have to eat that bitter pie after all.

Standing at the back of the room, he noticed the white of her dress when she neared the top of the rise. She wore her shoes again, obviously no longer worried about fleeing from him. By the time she knocked upon the door, the buggy was growing near.

"Mr. Fraser," she called quietly through the screen of the door. "Mr. Fraser!"

He paused from stacking wood on the grate and said, without looking her way, "Ye've broken in before, lass. Why let a thin door stop ye now?"

She paused not at all and threw the screen wide, then pulled it shut behind her and closed the larger door besides. He stood to face her just as she finished with the locks.

"Um," she began, but he cut her off with a raised hand.

"No need to explain, aye? Hide where ye will. And when they've moved on, we'll find some food."

She gave him a relieved smile, then started for the bedchamber. But she stopped and laid her hand on his forearm. "Thank you." She gave his arm a squeeze, then hurried away. And while the buggy drove past the house, he stared at the spot where his flesh still showed the imprint of her hand. A minute later, there was a firm knock on the door.

He chuckled to himself as he unlocked all the latches and chains, but he sobered quickly when the one called Rick faced him alone.

"Found her, did ye?" Alexander asked.

The man frowned. "We didn't." Then he tried to look past Alexander, but he was nigh unto a door himself, not easy to see around.

"Pity," he said, "unless ye'd rather *not* find her of course."

The canny man understood and narrowed his eyes. "He just wanted me to check one more time," he said, then turned aside to give Alexander a clear view of a distraught groom seated in the vehicle, looking both hopeful and forlorn. Rick shook his head at his friend and the poor lad bit his lip and looked away.

"See what she's done to him?"

"As I said, pity." Alexander offered nothing more and stood his ground even though Rick looked past his shoulder and made the smallest faint, expecting him to at least take a step back. But he was no fool to be easily manipulated by a scunner like that. "Better luck…to yer friend," he said, then leaned forward slightly.

The man stepped back, then adopted an amiable smile. "Sorry to bother you again," he said loudly for his audience in the cart. "You've got my number, if you see her."

"Aye," he said. "Godspeed," he called to the groom who then gave a kind wave. As soon as the cart moved into the road, Alexander turned to find a weepy woman at his back.

"Did you see him?"

"Aye. He's a pitiful mess, lass. Would ye like me to call him back? Or rather… Do ye have a mobile in yer purse? I can hardly go collect the man, since I canna seem to leave, but perhaps ye can dial the number and I can ask him to come. You wouldna need to speak to him yet, if ye're nay ready—"

"A mess?"

He nodded. "Pitiful." And his own chest constricted knowing the lass was weeping over another man. It stirred up memories that he would rather leave buried on the moor. And he had to turn away from her to stop the rest from flooding in.

"I promised ye food, did I not? And a generous Mr. Muir arranged for a bottle of wine and a roasted fowl. If ye'll sit to the table, I'll see what manners I might be able to summon from the past."

Yes. Manners, not memories.

Thankfully, he was occupied with domestic details for the time being and when he had time to think, he was careful to keep those thoughts on the woman he was there to help. He hurried a bit since there was a chance he had already helped her enough by simply keeping that Rick character away from her, twice. And if his duty was finished, he wanted a chance to taste the food and the wine before the wee witch came to gather him up and take him away.

And it was for that reason he snuck a few mouthfuls of chicken and half a glass of wine while he moved about the kitchen area making his preparations.

"Elbows from the table, if ye please," he said. He handed her a small box of tissues to occupy her hands while he spread a cloth. Then he returned with plates, wine glasses, and utensils. He set them out as he remembered, then plucked the tissue box away again. "No more tears until the meal is finished, do ye ken?"

"Aye," she said, grinning with damp cheeks. It took all his fortitude not to bend and reward her with a kiss.

He gave her a frown for tempting him, but she continued to grin. He shook his head and went back for the food. Upon a long platter, he placed one of the roasted chickens. To one side, he positioned tomatoes and on the other, some of the mushrooms he'd sliced and cooked briefly in a pan with butter and garlic. His bungling fingers had ruined them, but he would serve them just the same.

When he returned to the table, those lovely cheeks were dry once more and the smile was less obligatory.

"You'll have to forgive the mushrooms. I spilled a tin of parsley flakes all over them. If ye'd care for the recipe, I call them Mushrooms in Parsley Mud."

Her laugh was delightful and caught him off guard. It bubbled around him like music amplified on speakers and he winced, suddenly pained by all that her laughter implied.

He was sitting down to dinner with a woman who belonged to another man. Tempted to kiss another man's woman—a man who mourned the loss of her while Alexander prepared her meal and cajoled laughter from her.

He had no right.

"Excuse me, lass. I suddenly doona feel so well, and I need a bit of air." He avoided her concerned gaze. "Eat up. I've not cooked for naught, aye? But if the mushrooms go untouched, I'll not feel slighted. Ye have my word."

He stepped into the living room and scrubbed his face with his hands. A second later, he was out in the fresh air determined to think of nothing more than identifying the limits of his barrier. Then he'd find the point farthest from the cottage door and spend some time there—*not* thinking about the bride inside.

CHAPTER NINE

Chelsea was starving.

It was the only excuse she could think of for diving into a meal prepared by a stranger, drinking some of the wine from a bottle that had already been opened, and ingesting both the chicken and the wine after the stranger who prepared it suddenly came up with an excuse not to have any himself.

She was going to die!

She wiped grease from her fingers onto the plaid napkin and sat perfectly still for a minute, trying to notice the second the drugs started taking effect. Then she waited another. Her stomach felt… To be honest, it felt relieved that there was finally some food in it.

She'd been way too nervous that morning to eat anything, and the little drink of orange juice had burned more than it soothed. So, yeah, she'd been starving. The wine was strong so she hadn't had much. If the Scot had drugged the bottle, she obviously hadn't had enough to affect her. She didn't drink often, so she was always careful not to overdo it. This time, it might have saved her life.

Only she didn't feel funny. The wine barely warmed her throat. That was it.

Okay. Two more minutes, and if I feel okay, I'm eating a miniature tomato... And a little more chicken.

She didn't last another minute. He'd promised he wouldn't harm her, and she had believed him. As she ate the meat off the second leg, she started feeling guilty for enjoying the food at all when he was clearly in distress.

Reluctantly, she put the chicken back on her plate and cleaned her fingers again. She was just going to have to wait until they could eat together.

She paused at the door to listen for the golf cart but heard nothing. And the entire time she'd been inside only two real cars had passed the cottage. For all she knew, Austin and Rick and the entire wedding party might have left the castle and gone on with their touring plans. And if Rick stayed true to form, he'd either be running around with Austin on their honeymoon itinerary, or he'd drag Austin off to France and the rest of Europe.

And wouldn't Austin be surprised when Erica Winston just happened to be joining them?

It was all so ridiculous! She should have never run off, never let the bastard win! She should have marched up the aisle, grabbed Austin's hand, and hauled him out of there for some privacy. All she'd needed was a little assurance that he really did want her more than he wanted a career in politics. It was a conversation they'd had a dozen times, but she'd just needed to hear it once more.

And then she would have been fine.

Wouldn't she?

She held onto the door jamb and tried to tell whether it was emotion or poison that made her question her own reasoning. Or maybe it was the distraction of the Scottish magician who was able to make it seem like he could change the trajectory of a rock after it left his hand.

She had tried for nearly half an hour to recreate what he'd done, but she couldn't do it. In the end, she figured he had to have been using a mirror, or a piece of glass she never saw. Who knew what a man could hide beneath one of those kilts, or in the folds of material draped over his chest.

Or maybe it was that chest that distracted her. Holy cow. If she looked at him for too long, he took her breath away—and with it, some much-needed oxygen.

She took a deep breath to prove she could, then went looking for the Scottish heart-throb the rest of the world may or may not have discovered yet. There was no use worrying too much about the dress. Either it could be cleaned well enough for another bride to wear it, or it couldn't. All she had to do was keep from snagging it on some gnarly looking bushes, and there would still be hope. But luckily, the lower plants had lots of yellow blossoms on them, warning her to stay away.

She was careful to stick to the center of a path that wound around the side of the cottage and down into a ravine behind. But she was so absorbed by keeping her dress away from the branches, she hadn't noticed what she'd walked into until she was smack dab in the middle of it.

A fairy glen!

Or at least, if there were such things as fairy glens, she was standing in one. The ravine was covered by a high umbrella of tiny leaves that only let the mildest light through them. And the trees themselves were covered with a thin layer of bright, spring-green moss that looked like it had been sprayed on like a coat of paint. She could almost imagine tiny, winged figures flitting around with miniature paint sprayers making the world match their favorite color.

Like so many scraps of delicate, fragile lace, a lovely species of moss draped from branch to branch. And in places, morning dew still dripped and clung, waiting for a sharp point of light to burst its glistening bubble.

The water of a small creek percolated between rocks that had also been sprayed by the fairies, and, sitting on a bank of thick, soft ferns sat the Highlander, picking pebbles out from under the fronds and tossing them into the water. As far as she could tell, he had no magic trick set up. Clearly, he wasn't expecting her to find him.

"No force field on this side of the house, huh?"

He started and turned with his hand raised, then relaxed when he saw it was her. "The barrier? 'Tis over to the left there," he said.

She rolled her eyes, but he didn't notice. When she stepped closer, however, he seemed leery. A big man like him, afraid of her?

She laughed. "I promise not to toss you over my shoulder again."

He smiled at the joke, but it wasn't convincing.

"What's the matter? Do you really not feel well?" She reached forward on instinct, to touch his forehead and check for a fever—maybe it was just a female instinct—but he flinched.

She straightened and stepped back, feeling like a leper.

"I'm not unwell," he confessed, and she started worrying about the whole poison scenario again.

"Then what's wrong?"

He pivoted away from her as he stood and she resisted the urge to sniff her armpits. If she stunk after running two miles in a wedding gown, she shouldn't have been surprised.

"What is wrong, lass, is that ye're the betrothed of another man and I should keep my distance, aye?"

She exhaled more than just the air in her lungs. She felt her entire body deflate with the realization that she had given up that fiancée status. And now she was just someone's…ex.

"That's funny," she said, trying to keep her tone light. "I don't feel like I belong to anyone anymore."

His right brow rose into a high peak. "Truly?"

She shrugged and sighed again. "Truly."

A slow grin spread across his face and she stepped to the side, prepared to hustle up out of the ravine if necessary. But he waved his fingers. "Come." Then he pointed to the bed of ferns he'd crushed flat. "Sit beside me and listen to the water for a mite. 'Tis a magic place, is it not?"

She nodded and stepped onto the ferns, relieved he hadn't tried to throw her over his shoulder and carry her into the house like some barbarian. She was also eager to move closer to him just to prove to herself that it wasn't the smell of her that made him back away.

She sat carefully and smoothed her skirts like she was getting ready for a photo. He plopped down beside her, his thigh pressed close to hers and his kilt spilling onto the white satin. And while she tried not to overreact to both those facts, he dug through the leaves on his left and came up with some rocks.

He held them out to her on his hand like he was offering hors d'oeuvres. "Go ahead, lass. Tossing rocks in the water is good for the soul. And besides, they weigh much less than a man, aye?"

She laughed and took a stone, then tilted her head and narrowed her eyes at him. "Where did you say that barrier was?"

He bit his lip for a minute and she completely forgot time and place until he finally released it. His arm rose and he pointed to a path that rose up the far bank and disappeared between two trees.

"Over there, lass. I've already tested it."

She grinned and held up the little stone. "Here. Spit on this." She looked him in the eye, daring him to refuse.

He studied her for a second or two. His cheeks dimpled and she knew she had him. She had to bite her own lip to keep from grinning like an idiot. And after he stared at her lip like she'd stared at his, he wrapped his hand around hers and pulled the stone close. But instead of spitting on it, he licked it.

She snapped her mouth shut when she realized it was hanging open. Then she hauled back and chucked the rock, aiming as well as she could for the space he'd pointed to. It flew straighter than she even hoped, but before it passed between the trees, it shot straight down to the ground and bounced in the dirt before rolling backward and landing unceremoniously in the creek.

Chelsea jumped to her feet and hurried down to the water. A quick glance over her shoulder proved he wasn't trying to follow. Her skirts had to be held high to keep them dry, but she found enough sturdy stones to make her way across the stream without slipping in. Her shoes left prints on the stones where they had crushed the moss, and a fleeting twinge of guilt—for destroying even the thinnest layer of fairy moss—made her pause. But she wouldn't be stopped. She was determined to find the mechanism he'd set up for his trick before he could hide it from her again.

But there was no mirror. No glass. And if she was honest with herself, she'd heard no thump when the rock had suddenly stopped in mid-air and changed direction.

Maybe a magnet!

She hurried to the water's edge and tried to find the little rock he had supposedly pulled from the forest floor. But there were hundreds there that looked just like it.

"Fine," she said in a huff. "Come over here. You're going to have to prove to me you can't cross this barrier."

He let his head fall back and closed his eyes. "What ye propose, lass, is much less good for the soul. Wouldn't ye rather come back and be at peace for a wee while?"

Of course he'd say that.

"No. I'll be at peace when I know how you did your trick."

He climbed to his feet, tucking his kilt around his knees as he did so, then crossed the creek by stepping on one stone in the center. There wasn't much room for them between the slope and the magic barrier, so she had to stand close.

"Keep walking, buddy," she ordered, and gave him a little nudge.

He moved his foot forward, but never put his weight on it. "I canna."

She rolled her eyes, then tapped his arm. "Hang on. I'm going to give you a shove. And I want you to stand on one foot so you can't brace yerself, okay?"

He closed his eyes again like he was praying for patience. "I'll do it. The once. I'll not have ye harming yerself trying to prove me a liar, aye?"

"Yeah. Sure. Okay." She had him stand two feet back from the invisible line, then stood behind him and waited for him to lift one boot off the ground. He wasn't leaning back against her either, so it should be an easy thing to do—push him off balance and force him to stumble forward.

So she pushed. Hard.

He fell forward and put his hands out to catch himself. She stepped to the side and found that he wasn't bracing himself against the trees…

He was bracing himself against…the air.

CHAPTER TEN

Alexander knew the moment Miss Chelsea understood that there was something otherworldly going on. It was almost as if he heard the pop of a bubble, warning him.

"You..." The lass pointed an accusing finger at him and stepped backward into the brush. "You," she said again. Her attention turned to the side as she checked her footing and took yet another step away, but the finger still pointed. "You—"

She tumbled sideways before he could get his feet under him and reach her. And for the third time since they'd met, he failed to catch her hand in time to prevent her from toppling into the burn.

The pitch of her surprise mirrored the chill of the Highland water, but when she spoke again, it was the same. "You..."

"Aye," he said, nodding to placate her while he bent and scooped her person away from the tide rising against her gown.

Her unexpected weight was due to a few gallons of water clinging to her skirts, but he didn't complain as he carried her up the rise and continued to answer every "You" with an "Aye."

"Stand on yer feet," he ordered as he put those feet to the tiles in the shower.

She obeyed. And though her teeth chattered, he reckoned it was more from shock than from the icy cold of the mountain runoff.

"Turn," he said firmly.

She obeyed again. He pushed her tumbling hair to the side and tugged on the zipper.

"You..."

"Aye."

He pushed the heavy cloth away from her sides and forced it into a puddle at her feet while he tried to ignore the flesh of her derriere pressed against the wet and delicate shift she wore beneath it.

"Step out," he said more gruffly than he wished.

She lifted one shoe and held it until he pushed it where it needed to go. The second shoe did the same and he slid the mass of white free. While keeping a hand to the lass's lower back in case her knees failed, he whipped the gown up over the edge of the glass cage and allowed it to hang there. Then he guided her to a wide ledge of tiles and told her to sit.

She crossed her arms in front of her and hid her gaze behind damp clumps of hair. He turned on the shower, adjusted the temperature of the water, then aimed the showerhead her way.

"Warm yerself," he said gently. "I will find something passable for clothing. Call out if ye need me. Can ye do that?"

She started to shake her head, but then recovered and nodded firmly.

He left her to her own devices and tried to keep his mind from lingering on the body he needed to clothe and simply focus his attention on locating the garb to do it with.

In the kitchen, he found an apron, five dish towels, and three wash cloths.

In the living room, the pelt of a deer on the wall, a small thick rug what would hardly roll, let alone conform to her...form, and a loosely woven blanket that would show more than it covered.

Back in the bedchamber again, the closet was bare. The small pile of towels wouldn't do. The drawers were empty but for small vials of shampoo and small cards of soap. He had only one alternative.

A minute later, after a quick pop into the kitchen for a bit of rope, he knocked on the door to the bathing room.

"Did you find clothes?" she called.

"I leave ye a dress and a belt on the bed, lass. Do ye need help?"

"No," she said firmly, giving him cause to hope she was recovering from the shock, at least for the moment. "Thank you," she added.

He ate a bit while he tidied up the kitchen. The wine was better left alone, he reckoned, and drank water from the pipes instead. When the bedchamber door opened, he jumped like a guilty child, then stepped into the living room to see what she made of his improvisation.

She stood shyly by the door for a moment, then stepped into the room and turned in a circle. "Not bad," she said. "Thank you."

The belted poncho he'd made from one of the bedsheets suited her better than the wedding gown had done. At least she could move about in it without causing a ruckus. He'd sliced a small hole for her head. Then, about a foot or so away from that hole, to either side, he'd cut an even smaller hole for her arms. Through those holes, her hands and forearms protruded and she was free to move them about without revealing any more of her.

She'd bunched it up, however, and left a disturbing expanse of her calves showing beneath. Of course he'd seen women in shorts all through the summer months, but not while he was burdened with the weaknesses of the flesh.

He would simply have to keep his gaze away from the floor, was all.

She gave him a wide grin. Her approval was a relief. The only other option he had to give her was the kilt off his back, and she wouldn't appreciate him walking about the place in nothing but his long shirt. At least, he didn't believe she would.

Their smiles faded in unison and they stared at each other. A shiver started at her elbows and shook her shoulders. He looked to the hearth and grimaced.

"Forgive me, lass. I should have lit the fire afore now."

He pulled a wooden rocker close, insisted she sit, and bent to light the fire. He'd desired to light a match for half a century and was happy to find a box of them on the mantle. But it was almost a disappointment how little effort was needed to get a good cook on the wood. His efforts, however, would be better spent in conversation with a lovely lass who might well be the last one he would ever see in the flesh.

She declined a glass of wine or water, so he finally settled into a large, comfortable chair facing the fire.

"Are ye feeling sound, then?" he asked politely, dreading the conversation to come, hoping she'd forgotten all about the silly rock and the barrier. Perhaps her mind would find a way to hide the memory from her, as had happened in one tellie program or another.

"I turned on my phone long enough to send Austin a text." She stared at her fingers. "I told him I'm safe, not to worry about me, and that I'm not ready to talk about it." After a minute, she looked up. "But I am ready to talk about that rock. But first, I want to know if I'll be able to leave here. If I got up and walked out of here, how far would I get? Am I trapped here too?"

He quickly shook his head. "The barrier is for me alone. Ye're free to leave whenever ye wish."

She leaned forward until her bare feet were flat on the floor and her elbows rested on her knees. Thankfully, the sheet draped low over her calves. "All right. Tell me. Why can't you leave? And what kind of magic..." She waved toward the kitchen, but he knew she meant the glen beyond it.

"If ye think ye can stand to keep yer eyes open for a long-winded story..."

She nodded.

"Then I'll start at the beginning."

Her toes poked at the floor and got the chair to moving. He supposed the motion had a soothing effect on her much like Rabby petting old Dauphin, for which he was glad—she would need soothing by the time he was done.

He pretended not to notice the way her fingers bit into her own arms when he told her he was born in 1718--and died on Culloden Moor in 1746. She sat back quickly when he explained how he'd risen on Culloden the day after the battle...a ghost. She never interrupted, though, even when he skimmed over the happenings of the past two hundred and nearly seventy years since that day. She leaned close again when he told about Soncerae, how she had been a witch all along but they'd never known it, and why he'd been sent to this grand cottage, to await the moment when an impressive, heroic action would be needed.

He omitted the detail of how much time he might have to accomplish this deed, and if he fails, that he'll miss the chance to help wee Rabby summon the courage to escape the moor. All he'd said about it was that he'd already given away his boon in exchange for the chance to help the lad.

She sniffed and wiped at her eyes with the edge of the sheet. "Well, that's just stupid. Waiving your right to your boon, or whatever you call it, should be heroic enough, don't you think? The witch should have called it good and let you...be...done."

He shrugged. "I've never been gifted with knowing a woman's mind, lass. I'm not Jamie Bloody Fraser, am I?"

"Sorry?"

He shook his head, disgusted with himself again. He'd let his bitter past slink into his mind much as the weather creeping up on them. The natural light dimmed and the smell of rain seeped through the screen and around the edge of the inner door. When the rain did come, he would go outside and stretch his arms wide, look up at the sky, and feel the drops splash against his skin. For too long he'd been immune and unfeeling to Scottish weather. The chance to touch the Highland rain again was a boon in itself.

"Never ye mind," he told the lass. "Just a popular character from fiction. I thought ye might be familiar..."

"Popular, huh?"

"Aye."

"And knows how to understand women?"

He smiled at the tease. "Auch, aye. And a braw Scottish laddie to boot."

"Mm hmm."

"Of course, he was created by a woman, so..."

She nodded. "Oh, I see. About as popular and probable as unicorns?"

"Exactly that. And if the television actor farted rainbows, I wouldna be surprised."

After she stopped giggling, he then confessed to trying to use his own name of Fraser to lure her back to the house when he worried she might leave him in truth.

She sat forward again, as did he, feeling a need to be closer to the lass, but not bold enough to move his chair for fear of frightening her again. Her charming toes pinched at the floor and he wondered if they were cold.

"So, you think you're supposed to save me from something? You think I'm your damsel in distress?" The sparkle in her eyes made him believe the idea intrigued her. Many a lass might have been offended by the idea of needing any man's help.

"Perhaps," he said.

"It couldn't be from Austin, but maybe from Rick?" She laughed then. "Or maybe from a bear?"

"It has been centuries since we've had bears in Scotland, lass."

She sucked in her bottom lip and studied his face for a moment. He could hardly wait to discover what was going on behind those clever eyes. "Maybe," she finally said, "you're supposed to save me from you."

He came very near to closing the distance between them, taking her in his arms, and showing her how a mortal man might truly pose a danger to her. But from the look on her face, she had understood the message in any case.

CHAPTER ELEVEN

At long last, Alexander could appreciate the term *awkward silence.*

Seconds ticked by while they gazed at each other, waiting for the other one to disrupt the quiet. A slow smile stretched across Chelsea's blushing face and she chuckled. He laughed along with her to try to dispel the discomfort of the moment.

"Well," she said, "since I don't have anything else on my calendar, I think I can stick around for a little while and see what happens."

He inclined his head. "I'd be much obliged to ye."

"Maybe you can tell me more about your ghost friends."

A pleasant change to be sure, speaking of things other than themselves. It was evident she wished to avoid the subject of her own wedding just as he wished to avoid the memory of the day when he, too, came close to marrying. Or at least he thought he had...

She rocked the chair on and off, stopping when the conversation grew serious, rocking while he told her of silly things, like the color of heather, gorse, and the enchanting glen behind the cottage—all more beautiful now that he could see them with mortal eyes—and how he would like to see Culloden one last time in full light.

When there was little else to tell, her legs seemed to grow weary and the chair settled. A sigh escaped her, heavy with regret. She tried to smile, but failed. "I can't really believe any of this, you know."

"Oh, aye." He knew her easy acceptance of his tale had been too good to be true. "I can only guess at how impossible it all sounds. It would have seemed outlandish to me had I not been witness to my own death, felt the blood drain from my body and leave me cold as the moor itself." A shiver passed through him at the memory.

She wrapped her arms around herself as well. "And supposedly, when you…go again, you'll die again?"

The idea was sobering and brought him to his feet. He bent to stoke the fire to excuse the action. "I dinna ken what will happen, lass. I can only hope that Soncerae, a lass I've known nearly all her life, would not put me through something as violent as my first death."

A second death? *Please, God, spare me that.*

It suddenly occurred to him that such a fate was likely what made Rabby hesitate. Before he assured the laddie it was safe to move on, he would have it from Soni's own lips that there would be nothing frightening awaiting Rabby if he did as he was bade.

Laughter filled the room and he turned to find Chelsea with her head thrown back against her chair and her hands gripping the carved arms as she laughed herself silly.

His own thoughts were far too sober to laugh with her, though he could not help but smile at her delight. He scooted his arse onto the hearth and waited for her to finish. It proved to be a fine maneuver to get closer to the lass, so he was in no hurry to have his curiosity satisfied.

When she finally wound down like a child's toy running out of battery power, there were tears in her eyes that couldn't all be blamed on amusement. His smile fled and he reached out and took her hand in his.

"What is it, lass?"

She bit at her lip and her brows worried together. "Are you even here? Maybe I'm… Am I going crazy?"

He was finally able to chuckle, though lightly. "Nay, lass. Ye're not mad at all. Any sane woman would balk at what I've said, at what you saw in the glen. Nothing natural about it, to be sure." He squeezed her hand. "Do ye feel that?"

She nodded, relieved.

"I'm real enough, then. For the moment."

She seemed much calmer, though still a bit worried. "Then what do we do?"

We? "Auch, but the dilemma is nay yers, lass. I alone must prepare for what may need doing. Nothing for you to worry over at all."

She was the one to squeeze his hand then, and he felt it all the way to his heart. "But you'll go away as soon as this quest is over?"

"Aye, lass. Straight away, I would hope. For every minute I can spare the laddie from his tenure on the moor is a victory, is it not?"

She nodded. Could he dare imagine she might regret never seeing him again?

"Let us not worry o'er it," he said cheerfully. "Tell me about yerself while there is time to tell it. Later, I will wish I knew more about ye than the curve of yer cheek and the bow of yer lips."

Her hand flew up to cover her mouth and she blushed. "You'll remember my lips?"

"Auch, aye. I've stared at them long enough, haven't I?"

She giggled and forced her hand to her side, then bit her lip to keep from smiling. It was the dearest sight. And a moving one. In fact, it moved him off the hearth to kneel before her knees. She sobered instantly, and though she appeared uneasy to have him so close, he couldn't drag himself away. At least, for a moment, he wanted to be near enough to feel the warmth of her, to see her face clearly, to absorb the sound of her voice into his bones.

It would all make a fine memory…no matter where he went…*after.*

"Well, that's a pretty sight, isn't it?" Rick stood on the small porch holding the screen open. He'd already pushed the inner door wide, but Alexander hadn't heard so much as a squeak. And sitting before the fire, he'd not felt the air move.

He was already on his feet, ready to defend the woman with his life, as he'd been prepared to do all day. It seemed a quiet moment alone with her, a kind word and a gentle touch, were to be fleeting things, but he was glad the gifts had come before it all ended.

It took all his concentration to keep from glancing at the weapon mounted just above the doorway. If the man charged, there would be no time to reach it. He needed to keep the man outside.

He hurried forward, blocking the villain's view of the lass, demanding his attention. He only hoped his expression promised pain if the man had ill intentions.

"Wait!" Chelsea's voice stopped him in his tracks.

He turned sideways to divide his attention between her and the one who so upset her.

She stood and crossed her arms over her chest. The defensive move was telling. This man had hurt her before. "Is Austin with you?"

Rick sneered. "No. He's sleeping, hopefully."

She stuck her chin out like the brave lass he knew her to be. "Then what do you want?"

"I want your promise that you'll leave him alone. But now that I've got these pictures," he waved his camera back and forth, "I don't need any promises from you. I'll let these do the talking, and there will be nothing you can say that will make him want to listen." He laughed and walked sideways down the steps. "You have a nice weekend, *Cheese*."

He strode arrogantly down the drive, then began jogging at the bottom, no buggy in sight. Alexander prayed for the clouds to unleash their load and humble the blackguard.

The lass stood rooted to the spot, staring at the open doorway. Alexander had no idea what might soothe her, so he waited for her to give him some hint. A long minute later, they heard a distant engine turn over. With the door mostly closed as it had been, it was no wonder they hadn't heard the man approach.

Finally, Chelsea met his gaze. "That should put the nail in the coffin, right?"

He winced at her choice of words.

"Oh my gosh!" She hurried to him and gently squeezed the sides of his arms. "I'm so sorry. That was a horrible thing to say! Please forgive me."

There was the gentle touch again. A kind word. Another private moment. So he wasted no time.

"Tell me, lass, do ye still feel the same as ye did in the glen?"

"You mean, petrified?"

"Nay. Like ye dinna belong to any man?"

Her hands fell away as she released a drawn-out breath. "Yes. I do."

He nodded sharply. "Good." With gentle hands, he tugged on her arms, then gathered her close. "For I believe the balm that will solve both our woes...is a kiss."

Surprise parted her lips and he took advantage. At least, if she wasn't prepared, she couldn't send him arse over teakettle into the fire. Her lips were sweet and soft as he knew they'd be. And the tang of her skin nearly intoxicated him after so many years without any sense of taste. His memories of most things had faded and jumbled, and he imagined, if he sipped whisky again, it would pale in comparison to this lass's kiss.

As would roses, violets, honey on his tongue…

Chelsea seemed taken with the kiss as well. For a long while she played give and take with him. But when the toying ended, he should have stepped back. He held her close just a moment too long and her thoughts must have found their way through the lovely haze he'd tried to create around them—for her tears tumbled down her face and onto his chin.

She tried to retreat, but he pulled her against him, cradled her head gently to the side, and straightened so she could greet against his chest and catch her tears on his shirt. She ceased resisting and waves of sobbing broke over whatever barriers she'd erected for herself.

Listening closely with all his soul, he heard it—that moment when her heart well and truly broke.

If the groom and his henchman were lined up at the door just then, he would have run them both through in a single thrust of his spear.

CHAPTER TWELVE

Dear Diary,

If I ever fall apart again, I mean really fall apart, I'm going to find a Highlander first. I mean, if I'm going to bawl my eyes out, what I really need is for the skies to unload millions of gallons of water and for the rumble of thunder to match the exact tone and vibration to the guy petting my head and saying soothing things in a language that could not possibly be real.

Chelsea smiled into her tissue. Yeah. That's what she'd write, if she was the type to keep a journal. Oh, and she would have to remember to add in the part about having a nice soft sash of plaid wool to discreetly wipe her nose on in an emergency situation.

Only, she kind of got busted on that one. He had to have suspected what she'd done because a few seconds later, he excused himself, went to the kitchen, and came back with a box of tissues. He didn't look too disgusted, though, so maybe he hadn't noticed after all. Or maybe he was just a good actor.

"Better now?" he asked softly.

She nodded and moved to the small fire to toss the tissue into the flames.

"I do regret the pictures the man was able to take. I should have never moved so close to ye, aye?"

She shook her head. "Don't worry about it. Rick's a patient man. He would have waited as long as he had to for what he needed. If he meant to ask me to leave Austin alone, he would have parked at the bottom of the hill. But he didn't. He knows that being sneaky always pays off, eventually."

"Just the same," he said, "I am happy to stand as witness if ye'd care to call Austin to come to the property, to hear our side of things."

"No. If I can't forgive myself for what I've done, I won't ask him to forgive me."

"Is that it, then? The reason you greet so? Because ye canna forgive yerself?"

"I guess. No." She shrugged. "I don't know." She had no energy left for thinking.

He nodded knowingly. "Ye've had a long day of it. Ye need to close yer eyes and rest a bit." He took her by the shoulders and turned her toward the bedroom. "Go ye now and lie abed. Nothing will change but the weather while ye sleep. And I'll give ye privacy, I vow it."

"You *vow* it?" She giggled, then remembered the conversation they'd been having before Rick interrupted. He wasn't even real. She spun around to face him. "Wait!"

He closed his eyes, shook his head, and turned her back around before pushing her through the door. "No waitin'. No thinkin'. Just sleepin'. I promise to be here when you wake."

"But—"

"I said no thinkin'. We'll talk later."

"Talk?"

"Auch, aye. And we'll maybe kiss a bit." He didn't allow her to turn. "But if ye think much about it, neither of us will sleep, will we?"

"What time is it?" She allowed him to steer her to the side of the bed. With the storm outside, she couldn't even make a guess. Time had gone by at a dozen different speeds since the moment she woke up at Castle Murray while it was still dark outside.

"Time to sleep." Her protector pulled back the blankets and covered her up after she tucked her feet in. Then he bent to kiss her. But instead of her lips, he swooped up at the last second and kissed her chastely on the forehead, then chuckled as he left.

She threw a pillow at him too late and it hit the door as it closed.

He peeked back in. "Sleep, lass. Through 'til tomorrow if needs be." Then he was gone.

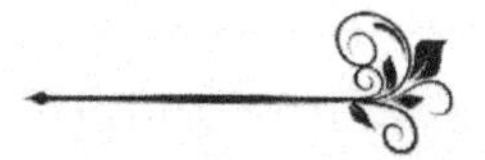

Chelsea was wrong—it was possible to tell exactly what time it was when she woke up. No need for clocks or to see the position of the sun or stars. It was absolutely, straight down the middle, the dead of night. She couldn't see her hand in front of her face and she panicked the way people did when they think there might be the slightest possibility they've gone blind.

She felt a good old-fashioned freak out coming on for a wholly unique reason.

Instantly alert, grogginess was not her problem. She knew where she was, so there was nothing wrong with her memory, or no after effects of the wine she'd had whether or not it had been drugged. And she wasn't afraid due to the possibility that a real ghost might be in the next room—the ghost of a Scottish soldier from Culloden Moor, one of the most haunted places on the planet.

No. She was on the verge of freaking out due to the chance that said ghost might be gone!

"Mr. Fraser," she said. Her voice sounded funny in the dark, so she cleared her throat and tried again. "Alexander!"

The door flew open before the echo of her voice died against the bathroom tiles, so he must have heard the first thing she'd said. The light from the next room was enough to prove she wasn't blind. And the man breathing heavily, with one hand on the wall and the other holding the door open, proved he hadn't left her.

With her biggest fear put to rest, she couldn't think of what to say.

He continued to stare at her while his breathing calmed. "Aye, lass. What is it I can do for ye?"

"Uh... I woke up... And it was really dark... And I was afraid you had...gone."

He walked quietly toward her. Her heart jumped and started pounding so loud she thought he might be able to hear it too. But he faced the bureau and pulled out the top drawer. After rummaging around for a few seconds, he closed the drawer and left the room, but didn't shut the door.

So she sat there and wondered what in the heck was going on.

He appeared a minute later with a lit candle in his hand and it was then she realized he was missing his kilt! His shirt was plenty long, however, like an old-fashioned night shirt that went halfway down his thighs.

"If you had a long pointy cap hanging off to one side of your head, you'd be a younger version of Ebenezer Scrooge, waiting for the three Christmas ghosts to visit."

"I am familiar with Dickens, and the plays on the television." He didn't sound too pleased about it. In fact, he sounded a little gruff.

"I'm so sorry I woke you. I should have gotten up and turned on a light. I just...kind of panicked."

"Lass," he said, bending to set the candle into a candle holder on the nightstand. "Ye didna wake me. I'll not sleep away the two days I've been given. And I'm happy to be of some service to ye."

Her head shook quickly all on its own. "You never said anything about two days! You only have two days?"

He tipped his head back and grimaced. "I didna mean to worry ye. Besides, I've an entire day left now. I'm certain I'll manage something before my time is at hand."

She scooted her legs to the side and patted the bed by her knees. He hesitated, then sat. He put a hand on the bed on the far side of her legs and leaned over her lower half.

"And what happens if you don't do something heroic before your time is up?"

He tilted his head but said nothing.

Was the answer obvious? If he *did* succeed, he was going to go get the boy off the battlefield, then...move on to the next life.

"If you fail, you won't be able to help the boy? Or you won't be able to move on? Will you be trapped at Culloden Moor forever?"

He frowned and used his free hand to pick at the white tie in the center of a dark quilt square. "I reckon I won't be able to see Rabby again, to ease his mind. I ken Soni will take great care with the lad, but he...trusts me."

"Who wouldn't?" She said it quietly, but his head snapped up. She'd just confessed that she trusted him too, she supposed. But he really shouldn't have been surprised. After all, she'd called out for him in the middle of the night.

"Truth be told," he said, and dropped his attention back to the quilt. "There was a lass, nearly three centuries ago, who couldn't put her trust in me, even though we were to be married."

Holy cow! She'd never asked him if he was married before. Of course, if any of this twisted fairy tale were true, his wife and family would have died a long time ago, but the idea of kissing a married man made her feel horrible!

"But you didn't? Marry?"

He shook his head half-heartedly. "Her sister waylaid me in the barn, kissed me. I thought it was my Meredith, but it was Fiona. And the mean lass must have told her sister I'd intended it. Of course, I had no ken of what went on between them. But the next day I was given a note by Merri's own hand, to meet her at the kirk wall at six o'clock that evening, that she could no longer wait to be married.

"The kirk wall was the place we often sat and spoke of how our lives would be after we were man and wife. It was natural she would wish to meet there. In any case, I bathed and put on my finery, prepared my cottage for the woman of the house, and got myself to the kirk wall." He swallowed and stopped talking.

She didn't want to ask the question, but how could she not? Now it was clear, by the reaction he'd had when he found out she was a runaway bride, that he'd been left at the altar himself.

What had he said, that all men are too trusting, until they've been betrayed?

She didn't want to hear the rest, but she deserved it. So she asked, "What happened?"

He nodded, looked her in the eye, then leaned away just a little. The message was clear. He was back to disliking her again.

"I waited what seemed an hour," he finally said, "but it couldn't have been half that. And suddenly the church bell rang and the doors swung open. And there was my Meredith, clutching the arm of Paddy Ewing who smiled like the cat who'd spilled the cream. Merri craned her neck to see me, waiting where I'd been told. And the look in her eye was unmistakable. Pure hatred, it was.

"I was stunned, of course. Unable to move while the wedding party paraded past me. Her family avoided looking my way, but

Merri stopped. While her new husband looked on, gloating, she tossed a small bouquet of flowers into my hands. Then she stuck her nose in the air and walked on. At the back of the pack was Fiona. She blew me a kiss and wink, and to this day I canna say whether she expected to have me for herself, or just didna want her sister to be happy."

"Alexander! That's horrible!" Chelsea leaned forward and gave his arm a squeeze before she remembered he wouldn't welcome it. She pulled her hand back quickly and folded her arms. "Neither one of them deserved you. You're such a great guy! Meredith was out of her mind not to trust you!"

Finally, he smiled, but it was a very sad smile. "And your Austin? Ye've nary an unkind word to say about him, lass. And I've been listening for it...with all my heart."

He dragged himself to his feet and walked slowly to the door. With a hand on the knob, he faced her with a wide, fake, have-to-be-nice-to-the-tourists smile. "In only an hour or more, dawn arrives. I'll fix ye a grand Scottish breakfast and we'll...we'll hammer out a plan for getting you back to your husband-to-be."

Chelsea stared at the closed door for at least a minute before she lay back down. As she watched the candlelight dance on the ceiling, she had just one thought.

Meredith, honey, you were an idiot.

And from somewhere deep in her brain came a response.

Chelsea, honey, so are you.

CHAPTER THIRTEEN

She woke to the sound of singing.

The voice belonged to her host. The deep rumble of a baritone poured out from under the bathroom door accompanied by the spray of the shower. It didn't matter what the tune was supposed to be, there was no question it was off. And the words were sung in that impossible Gaelic language that she couldn't believe anyone could understand—unless they lived hundreds of years ago.

Yesterday, she thought it was a fairy tale meant to distract her from her heartbreak, but by the time she went to bed, she was pretty sure it was true. In the bright, glaring light of morning, she didn't know what to think.

The guy didn't act crazy.

Okay, so his clothes were eccentric, his speech patterns, including his *vows* and words like *mayhap*, could just be a Scottish thing that wasn't unusual at all. Heck, for all she knew, he was just an Outlander fan gone rogue.

Of course, she wasn't about to let him know that she was familiar with the books and the cable show. She'd pretended not to know what he was talking about once, so she had to stick with her story. But damn! He could have walked off the set and decided to spend his vacation in character, to see if he could get some American chick to go all gaga for him.

Well, she nearly had. When he'd come into her dark room and headed for her, in that split second before he turned to the bureau to find a candle, she couldn't admit what she'd been hoping for. Of course she wouldn't have slept with the guy even if he'd been the star of the show. But she wouldn't have minded some lip action worthy of the big screen.

She shook her head and tried to dispel the shadows and images of the night before. The way he'd stared at her, all out of breath, when he'd first burst through the door. The backs of his legs, below his long shirt, when he'd walked away. The way her breath had caught when he leaned down to kiss her goodnight, then planted his lips on her head. And that sexy little smile as he'd turned his head, knowing what he'd done to her.

Yeah. She'd come up with a perfectly logical reason for his odd actions. And if he had walked off the set of some Scottish film—Macbeth, maybe—that would explain why he was so convincing when telling his sad story. I'm a ghost from Culloden who was jilted at the altar.

But that wouldn't explain what she'd seen—a guy leaning forward at maybe a 30 degree angle, supporting himself on nothing. It wouldn't explain the rocks. And it wouldn't explain why she felt, deep in her gut, that there was a clock ticking somewhere that would determine whether or not the spirit of a little boy would be able to finally leave a gruesome battlefield.

Even if it was all bull, even if someone came to the door and said, "Ha ha, the jokes on you," she was pretty sure that clock thing wouldn't go away. She would probably never be able to explain it.

Of course, she still had her own problems to deal with. It was mean of her to keep avoiding Austin, but their problems didn't have a time limit attached to them. If Austin really wanted to marry her, to stay married to her for the rest of their lives, like he'd promised, then they'd be able to work things out once Rick was exposed for the snake he was.

But the fate of Alexander and the little boy would be determined in a day. If she was able to help, she was going to help.

Of course, other people would see that as an excuse, but she didn't care. Until time ran out, she would just have to trust that Austin would understand. Eventually. And at the moment, trust seemed to be the magic word of the day.

The singing stopped and her heart started pumping overtime. What would she see when he opened that bathroom door?

A coward to the end, she scooted back under the blanket, pulled it up to her chin, and turned her head away.

The doorknob clicked and she froze.

"Good morrow, Chelsea," he said, and chills shot through her from her feet, which were closest to him, to her ears. She glanced at the mirror and realized his reflection was looking her in the face. Wrapped only in a towel, he carried a pile of clothes in his arms. "May I have use of the bed, lass, to don my plaid?"

She sat up and sprang to her feet, averted her eyes, and hurried through the bathroom door behind him. She had to pee anyway.

When she turned the lock, she could feel the vibrations through the wood.

He was laughing at her, and what his laughter did to her insides turned all her newfound trust into a bowl of warm, melting Jell-O that couldn't even be trusted to stay on the spoon.

CHAPTER FOURTEEN

Alexander used all the knowledge he'd gleaned from the tellie to cook Austin's bride a proper Scottish breakfast. There were no mushrooms left, and he'd been unable to find any edible ones outside to replace those he'd used for *Mushrooms with Parsley Mud* the night before. He only hoped she would be thirsty, for he had plenty of juice, milk, and tea.

"You sure don't cook like an eighteenth century man," she said when she came to the table. "I kind of expected you to be roasting it all on a stick over a fire in the backyard."

She was wearing the sheet again, but her shift poked out the bottom. Another layer between them, for which he was grateful.

"I know the clothes aren't all clean, but the body is," she added cheerfully. But she must have read his discomfort on his face, for she cleared her throat and tried again. "I mean, I had a shower and washed my hair. So, you know, I won't stink or anything." She ultimately dissolved into a blushing mass of damp curls and hid her face behind her hands.

He couldn't seem to stop his hand from reaching for one of those curls and tucking it behind her ear, revealing part of that lovely face and inviting her to come out from behind her hand.

"We'll neither of us stink, then."

They shared a laugh while he put the plate of back bacon on the table. When he folded his hands together for grace, she followed suit, then peeked at him the entire time he recited the prayer.

They ate in companionable silence while he waited for her questions. He was so certain she would have some. But he was wrong. When their plates were clean, he wondered if she had forgotten all that had transpired the day before.

"I've been thinking." She stood and began clearing the table. "What if I climb up on top of the roof and, you know, fall off or something? You can catch me. Save me from breaking my neck. Do you think that would work?"

Well, she'd at least remembered his quest. But what did she think about returning to Austin? He dared not ask until his breakfast had settled in his stomach.

"Soni's a canny lass," he said. "She'd recognize a set-up in a trice, I'm fair certain of it. Besides, she likely has a plan. I must simply wait to see what that plan entails."

Chelsea nodded and bent to the task of washing the dishes. "I'm good with waiting."

A short while later, they strolled down to the glen to see about catching a fish for lunch. He used the fishing tackle he'd found in the house, added a worm to the hook, and dropped a line in the water just above a shadowy spot that ran deep and smooth.

"I was thinking." The lass perched on the flat top of a large mossy stone. "This Meredith chick sounds pretty mean. It's one thing to marry another guy, either because she liked him better or she was mad at you." She toyed with the edge of the water with her bare toe. "But to invite you to watch? That was so mean! I think you dodged a bullet."

Her gaze flew to his and she grimaced, no doubt sensing she'd said something insensitive to a man who had probably died from a bullet he hadn't dodged. But he waved away her concern. His own death didn't bother him much after all that time. Not nearly as much as the wound to his heart had, at least.

"Women are mean creatures by nature, of course." He grinned when she gave him an indignant gasp. "Men are much more forthright."

She rolled her lovely eyes. "And this is coming from a soldier? Men kill each other all the time. How can you say women are meaner than that?"

To avoid scaring away their lunch, he moved closer to the lass and lowered his voice. "To kill a man in battle is not so mean at all, to my way of thinking. There is something honest and simple about it. One man says *I will fight to the death for what I believe.* The other says *I will fight to the death to prove ye wrong.* And they fight. A promise given, a promise kept. One man survives and has proven his point. The other man proves himself with his own spilt blood. There is nothing mean about it."

"The mean part is what happens to the women who loved the ones who don't come back."

He gave her a wink. "Perhaps this is what turns them mean."

She laughed and the clouds seemed to part. And if more light did not make it through the treetops to shine on their little idyll, it made no matter. He'd drawn the laugh from her. A victory he would cherish.

"Well, if I'd been Meredith..." She found a stick and began drawing in the mud at the burn's edge. "Losing you to someone else would have made me mean, I guess."

"Auch, aye. The lass was mean, no question. She took something very precious from me."

"Your heart?"

"Nay. My right to love her. Nothing is quite so mean as to be forbidden to love." He grimaced, embarrassed by the lass's rapt attention. He had no choice but to go on. "Meredith stopped me from loving her. She smiled and walked away as if my love was as meaningless as the rain. The right—nay, the ability—to love someone is the freedom granted to all. But she deprived me that freedom. There are some things you cannot take from a man if he will not give them. But there are also things you cannot give a woman if she will not have them.

"In the beginning, yes. Meredith did take my love. But what she did with it, without trusting me, without giving me a chance to challenge whatever her sister might have said, was mean indeed." He bent and plucked up a wide pink flower. "She took my love and let it fall from her fingers, to shatter like the petals of a crushed rose as she walked away. And they fluttered in her wake and fell dead and lifeless on the ground." He did the same with the pink blossoms. "So, when they turn their backs on ye—if they know they hurt you, and they take joy in the hurting—your love dies quickly like a fish denied the ocean. A few surprised gasps, an accepting, and it's over."

A sharp clap drew their attention to the top of the ravine. Then another followed, and he realized it was the sound of car doors closing.

Chelsea paled and started to stand, but he waved her back down.

"Stay where you are. Let me see who it is."

She was already shaking, and he realized she truly was not prepared to come face to face with Saint Austin as yet.

The fishing pole was forgotten and he hurried up the path and around the house. He saw the front of the car first. Someone had pulled all the way up the drive to park at the top. It wasn't the blue vehicle of the proprietor, but a new red SUV. Since he'd heard the slam of two doors, he prepared himself to face both Austin and the dastardly one, possibly more.

But there was no one about. No one waiting on the steps. The door, however, stood wide when he remembered closing it behind them when he and Chelsea had come outside.

He hurried up the steps as quietly as he could. But it was imperative that he get his hand on the lance before he was noticed. The screen door opened silently. His weight caused no squeak of the floor. He turned and reached above his head, but the weapon was gone.

CHAPTER FIFTEEN

Chelsea heard the surprised, high pitch of a woman and jumped to her feet. Suddenly, all her nervousness about facing Austin was gone. If he'd brought Emily along for a front row seat to their confrontation, Chelsea was going to toss her out on her ear. And if that wasn't ladylike enough for Austin, she knew a big handsome Scot who would probably appreciate her combat talents!

At least he would…for another day.

It didn't matter. Alexander was there now, and with him at her back, there was no need to sit and quake in the shrubs and wait for the visitors to leave again. She could handle just about anything.

The red car was a surprise only because it was parked so close to the house. Voices, including Alexander's, came from inside.

"It looks like a giant pencil," said a woman from the kitchen, so Chelsea headed in there. Her hands were on her hips before she rounded the corner.

"Aye. A pencil. Now, if ye doona mind, I'd like my pencil back." Alexander stood with one hand outstretched.

A woman around 50 years old sat on top of the table with her legs crossed, smoking a cigarette, and talking out the other side of her mouth. "Why do ye need a giant pencil?"

Alexander let out a pent up breath. "It's nay a pencil, ye daft woman. It's a spear."

The woman snorted smoke out of her nose, then choked. Another woman who looked just like the first one came around the corner from the dining room. "You're not supposed to be smoking in here, Lorraine. Wickham will have to pay a fine if you do."

"Who's Wickham?" Chelsea demanded. She was upset because Alexander was upset. But she also thought it would be a good idea to keep up a bold front in case these two thought the rental house was theirs for the day. With only a day left before that internal clock ran out, she wasn't going to let two strangers push them around.

"You must be Chelsea," said the one on the table, her cigarette wagging. Her sister reached up and plucked the thing out of her lips, walked it over to the garbage can, lifted the lid and chucked it in.

"Who's Wickham?" she asked again, ignoring the fact that they knew her name. Alexander could have told them.

"Our brother," answered the one while she washed her fingers in the sink. Her sister, on the table, was still giving her the stink-eye. "He rented this place for Alexander, here. Soncerae is our niece. He's told you about her, hasn't he?"

"I only have one cigarette a year," said Loretta. "And since you didn't let me finish it, that one doesn't count."

Loretta rolled her eyes and waved a hand. "Ignore her."

"Aye. I told her about Soncerae. Now, may I have my pencil—I mean to say, my spear!"

The one called Lorraine shrugged and tossed it to him, which was surprising considering how heavy the branch was.

"I'm very sorry we're late," said the sister.

"Late?" Chelsea said it in unison with Alexander.

"Yes. We were supposed to be here yesterday, but we got lost."

"Yesterday?" He frowned. "Why?"

Loretta laughed. "Chaperones, of course."

Alexander smiled and nodded, but his lips were slightly pinched as he came toward her, took hold of her forearm, and led her back outside. They strolled around to the back of the SUV where he spun around to face her. "I have no ken what they are about. I ken only that a man named Muir paid for my lodging here. They said it is this same Wickham. And the name Soncerae is not a common one, aye? So they must ken the witch."

"Did you tell them my name?"

He leaned close and whispered. "I did not." He shook his head in frustration. "Ye're certain they were not members of yer wedding party? Perhaps it is a cruel jest orchestrated by that Rick fellow."

She laughed. "No. They're not Austin's family. And Rick certainly wouldn't have known about Soncerae. But it is kind of funny that Soncerae sent chaperones, right?"

One of his brows lifted. "Aye? You think so? And where do you suppose everyone will sleep this night? And how much privacy will we find to... To discuss how to get you back together with Austin?"

She was pretty sure that whatever privacy he had worried about didn't involve Austin at all, but he was too embarrassed to admit it. He was obviously still caught up on that "kissing another man's woman" idea, which only made him sweeter. But she was still in denial about belonging to anyone, no matter how their conversation had ended the night before. And if the man decided to kiss her, she was pretty sure she wasn't going to stop him.

But those women might...

“I see what you mean.” Her gaze caught on his bottom lip and couldn’t seem to move on to his eyes.

His tongue came out and swept moisture across it. “Do ye now?”

She lifted her chin without thinking, and his mouth quickly found hers. The kiss was as frantic as she felt. Crushing and desperate, like they were saying goodbye.

“Hoohoo!” The woman’s voice came from the porch. *“Alexander?”*

He closed his eyes for a few seconds, then hollered, “Aye?”

“Are ye going to bring that fish in for lunch, dear? Or do ye plan to leave it thrashing on the line?”

Chelsea frowned up at him. “How can she know there’s a fish on the line?”

He shuddered and shook his head. “I’m afeared to ask.” After squeezing her hands briefly, he walked around her and headed back to the fairy glen. She quickly followed.

“Chelsea, dear?”

The woman smiled innocently, leaning back against the open screen. “If you’d like to come back inside, we’ve got some clothes for you.”

She nodded and gave up on following Alexander. But as much as she wanted to get dressed in real clothes again, she couldn’t help suspecting that the sisters planned to take their chaperoning duties very seriously.

CHAPTER SIXTEEN

Alexander would have preferred to eat his meal out of doors, but the sisters wouldn't hear of it. They'd gone to a lot of fuss, they'd said. So the four of them sat down together. With a sister to each side of him, he waited for Chelsea to reappear. The last he'd seen her was when they'd exchanged a hurried embrace behind the SUV.

"Chelsea, dear! Are you coming?"

The lass's head appeared around the corner with a scowl on her face. The bright pink on her shoulder proved she'd found clothing. Had Austin brought it to her? Or that other bastard?

Alexander shot to his feet. "Is something the matter?" He looked over her shoulder while he reached into his sock for his skean dhu, but left it put when the lass held up a hand and shook her head.

"Nothing's wrong," she grumbled, then stepped away from the wall. She was covered from shoulder to foot in the same thick fuzzy cloth that covered the sisters. But where the other women wore blue, Chelsea was ensconced in the pink. She had rolled the sleeves up to her elbows but there was no question, the clothes had come from their unwelcome chaperones.

"A...leisure suit, is it?" He tried not to grin too broadly. It wasn't that the clothes were less than flattering—which they were—it was that Chelsea seemed so unhappy to be wearing them. Of course, he'd prefer she wear nothing but her shift, but no one would hear that thought leave his head.

The woman to his right gave him a sharp scowl. Loretta, if he remembered aright.

"Pardon?" he said to her.

She shook her head at him, then turned a smile on the lass. "The pink suits you."

When the second sister started inquiring about underwear, Alexander shot to his feet. "I must check the perimeter."

"No. You mustn't," Loretta said firmly. "Would you waste what time ye have?"

He relented and walked about the table to hold the chair for the lass. She leaned back against his hands as he reluctantly pulled them away. He had to force himself to return to his seat. But the women were watching them closely, even while they chatted about things he had no attention for. His ears were finely tuned to every word that fell from Chelsea's lips, however.

"Really? A tea shop?"

Loretta mumbled something about Edinburgh and Cockburn Street.

"I've never been a fan of tea."

That explained why she hadn't partaken of the tea he served with breakfast.

"I'm a waitress. Or at least I was a waitress, until Austin insisted that I stop working. It was a scary part of town, actually. So it was probably for the best. I don't know what I'll do when I get back." She suddenly locked eyes with him and the rest of the world slipped away.

Her expression said everything he was thinking himself. *Why can't we talk privately? When will they leave. We have no time to waste!*

Someone tapped his arm. Lorraine. She was saying something.

"Pardon?"

"I said, it's a fine fish you caught."

Chelsea looked down at the platter and frowned, then looked up at him with raised brows. "You caught this?"

"Aye," he beamed proudly.

"In that little stream?"

Her evident doubt took a bit of that pride away. "I must admit, it doesna seem likely." After all, the fish was larger than the sole of his boot.

The lass swallowed uncomfortably, and he could only imagine what she must be thinking.

"And you two are related to Soncerae?"

"Yes, dear." Loretta smiled sweetly and outright ignored what Chelsea implied.

"So," she pointed a fork at him. "You know that he's… Or he was…"

Loretta looked him over. "A ghost?" Then she nodded and turned back to her meal. "Yes, dear. We know. Our Soni can't do everything on her own, now can she? With so many to chase after?"

Lorraine shook her head and took a sip of wine that painted her red even outside the confines of her lips. "She's having a devil of a time with that MacGregor fellow. Of course, we knew she would but, well… We promised to step in and help the pair of you."

"Help us to do what?" His instincts had him wrapping his left hand around his dining knife.

The woman shrugged and wrinkled her nose at her sister. "You know, just…help."

Something wasn't right about the women, but he couldn't say why. Of course, they would have to be witches. After all, they were Muirs, and twins to boot. But there was something else at play that he didn't understand. Were they there to make certain Chelsea went back to Austin? That she didn't throw her future happiness away for a brief triste with a man who would only be mortal for a few hours more?

Loretta laid her hand over his and gave it a little squeeze. The look in her eye was all pity. So, she'd read his thoughts? And she was telling him what? That his suspicions were correct?

He was affronted by the idea, truly. What kind of man would he be to allow the lass to be deprived for the rest of her life due to his selfishness? And yet, each time he succumbed to the temptation to kiss her, he was luring her heart away from her true course.

He studied her while she listened to the older women. She was a kind lass to be sure. Quick to apologize when she'd said something insensitive. Quick to return his attentions, but also quick to excuse Austin-who-walks-on-water of all blame in the matter. But what kind of man would allow this lass to slip out of his grasp in the first place?

A fool, obviously.

And what kind of man was Alexander Fraser, to spend the day trying to woo another man's woman when he would not be around a day from now to see to her care?

Begrudgingly, it seemed that he and Austin had much in common.

CHAPTER SEVENTEEN

Alexander checked the perimeter again.

Still solid. Still unforgiving. His destiny was still contained within its limits. He'd done all he could do. There was nothing left but the waiting. But it was cruel indeed to leave him wondering what he was waiting for.

He let his mind wander back to the moor and wee Rabby. What would the lad be thinking? Or would he be lying in his grave again, next to the dog, waiting for Soni to rouse him again? Alexander could only hope.

And the others? What were they making of Soni's bargain? Would they be plotting for ways to resist her? Or would they be drawing lots and deciding who would be next.

No matter. Wee Rabby would be next and there was none that would challenge it. What happened after was none of his concern. He wouldn't be present to see it.

All those years on the moor, he'd kept his imagination at bay, refusing to wonder what waited for him in the next life, afraid he would never have the chance to see for himself what God had in store. But since Soni built her great bonfire and summoned the strange ring of green light to protect her—from demons, no doubt—Alexander had allowed himself to finally wonder. To hope. To want.

Only what he wanted had naught to do with the afterlife.

Heaven help him.

One of the sisters caught Chelsea peeking out the bedroom window, watching Alexander stomping around the fairy glen.

"He's a lovely thing to watch, isn't he?"

Chelsea laughed. "Yes. He is. I can't…help it."

The woman patted her on the velour-covered shoulder. "I'm so sorry, dear. If we'd have come yesterday, maybe the two of you wouldn't have become so attached."

She turned and shrugged the hand away. She didn't want anyone's comfort. She just wanted more time. And she was feeling a little angry with the guy in the glen. It was like he was wasting time on purpose.

The woman's smile was full of pity. "I'm sure it's the right thing to do, to stay away from each other. After all, if you get to liking each other too much, you'll suffer all the more when he is taken away." Her patronizing smile dropped from her face when she took a good look at Chelsea. She patted the towel she had hanging over her arm. "I believe I'll take a shower." Then she hurried into the bathroom.

Stay away from each other? Who the hell were they to tell two adult strangers what to do? And for that matter, how dare Alexander avoid her? She was the one he needed to save, wasn't she? His damsel in distress? He should stay close to her or he might screw up and miss his chance! Then where would he be?

The bathroom door opened abruptly. "Uh oh," the woman said and hurried to the door to press her ear against it. Chelsea had just decided the twins needed psychiatric help when she heard a commotion from the living room.

"Get out of my way, woman!" It was Alexander's booming voice. She would know it anywhere.

Lorraine stepped back from the door just before it flew open and she cowered at the sight of an enraged Highlander in all his glory. He glowered at her, then looked for Chelsea and pinned her to the spot. "Dinna move, lass."

She nodded quickly and wrapped her arms around herself to keep from shivering to death. But inside, she was jumping up and down, cheering him on.

"You." He glared at Lorraine again. "Gather your sister and your groceries and leave this place. I dinna care if God Himself sent ye. Ye have no place here."

The woman swallowed and nodded. Then beamed at them both as she scooted around him and out the door. She didn't act like her feelings were hurt. In fact, she looked a little pleased.

While the sisters shuffled around in the next room, Chelsea stared into Alexander's eyes and waited. She still hadn't moved and hoped she would get credit for that. His gaze dropped to her mouth, then up to her eyes again and a fresh wave of shivers crashed through her. The pink velour wasn't doing anything to stop them.

"You can keep the clothes, dear!" one of the sisters called out. "And Alexander? Be sure to tell Soni that we did what she asked."

His brow furrowed, and finally, their curiosity got the better of them and together they stepped back into the living room. Alexander wrapped his hand around her wrist and held on tight, like he was afraid she might be taken from him if he wasn't careful.

"Just what is it the lass asked of ye?"

Lorraine pushed the screen open and stepped out, then turned back with a grin. "Let's just say that, with particularly stubborn people, if you need to get them moving in a certain direction, you have to tell them they can't go that way."

Her sister wasn't nearly as amused and stepped close to Alexander while Lorraine held the door. "Please, son. Don't be too hard on our Soncerae. She agreed to the rules and must stick by them."

"Dinna worry o'er it, madam. I will always bless the ground she walks upon."

Loretta reached up and patted his cheek, then left smiling, nearly as pleased as her sister.

She was so afraid she'd jinx things, Chelsea didn't dare move until she was sure the car was gone. It was torture watching through the screen while the sister behind the wheel backed the SUV down the drive at about a foot a minute. And it was a long drive!

When she couldn't hear the engine anymore, she jumped in the air like the Patriots had just won the Super Bowl again. But she stopped jumping as soon as she saw the look on Alexander's face. A million years of instincts told her to run. A couple dozen years of being an American told her to stand her ground. She couldn't seem to suppress either and ended up backing slowly away from him.

He took a step for every one of hers, but since his stride was a lot longer, he'd closed the distance between them just as she reached the wall. He captured her hands and pressed his mouth to hers in a demanding kiss that she needed as badly as he did. Then he released one hand and pulled her along behind him into the bedroom where he pressed her up against another wall and kicked the door shut.

He watched her closely, waiting for her to protest, but she didn't. She was still in the mood to celebrate the fact that they were alone again, and that Alexander was done wasting time.

He lowered his head and kissed her collar bone, and she giggled.

"Thank you for saving us from those women—"

His hand clamped over her mouth. "There will be no talk of savin', aye?" He looked up at the ceiling like he was looking for cameras, for anything that might prove someone was listening in.

She nodded.

He slowly removed his hand but let his fingers drag across her lips just before he kissed her again, inhaling like he was trying to pull her into his lungs. It was intoxicating, being wanted that badly. Austin had never wanted her that badly.

"Just so you know," she said, between kisses. "I'm not going back to Austin."

His lips pressed against her collar bone again and held there for a long moment. He then pressed his head to her shoulder and every cell in her body started to vibrate to the frequency of his laughter. But it wasn't a celebratory laughter at all. He was laughing at her.

Hurt, she tried to push him away from her, but he put his hands on her hips and pulled her closer.

"Nay, lass." He still chuckled. "Forgive me... It's just that, I've only just banished the two things keeping us apart, and now, minutes away from claiming ye as my own—or so it seemed—ye've landed on the one thing that could cut through this lovely haze and speak to my sense of reason."

"Reason!"

"Aye." He took her arms, one at a time, and encouraged them to wrap over his shoulders and around his neck. "The reason we're here in the first place. The reason I must not claim what cannot be mine in truth."

She knew it was a risky thing to say, but she said it anyway. "My heart can be yours."

He smiled sadly into her eyes and held up his finger and thumb with about an inch between them. "A small corner, perhaps."

She forced his fingers farther apart and nodded.

He laughed and swatted her on the butt. "Come, Chelsea. Let us go see how small are the non-enchanted inhabitants of the burn, aye?"

"So you think those twins were witches too?"

"Nay, my lass. For the rest of our time together, I choose not to think of them at all."

CHAPTER EIGHTEEN

So. This is my noble deed.

Alexander laughed down at the lass while she spoke to a wee frog she held captive on the knee of her peculiar pink suit. No matter what she wore, she was the most endearing lass he'd known in his life. And he'd seen thousands upon thousands of them cross the moor. Some even came back regularly, like Soni did. But none so charming as Chelsea.

And giving her up, sending her back to the man who would treat her well and care for her, would require heroic effort indeed.

Though he still kept his spear near and his blade in his sock, he no longer worried about Austin's self-appointed henchman. The man had made no trouble that day, and Alexander surmised that the photographs he'd taken to sully Chelsea's good name were enough to soothe his need for vengeance. He also believed that if Austin was worth his salt, he wouldn't question the lass when she explained what truly happened here.

Hopefully, she would see the wisdom in leaving out a few details.

When Chelsea placed the wee frog into his hand for safekeeping and ran back up to the cottage to fetch some things, he took the opportunity to attempt contact with Soncerae.

"Soni, ye wee thing," he called out to the glen as a whole. "If ye can hear my voice, heed me. I will not send the lass back until the morrow, when my days are done, aye? Not until the morrow. I beg ye."

A slight breeze wove through the leaves high above his head and on that breeze, he heard the laughter of a dear and familiar voice.

Laughter. It was a fine answer. And he was finally able to take a deep breath into his belly and release the tension he'd been holding there all afternoon.

Tomorrow. He had until tomorrow.

The lass returned with a large glass jar and into its depths she placed the wee frog. She was pleased he hadn't allowed it to get away. He didn't tell her how tempted he'd been to use it as bait. It might have broken her heart. And he preferred to end as a fond memory for her.

The creature struggled to find its way out. And with her tapping on the glass and offering soothing reassurance, the frog only panicked more. All at once, Chelsea burst into tears and apologized a dozen times—to the creature—while she took the glass to the water and freed it.

He set his pole aside and joined her. "What is it, lass?"

She straightened and smiled through a sheen of tears. "It was the glass. An invisible barrier to him, right? I just felt so awful for scaring him like that." Her eyes began to leak again despite her brave smile.

He chuckled and pulled her against him. “Wheesht, now. I’m no frog, aye? And this is no bottle to imprison me forever. It was a means to bring ye to me, to keep the pair of us together so… So both our hearts could mend, I think.”

She nodded against him.

“The gloaming comes. Let us go inside and talk of cheerful things, aye?”

He cut his bait, gathered the tackle, and put it all back where he’d found it while the lass put the kettle on. They settled in front of the fire and he tried to teach her how to appreciate tea.

Rain pattered gently on the roof and she wondered how the traumatized frog was fairing. When the topic of frogs and what might make them happy ran its course, their conversation became a complicated maze.

Any talk of his village invariably turned to Meredith. Talk of her own life included too many stories that involved Austin. She grew instantly sad at the mention of Culloden, likely for the reminder that he’d died there, and that he hadn’t been flesh and blood until he’d been sent to the cottage.

The only safe discussions were general in nature. She seemed to appreciate his country. He could appreciate American cinema.

The fire burned low and reminded them that time was running short. But no matter how desperately he wanted to take her into his arms and hold her until dawn, counting every last heartbeat between them, he would not.

He went to the hearth and picked up a thick log.

She put a hand out. “Don’t,” she said. “No more.”

But he didn’t think she referred to the wood, or the conversation. He was fairly certain she was wanting an end to the torture.

He dropped the log back on the pile and spread the coals so they could die in peace. A pair of glass doors, closed over the opening, finished the job. And they were suddenly facing each other in the darkness. He groped behind him for the box of matches and breathed carefully as she stepped toward him.

"Pleasant dreams, lass. Take the matches to light yer candle, aye? And I'll see you on the morrow."

He reached for her hand, to place the matches in her care. But the lass took hold of his hand and headed toward the bedchamber with him in tow. Her speed denied him of the chance to set his feet and resist. When they were inside, she tried to close the door, but he blocked it with his body.

"Nay, Chelsea. I must sleep on the couch. You must bide the night alone." He flipped up the light switch and hoped the harsh glare of the lightbulbs would help her see reason.

She blinked, rolled her eyes, then went to the night stand to light the candle. After the fire caught, she waved the match out and gestured toward the bed.

Heaven help him, his heart tripped in his chest and bid him stay. But he could not.

"Just because you're in here doesn't mean we have to *do it*," she gestured again. "And I'm not going to waste our last hours together with a stupid wall between us. I mean," she shrugged, "what if I think of something important I need to say? And I'll forget it by morning? Huh? What then?"

She shook her head and pulled down the blankets.

"Nope. You're staying in here, or I'm going out there with you. But my way, we both get to be comfortable."

"Dinna bet money on that," he muttered to himself.

She snorted, then went into the restroom. "You better be there when I come out."

It was a tricky promise to make, so he said nothing. By the time she emerged, however, he'd created a lovely pallet on the floor next to the bed, and he lay on his back with his hands behind his head, grinning like a cat.

She grinned back, not nearly as disappointed as he expected her to be. And he sobered a bit himself when he realized she was wearing nothing but her shift.

"Okay," she said, and jumped onto the bed. Then she hung her head over the side. "If your back hurts in the morning, don't blame me."

"If my back hurts in the morning, lass, it willna be hurting for long, will it?"

Her head disappeared and he realized at once that his quip had been insensitive. He quickly sat up and leaned close.

"Forgive me, Chelsea. My lass, please. Had I taken a moment to consider—"

She cut off his apology with a kiss. Her hand wended its way around his neck and pulled him close. He was nigh crawling onto the mattress before he was aware enough to stop himself.

"Goodnight, Alexander," she whispered against his lips, then put only the slightest effort into pushing him away.

"Godspeed," he whispered back, then sank back down onto his pallet. And no matter how difficult it would be to stay on that pallet through the night, he was grateful she'd forced him to join her in the room. For that last kiss... He wouldn't have missed it for the world.

CHAPTER NINETEEN

In the darkest hour of the night, the candle sputtered and died. Chelsea could tell by his breathing that he hadn't slept any more than she had. But at least the dark didn't bother her at all, knowing he was close.

"Chelsea?"

His voice jumpstarted her heart.

"I'm here," she said.

"That's fine, then. I thought you might be awake, and I simply wanted to hear your voice."

"Oh. Okay. Um, do you want to know what I'm thinking?"

"Absolutely not."

And together, they laughed themselves silly.

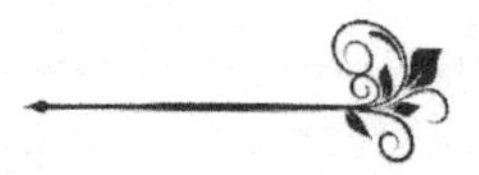

By morning, he was curled around her in the middle of the bed like a fox protecting its young. She only wished they could have stayed that way all day. But at least, if she held really still, it could last a little longer.

Of course, there was no chance she'd fall back to sleep, knowing that witch would be coming to get him soon. That was, if she wasn't really just imagining this all while she languished in a coma in a Scottish hospital.

Maybe she'd been struck by a car while running down the road in her wedding gown...

"Ye've a wondrous gift for snoring," Alexander murmured in her ear, and the vibrations of his deep, rich voice were too delicious to be imagined.

She gasped and scooted around to face him. "Take it back."

"I take it back." Then he winked.

She laughed and the delightful sound was as charming as the tinkling of bells—until she stopped her laughing and the ringing continued. Someone was at the door!

It took a handful of minutes before they were both dressed and presentable. It was hard to zip up her jump suit or help Alexander get his broach pinned when her hands were shaking so hard.

"Is this it? Is Soni here to take you away?"

He shook his head and gave her hand a squeeze. "Nay, lass. My sweet lass. If Soni was within a hundred meters of the place I would ken."

Only slightly relieved, she ducked into the kitchen and he went to see who was then beating on the door.

She stood with her back against the wall, straining to hear, and held her breath when Alexander pulled the door open.

"I have to talk to her." It was Rick. She'd almost hoped it was Austin. What was wrong with the man if he couldn't come after her himself?

"No." Alexander started to close the door, but it jammed, probably on Rick's foot.

"It's an emergency," Rick said. And even though she knew it was just his usual ploy, she decided to talk to him.

Alexander gave her a warning look, then stepped back and let her stand beside him. She noticed his right hand raise and wrap around his giant pencil. But he just let his arm hang there, like he was leaning on the door jamb.

Rick narrowed his eyes at her for a second and she smiled back, knowing that if the guy made the wrong move, Alexander would skewer him. Two feet away from her mortal enemy and she couldn't have felt safer.

"I won't believe a word you say, but say it anyway." She crossed her arms and waited.

"Austin has gone to the police," he said. "He's convinced you're being held against your will somewhere and that the text you sent wasn't from you. He's getting them to trace your phone. Where is it?" He tried to look past them into the house.

"That's bull," she said. "He wouldn't think that unless you said it. If he saw the pictures—"

"There were no pictures. At least, when I got back to the castle, they weren't there anymore. The video, everything, erased."

She shrugged. "Well, let him come. I'm not afraid to talk to him or anyone else. And this is Scotland, Rick. They won't surround the place and start shooting."

Rick growled. "Don't be stupid, *Cheese*. I can't believe you're still here in the first place. But if you go now, you can spare him some humiliation. Get in the car and I'll take you to the... What are you wearing?"

"Go away, Rick. I wouldn't get into a car with you if you were the last ride out of town and the volcano had erupted."

She nodded to Alexander and stepped back so he could close the door. But Rick rushed between them into the house. A split second later, he was lying on his back with the giant pencil poised above his throat. The sharp tip was pushed a good inch into his skin. He gasped like the wind had been knocked out of him.

Alexander really could protect her against anything. Maybe he really had come there to be her hero. But did that mean he was going to be taken away now?

Gravel crunched outside. The screen door was still propped open and she had a clear view of Austin getting out of a rental car and hustling up the drive. Her heart tripped at the sight of him. It wasn't exactly love that tripped it—more like the memory of love. It seemed like they hadn't seen each other for a month.

In jeans and a t-shirt, she nearly forgot they were in Scotland. It was just another day in her life with Austin stopping by after work.

She shook her head to clear the tainted image. But it was still Austin who walked through the door. And she felt her world crack down the center, like glass under pressure. There was no telling if it was going to hold, or where the pieces would fall if it failed.

"Hi, sweetheart," he said, but held up a hand like some signal guard. "We'll talk in a minute, okay? But right now, I have to deal with him." He gestured to Alexander and the idiot on the floor.

"His name is Alexander," she said firmly.

Austin shook his head. "Not him. *Him.*" He pointed to Rick, then put his hands on his knees and leaned over him. "Comfortable, Rick?" He glanced up at Alexander. "Can you keep him there?"

The big man nodded. "Aye."

"Good." Austin had a nasty grin on his face that Chelsea had never seen before. "Look what the staff delivered to me this morning, buddy!" He held up a small silver device. "Recognize this?"

"No," Rick whispered.

"Well, you should. You're always carrying it around with you, leaving it on restaurant tables. Remember now?"

Rick said nothing.

"Maybe this will jog your memory." Austin bit his bottom lip, sneered, and pressed a button. His own voice sounded in the room. *"Marrying her would have cost me a whole lot more than moving the wedding party to Scotland."*

"Yeah, but it would have been worth it."

"You think?"

Austin turned off the recorder. "Is that what you played for her, buddy, when you went to check on her one last time?" He straightened and faced her. "I can't expect you to forgive me, Chelsea, for letting this snake get between us."

"I like to call him The Worm. Weasel works too."

"He cut off the part where I said I could either marry Erica and be powerful, or marry you and be happy for the rest of my life. What idiot chooses power over happiness?"

She smiled. "That's just what I thought you would say. Just what I needed to hear. So I told that kid to ask you to come talk to me. I knew if you did, I would be fine."

"But I let Rick go instead." He shook his head. "I was so worried about what it would look like, if I walked out, that I jumped at his offer. I should have suspected something when it took him a good ten minutes to come back and say that you'd run off."

It sounded good. It always sounded good when Austin talked. He was just so...perfect.

"Look, sweetheart. I'm not making you do anything you don't want to do. I'm just letting you know," he pointed at Rick without looking at him, "that this scum is out of my life for good. There's plenty of room now, and I'm saving all the seats for you."

He then frowned and turned to face Alexander. "I think you can let him up now."

Alexander narrowed his eyes and studied Austin for a minute, then nodded and stepped back, taking his weapon with him.

Rick rolled onto his knees, then stood, holding one hand against his bloody neck. "You're going to jail," he told the Scot.

Austin stepped up into his face. "And when I asked you to call the airline, you said she'd already flown home."

He bent his arm and gave an uppercut to Rick's jaw with his very solid elbow. The guy went flying backward and landed on the floor in front of the couch, then he curled into a ball and screamed while holding his chin.

Austin turned to Alexander and held his hand out. The Scot moved his weapon to his left hand and shook Austin's. But Austin pulled him off balance with a jerk and planted a left hook into the side of Alexander's face.

"That's for falling in love with my fiancée. Don't bother denying it."

The Scot narrowed his eyes, picked Austin up, and rushed toward the hearth.

"Don't!" she shouted.

Alexander skidded to a stop and dropped Austin's butt onto the bricks, but the way her fiancé grunted when he bounced, she thought the Scot had probably given gravity a little help. When he turned to her, he wasn't happy.

She shrugged. "He might have hit his head on the fireplace."

Alexander nodded sharply. "That was my plan."

She laughed, knowing he must have been joking. At least, she was hoping he'd been joking. "What now?"

Austin got to his feet and stretched his back. "Now, you choose."

CHAPTER TWENTY

Austin gave her a sad little smile, then walked to the couch and pulled Rick to his feet. The guy was still moaning. "I'm going to take this garbage into town, and then I'm returning to the castle. If you don't come by sundown, I'll know you didn't choose me." He stopped in front of her, dug keys out of his pocket, and handed them to her. "Here. You can have the rental at the bottom of the hill. I'll take Rick in the one he parked on the street." He paused for a second or two, then sighed. "Believe me when I say I still want you as much—no, more—than I did a few days ago when I was standing in that chapel. And if you want, we can start over, see what the world looks like without Rick in the picture."

She bit her lip and nodded, but resisted the urge to reach out and touch him. She didn't want to hurt him any more than she already had, and a gentle touch would give him hope.

He gave her a wink and forced himself to smile, then turned and dragged Rick out the door. She turned back to Alexander and nearly jumped out of her skin when she found they were not alone.

A young woman in a long black robe stood next to Alexander with her arm wrapped around his waist. Obviously caught in the middle of a hug, the girl stepped back and let go of him.

"You're Soni," Chelsea said, but she hadn't meant to sound quite so snotty.

"And ye're Chelsea."

She had to admire the way the girl didn't sneer at the way she was dressed. It was obviously taking effort to keep her gaze from dropping to the pink monstrosity.

Finally, the girl giggled and pointed to the old-lady sneakers on Chelsea's feet. "I must apologize for my aunties. I told them to bring you clothes. I didn't mean for them to bring you *their* clothes.

Chelsea would have laughed along but it was sinking in—she was standing in front of a real witch, a girl who had known she was stuck in a cottage with only a wedding dress and a sheet.

And Alexander really had been a ghost since 1746. She thought she'd already come to terms with it, but apparently, she hadn't.

Alexander moved fast, got behind her, and caught her before she realized she was collapsing.

"There, ye see?" he said. "I finally caught ye before ye fell."

Yes. He'd caught her, and he felt very solid at her back. There was no way this guy was just going to disappear.

"'Tis time," said Soni.

Chelsea wished she didn't know what she was talking about. Alexander scooped her into his arms and carried her to the couch. For the span of a couple of heartbeats, he squeezed her tight while she held on to his neck for dear life.

"What if we never let go?" she whispered.

He pulled her shoulders close and kissed her on the forehead, then lowered her to the couch and stepped back.

She shook her head and tried to inhale the tears building up behind her eyes. "You lied, you know."

He grimaced and nodded.

"You said you wouldn't harm me, and you did. You're hurting me now. So if you mean to keep your promise, you have to stay."

"Nay, lass. Ye ken I canna be kind to ye now, for the kindness itself would be the meanest act of all. I'll put yer things in the car, and ye must go. Every breath ye take worries at the strings of my heart and I cannot endure much more of it. Go," he repeated. "And smile as you do, so I can know that a bonny lass will live happily ever after."

"And you'll go too?"

"Aye. I must."

"Then I will never come to Scotland again."

He tipped his head back and she watched his neck move while he swallowed once. Then twice. "Nothing for you here, lass." It ended as a whisper and he hurried into the bedroom.

Soni sat quietly on the hearth and stared out the open doorway while Chelsea counted the teardrops alternating down her cheeks. She lost track of the number before Alexander strode through the room with a wedding gown under one arm and his hands gripping her fancy shoes and her purse.

She stood and somehow made it to the door. He met her at the top of the steps.

She smiled like he'd asked. "Alright, then. I'm going," she whispered.

He whispered back, "And I was never here to begin with."

She let the tears flow as she made her way down the drive since no one could see her face. The footing was slippery due to the rains that had fallen all night. She wondered where she'd be the next time it rained...

Once she was in the car, she was careful not to look up the hill again. It took a second to figure out the controls. She hadn't driven on the wrong side of the road yet, let alone the wrong side of the car. She had worried that she would need to be left handed in order to pull it off well, but thankfully, not all the controls were reversed.

Thank goodness she only needed to go a couple of miles to the castle.

CHAPTER TWENTY-ONE

Alexander closed his eyes to keep Chelsea's retreat from being branded into his mind for eternity. Then he tipped back his head and prayed Soni would spare him.

"Take me now, Soni. Take me back to young Rabby. Spare the pair of us from another moment of this."

Chelsea's engine turned, but the hum of it was quickly silenced. The ground fell away beneath him and returned just as quickly as it had gone. He opened his eyes and found himself standing on Culloden moor, on the footpath near a vivid expanse of pink heather. The color immediately brought to mind a certain questionable jogging suit...

Soncerae stood next to him. "What will ye say to Rabby?"

"What would ye do with the laddie? Surely you'd not have his heart broken as ye've done to me."

"Nay, Alexander. And yer heart might not have been broken when all was said and done. But ye gave up yer boon to speak with Rabby again, remember?"

"Ye mean to tell me, Chelsea would have otherwise been my boon?"

She wagged her head neither one way nor the other. "Might have. For I might have been able to leave ye with her, had her love been strong enough. And had ye not forced that promise from me before ye left the moor." She winced. "Auch, I shouldn't have told you. No good will come of it, only to make ye sadder. Forgive me?"

He heaved a heavy breath in and out again, then shook his head. "Nothing to forgive, Soni. She truly did belong with Austin. She'll be happiest going back and claiming his heart. He seems a fine man."

The lass rolled her eyes. "Generous to the end."

A sudden thought twisted one of his cheeks with a sly smile. "Aye. Generous. Only the man won't think so when his bride thinks of me from time to time. And she will."

He looked about the moor for a moment, remembering the desire to see it in the full light of day while he still had human eyes to see it with. The mosses were bright and green. The turf around the clan stones was rich emerald. The stones of the cairn had been freshly washed with the night's rain, and the air filled his lungs with memories.

Rabby sat in his usual place petting the hide off Dauphin, but his attention caught on Soni and he hurried forward without hesitation. The rest, milling about in their pale forms, seemed not to notice they'd returned.

Soni tugged on his sleeve. "We've only a moment or two, lads. Say yer piece."

"Sir! Ye've come back after all! I told the others ye would. And I've told Dauphin a hundred times—"

Alexander turned to Soni and gave her a sober look. "I asked what ye had in store for the lad..."

"Everyone gets their chance to be a hero, each in his own way, aye? And only happiness awaits this laddie on the other side of tomorrow, I swear it." She grinned at the boy. "But ye dinna wish to hear it from me, do ye Rabby?"

The boy ducked sheepishly, then peeked up at Alexander. "Is it true, then, sir? Ye were able to prove yerself?"

He nodded firmly, only that moment coming to realize that it was true. If he'd have tried to keep the lass to himself, he'd have been a most selfish scoundrel and unworthy of her. But his heart wouldn't see reason and twisted in his chest to punish him for his surrender.

"Aye, laddie. I proved myself, and I've spent my boon. Now I'm away to better things, aye? So if ye're a canny lad, ye'll do as Soncerae suggests. She loves ye like her own. As do I. We'd not lead ye astray."

Misty ghosts of tears swirled in the corners of the lad's eyes and trickled down his cheeks. He turned to Soni. "I'll be happy to go now, miss. If I need not wait until dark, and your strange fire."

Soni nodded. "Ye go say yer good-byes to the lads, then, and I'll be right along. I need to finish with Fraser first, aye?"

Rabby threw his arms around Alexander's middle and to their mutual surprise, the lad was as solid as could be. Alexander felt the embrace all the way to his bones, and it gave him a peaceful satisfaction he'd never expected.

"Thank ye, sir, for watching over me all this while. It has been strange indeed to spend a day away from ye. I can only imagine—"

"Nay, laddie. I'll see ye on the other side. Ye just do what ye can to prove yerself so I willna be waiting long, aye?"

"Aye, sir."

Soni waved the lad away toward the clan stones and after a quick wave of his own, he hurried away.

"Thank ye, lass."

"A boon well-spent, I'd say."

"Aye."

Soni stepped forward and gave him a heartfelt embrace as well. It made him feel as if he were king for a day.

"Do you know the problem I have with a man like you, Alexander Fraser?"

"Nay, lass. Tell me."

"You do nothing but earn boons, aye? Ye never cash them in."

"Pardon?"

"Ye do a noble deed, looking out for Rabby all these years, for example. Ye help mend a lass's heart and remove a nasty thorn from her life, aye?"

"Aye."

"And instead of accepting a boon for such noble deeds, ye earn yet another boon for sacrificing more just to see a wee lad's mind set at ease, when ye ken full well I would have done right by him. Do ye see?"

He tilted his head, not daring to misunderstand. "What is yer point, Soni?"

She sighed. "Only that ye make it difficult to do my work here. I've only so many boons to offer, truth be told. And I find I have an extra one in my pocket, as it were. For apparently, the boon ye requested, to come back and speak with the laddie, cost ye no boon at all."

He took the muddled lass's head in his hands and forced her to look him in the eye.

"Boons in yer pocket? Discard the balderdash, Soni, and say what ye mean to say."

"I was stalling for time."

"Why? Must we wait until night to finish it?"

She shook her head and his hands fell away. She lifted an arm and pointed to the car park. "It's a full eight miles from here to the cottage. Ten to Castle Murray."

Still not understanding what distance had to do with the death he was about to experience, he followed her gesture. A red SUV pulled into a stall and stopped. Two vaguely familiar, but still unwelcome faces grinned his way. He said a quick prayer for patience and was just turning away when the back door of the vehicle opened and a pair of shocking pink legs appeared.

"My favorite shade of pink," he murmured.

"What's that?" Soni mocked. "Ye make no sense, Alexander. Get to the point."

He spared her a glance over his shoulder as he started toward the car park. "The point is I love ye dearly, ye soft-hearted witch!"

He didn't slow until he was within three meters of her. She finally slowed as well, but it was too late and they slammed into one another. It nearly took his breath away. He jumped back and looked her over, sure he'd broken something.

She only laughed.

His mind scrambled for the perfect thing to say, but he couldn't wait for inspiration. So he said the first thing that appeared on his tongue. "Chelsea, lass. How do ye feel?"

"Seriously?" She laughed again.

"What I mean is, do ye still feel as if ye belong to a certain someone?"

Her eyes widened. "Oh, I get it. You want to know if I'm still spoken for."

He frowned. "Aye. I wasn't there to see which way you turned."

She nodded. "Well, I headed back to the castle."

He held his expression and waited.

"I mean, I had to get my suitcase and get out of this get up, right?"

He nodded slightly, still waiting.

"But there was this red SUV parked sideways in the road. Apparently their "job" was to keep me from going back to Austin." She picked at her pink jacket. "They wouldn't even let me go back for my clothes."

He cocked a brow. “And a good thing too. Another minute or two and I might have been gone.”

All the teasing was replaced by horror and she clutched at his arms. “Really? I’m so sorry.”

He shook his head and pulled her closer. “A jest, my love. Apparently I had another boon I hadn’t cashed as yet.”

“The sisters…” She pointed to the car. “They said… Well, you are still here, and you don’t *feel* like a ghost…”

“I’m nay a ghost lass.”

“So the boon is?”

“The boon I choose is ye.” He sealed his pledge with the most sincere kiss he could muster, and yet she laughed. He gave her a frown for good measure.

“It’s a good thing I choose you, then, isn’t it?”

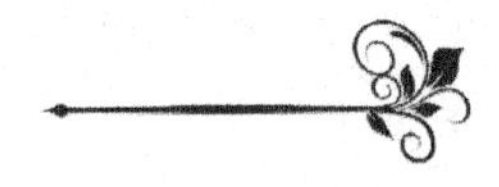

When Chelsea married him a few days later, surrounded by Muirs who honestly made them both nervous, it was in the small ancient chapel of his childhood village. There was no roof left of the church itself. The walls had worn down to half their original height, but the flowers blooming where the pews had once been made for a pretty picture.

The bride insisted that the location would give him closure. And while they stood there and waited for permission to kiss again, he decided that all he truly needed in his life was for the woman holding his hands to be content holding them.

For she was a boon he would never, ever surrender.

THE END

RABBY

CHAPTER ONE

It wasn't easy to rouse the soldiers from their deathbeds in the middle of the day. And an oddly bright day it was. But Miss Soncerae had instructed Rabby to go say his good-byes, and after knowing the men for two hundred sixty-nine years and two months, he couldn't simply leave without a *fare thee well*, could he?

He neared Number 32, Leif Lindsay, with dread in his heart, for it was Leif who sometimes awoke with half his face missing if he didn't take the time to right himself before moving about. Cor, but it was a frightening sight to look at a man and see what lay behind him at the same time, ghost or no.

The man lay on his back near the right end of the Jacobite line, where he'd served in Forfarshire's Regiment. A black and red corner of his Rob Roy plaid waved in the wind—though it was a windless day. He blinked up at the sky with just the one eye, but quickly righted himself and rose to his feet as he sensed Rabby approach. In the end, Rabby'd had no need to avert his gaze.

"Sir?"

"Aye, Rabby?"

"Dauphin and I are away, then. Miss Soni's come to call us on to some brave deed."

"Auch, aye?" The man frowned and his gaze lifted in the direction of the car park, then returned. "Look at ye then, so important and grown up ye're needed before the rest of us?" He chucked Rabby under the chin and gave him a wink. "Weel, get on with yer high and mighty self, then. Canna keep the lass waitin'. And when ye come face to face with that prince, ye give him one poke in the eye and a second in the snout. One for ye, and the other for Dauphin."

Rabby laughed along with him. "I will that, sir. And Godspeed to ye as well."

Leif nodded, patted Dauphin on the shoulder. He looked off, unseeing, into the distance, fading as he did so. "I'm content to wait until I'm called..." He was gone before he finished.

It sunk in then. This was the last he would see of Culloden's 79. And Leif Lindsay's imagined breeze sent a chill through him.

High time I moved on, he told himself. Besides, it wasn't the same now, with Fraser gone.

He picked his way toward the next man having a lie-in, as many seemed to be doing that morning. To a man, the rest were pleasant. Each one had a kind word to say when he told them Soni was there to fetch him and the dog away. But the sun, shining through their dimmed side of existence, cut their conversations short and sent many a man back to his muddy bed.

Others wandered off in the direction of their thoughts or made straight for Cameron, Number 7. After bidding Rabby farewell, the tall man was warming up to the sound of his own voice. And once Cameron started speaking, he could never seem to stop until he'd told a great long tale. One yarn would lead to another, and then another. And so it would go until he got round to recounting the days leading up to the battle of Drumossie Moor, as their resting place used to be called.

This was the part the other spirits enjoyed because, more often than not, in Cameron's telling, the war ended differently. Indeed, the truth was a stranger to Cameron most days, and it would be a foul-weathered evening or an evil moon that would dampen the tall one's humor and lure from his mouth the true version of that April morning.

But with the sun shining brightly, the men were guaranteed a lively account that would no doubt end with the Scottish army driving the Government troops south until every last one of them lost his footing and tipped off the white cliffs at Dover.

Rabby reckoned by the time Cameron's voice grew strong, he'd have at least seventy of Culloden's 79 gathered close, in spite of Miss Soni standing in their midst.

Odd, that.

Usually, when Soni neared the moor, every man was on his feet and alert, uncaring about weather, sunshine or no. Cameron himself would be shutting his gob and making note of where he'd left off, to take up his story again after the lass had gone.

But perhaps, Rabby reasoned, the witch had come only for him that day and the others were not invited to witness his going.

It made him feel a wee special. But he was also disappointed the rest wouldn't be gathered around the bright bonfire, watching him step forward and volunteer. They'd not witness his brave face before he would be whisked away in dramatic fashion, as the others had been.

Rabby took a deep breath and let it go. It was enough that he would never again wake to see Leif's missing face, never need to put forth a brave air for Fraser, even though he was greeting inside. He'd never again feel the weight of Kennedy's secret on his mind, or the secrets of others...

On the morning after the battle, Rabby had been the first to hail many of them when they'd risen, and some hadn't been able to hide those secrets quickly enough from him. But he'd kept his lips tight and carried those confidences about like the satchel at his back. The responsibility had been heavy at times, and he would be glad to be rid of it.

All those years, he'd reckoned it was that special duty that kept him there, on the moor. Keeping skeletons from escaping the cupboard—so to speak. But since Summer Solstice, the men had been in agreement that it was the thirst for revenge that had bound them together.

He'd nodded along, of course, loathe to lead any ghost into believing he didn't belong. But in truth, he didn't blame the prince. For he knew, good and well, the fault for his death on that battlefield…lay at his own feet.

Now that he had it from Fraser's mouth, that there was nothing to fear by taking up Soni's offer, he was anxious to get going. Although she'd promised he would not be facing a test, she would be sending him on an adventure nonetheless. If he truly did prove himself the heroic sort and win himself a boon, he hoped he'd be offered something much more gratifying than a meeting with the prince.

In fact, he wanted nothing more than what every ten year old boy wanted. Only, after waiting all those years, he was sure he wanted it more than any other could…

CHAPTER TWO

It took purpose of thought to resist joining the other ghosts headed in Cameron's direction. If ever Rabby had heard a true siren's song, it was the tall man weaving tales of happier times filled with victories and celebrating. But if he was a quick lad, he might be celebrating soon enough on his own!

He found Soni standing on the footpath with Kennedy to one side and a black haired gentleman on the other wearing jeans and a t-shirt. Fraser, sadly, was nowhere to be seen. So apparently their farewell had been a final one, just as Soni had said. He swallowed hard, forcing the truth into his belly. He was on his own now. His protector was gone. If Rabby was lucky, Fraser wouldn't be needed, but he would certainly be missed.

As he neared the group, he tried to keep from looking at Kennedy directly. He was always afraid he might betray that one's secrets with just a glance, so he averted his gaze when others were about. He slowed, to be sure he wasn't interrupting their conversation, but Soni waved him forward. The look on her face boded bad news.

"Rabby, lad," she said with a frown. Her hands twisted in front of her. "You ken Kennedy, but this," she pointed to the man on her right, "is my uncle Wickham. We'll need his help today."

The man looked him in the eye, just as Soni always did. Perhaps the ability to see spirits ran in the blood then.

Rabby nodded to the man but was greeted by an outstretched hand. He shook it firmly, as Fraser had taught him—in theory, not practice. But it wasn't until he felt the warmth of her uncle's flesh that he realized *he could feel!* And what was more, the grinning man could feel him as well.

"Cor!"

Wickham chuckled. "*Cor*, indeed!"

Rabby held tight for a moment longer, but the man didn't seem to mind. Once he let go, he looked about for what might be missing. Then he had it.

"Miss Soni?"

"Mm?"

"Where's yer lovely green circuit? That hoop of light that spins about ye when ye're sending the men away?" He tried not to sound too eager, but nothing about his challenge seemed to be unfolding as the others' had.

"Auch, laddie. No great mystery there. The green ring is for protection. I need no protection while Wickham is near. Does that satisfy ye?"

He didn't know how to mask his disappointment. "Aye. I just..."

"Would prefer the bright light and the big fire?"

He nodded, embarrassed she read his thoughts so easily.

"Yer wee adventure will be quite different from the rest, Rabby, but no less exciting. And ye'll be extended the same boon, of course, if that is what ye desire."

He bit his tongue to keep his own secret, then nodded.

Soni's frown returned. "I'm sorry to say, though, that Dauphin must remain behind for the now."

His fingers clamped around a handful of thick black hair and held. Dauphin was the only thing he'd been able to feel through the centuries. It was a gift from God it was, and grateful he'd been for the security he'd felt—and the chance to comfort the poor beastie that had been trapped on the moor by Rabby's own doing. To leave the dog behind seemed like an ungrateful thing to do.

But after a moment's thought, he supposed part of proving his bravery entailed proving it alone.

"I only worry about Dauphin," he said, and gave the beast a pitying look, imagining how lonely he'd be without Rabby as a companion.

"I've already thought of that," Soni said, and tipped her head toward Kennedy.

With a single pat on the leg, Kennedy proved that Dauphin was not so particular as Rabby believed him to be. But no matter. It was better the dog stayed with someone familiar.

"I'll be back," he assured the mongrel.

Soni shook her head. "No, Rabby. Ye'll see Dauphin on the other side—"

"But Fraser came back—"

"Fraser had made special arrangements. I cannot do the same for ye. And besides, I've no pixie dust in my pocket for the dog." She must have read something desperate on his face for she heaved a resigned sigh. "How about this? If ye find yerself in need of Dauphin's help, Wickham here will ensure the animal can come to ye. And if ye've no need of him, he'll be waiting."

"Waiting? Ye mean…" He gestured with his finger, up and over.

"Aye. On the other side," Soni said, then wrinkled her nose. "One last farewell then."

Rabby chanced a glance at Kennedy. Though the tears in those eyes were phantoms, the tears in his own felt real enough. He stepped forward, double-time, and wrapped his arms around Kennedy's waist and held them up as if they truly touched.

"Go with God, lad." A quiet whisper, and then Number 55 began to fade, along with Dauphin.

"Wait!" He dropped to his knees in front of the beast and Dauphin's form returned. "He must be given a chance to say goodbye, mustn't he? He's needed me all these years. It will be a shock for him, sure, when I'm not there when he wakes. I must at least try to help him understand."

No one argued.

He grabbed the sides of Dauphin's head and shook the fur, then scooted his hands up to ruffle his ears. The dog closed his eyes and relished the attention, but when those eyes opened again, they seemed to hold all the regret of the world.

"Don't carry on so," Rabby whispered.

Soni's hand came to rest on his shoulder. "Let him go, laddie. He understands."

Rabby nodded and climbed to his feet, and though it might have been his imagination, he thought the dog gave him a nod just before he faded completely.

The thought that kept him from crumbling into a heap of tears was this—if the dog understood so well, perhaps he also understood how Rabby regretted luring him away from home that day so long ago.

CHAPTER THREE

Soni made a noise in her throat. "Are ye ready, Rabby?"

He swallowed a bit of something lodged in his own windpipe, then swallowed again to be certain it was gone. "Aye."

She smiled warmly, nodded to Wickham, and stepped back.

The man moved to face Rabby and held out his forearms with his hands open to the sky. Bulging with veins and muscles they were.

"Push back yer sleeves, laddie," he said. "Bare yer arms and take a hold of my own."

Rabby did as he was told—pushed back the layers of loose clothing until his forearms were bare, pale and scrawny as they were. He laid those arms over Wickham's and gripped the thickest part of muscle, managing to wrap his fingers only half way round them, amazed once again that his own ghostly limbs didn't pass straight through to the other side.

Wickham's hands then took a firm hold of Rabby's arms just below the elbow, able to hold tight just as Soni and Simon MacLaren had been able to touch each other like true mortals.

The man gave him a nod of approval, took a deep breath, then released it slowly.

"Rabby," he said quietly, "hold tight until the end, aye? Dinna let go no matter how strange ye might feel."

His insides trembled with apprehension, but he nodded just the same.

Nothing to fear, Fraser had said. *Nothing to fear.*

"Good lad."

From the corner of his eye, he noticed Soni take another step backward off the footpath and onto the grass. He couldn't help wondering what she knew. But it was too late to question.

Wickham gripped him tighter and he was suddenly able to feel the pinch of it. After centuries of feeling no pain, the slight burst of it shocked him and forced his eyes shut, but still he held on.

He felt other things as well—a wash of warmth flooded his ears, his head and neck. His chest rose and fell again. The coolness of the late morning air lit his lungs from inside and made him giddy.

Scotland—a burst of taste in his nose, a sensation on his lips as he drew a breath over them. The salty tang of earth melted into his tongue and he wondered how he'd ever forgotten the flavor in the first place.

His stomach filled with teasing scents and grumbled from want of something more.

He thought the onslaught was over and slit his eyes open to peek at the man concentrating before him. Wickham's brow twisted, his frown deepened, and his fingers bit deeper into Rabby's forearms. Rabby was tempted to let go, fearing what the man intended next. As if he read Rabby's thoughts, however, he loosened his hold slightly and the bite of pain was gone.

Still he held.

The sensation of heat filled his hips and buttocks, then spread down into his thighs as if hot blood were pushing through his veins, forcing his puny muscles to accept and expand.

Through those slitted eyelids, he watched the man before him grow shorter as if he was sinking into the pavement. But it wasn't Wickham sinking, it was himself...*growing!* The man's grip hadn't lessened out of sympathy but because Rabby's arms had increased in girth. No longer were his arms puny bones wrapped in a thin layer of muscle and even thinner layer of skin. They were nearly of a size with Wickham's and still growing.

His eyes opened wide and he giggled at the ground as it moved away from him. But the voice wasn't his own. It was deeper, older. He cleared his throat to hear it again.

Wickham's eyes flashed open and one of his arms fell away as if the magic spell was broken by the interruption. Rabby opened his mouth to apologize, but Wickham shook his head. "It is done, Rabby. And we've arrived."

Arrived?

Rabby looked about him, still holding on to the man's arm, concerned that if the contact were broken, he might find himself small and scrawny again. But they hadn't gone anywhere. They still stood upon the moor, but it seemed as though many others had arrived as well. And in battle costume.

"Drumossie field," Wickham said, his voice hushed with reverence. "Do what ye must, laddie. But remember, ye cannot change the path of history, aye? If we could do such a thing, it would have been done already."

Culloden's battlefield hadn't been called Drumossie in some time. Neither had it been host to so many men.

Not since the battle!

Rabby turned back to ask Wickham if Scotland was ready to fight again for the reformation, but he found himself standing alone, his arms raised. But instead of holding two arms, he held the handle of a round wooden targe in one hand and a broadsword in the other.

Wickham was gone!

"You, there," a captain called out. "Take this to Lieutenant-Colonel Lochgarry. Left Front." He held out a folded bit of paper while he turned his attention back to his ledger.

When Rabby only stared, the man grunted in frustration. "MacDonalds of Glengarry?" He gestured to Rabby's knees which were, indeed, still covered in MacDonald plaid.

Though his father had fought with other MacDonalds, he and Rabby had come from Dalcross, very near Drumossie moor. It was why his father had been able to go home for supplies while the armies were still gathering. But when he'd left home the second time, Rabby couldn't bear being abandoned yet again. They'd had only a few hours together. It hadn't been fair.

So Rabby had found an excuse to follow…

"If ye doona ken the man's face, listen for a German accent," said the captain and slapped a letter against Rabby's chest.

"Aye," Rabby said. He slid his sword into the scabbard he found around his waist, then took the missive and hurried away. Toward the left. Toward the bog. And if the Battle of Culloden Moor was about to commence again… Toward the doomed.

'Twas no re-creation, no reenactment Rabby was witnessing. The odors were far too familiar to him—the last things he'd smelled in his mortal life. They were from long ago, of course, but there hadn't been many memories to replace them, no matter how much time had passed.

The lingering taste of morning dew was fading quickly in the midday sun. The trampled moss and crushed heather left a pungent bite on the air. And the fragrance of gunpowder and oil pushed its way up his nose, trying to displace all else. Soon, the taste of blood, char, and smoke would join in.

There was no question. He was back.

We've arrived, Wickham had said. Now Rabby understood.

And he wasn't to change history—not that he wasn't *allowed* to do it, but that it wasn't possible.

Well, he wouldn't fash over history. But if he was standing on the moor, if the battle hadn't yet begun, and if others could see him and hear him as they would any mortal man, then there was definitely something he could change. And if he died to make that happen, so be it. He was due to leave this world soon in any case.

Rabby knew he could make everything right again! He only needed to find his father...just as he had the first time he'd arrived on the battlefield, April 16th, 1746. He only had to keep on his current course...

CHAPTER FOUR

Do what ye must, Wickham had told him. Don't try to change history.

But standing on the moor as thousands of Highlanders lined up to face their sure deaths, how could he not at least give it a go?

Surveying the lines on the field, his own desires suddenly paled in comparison. Who was he to worry about one man when so many needed to know what he knew?

Someone shouted McGillivray's name and told him to return to the right flank. An older man shouted in answer. *So that was the great leader who had led and inspired so many—or rather, would inspire so many men in a wee while.* But if McGillivray knew the truth of what was about to happen, perhaps he could inspire them all to flee for their lives and live to fight another day. That wouldn't be meddling with history so much a postponing it, surely.

Rabby stepped in front of the famous man as he was about to pass. "Colonel McGillivray, sir?" The voice from his mouth sounded strange, as if he were plagued with a horrible illness that had set up camp in his throat.

The important man glanced at the letter in Rabby's hand. "You have something for me?"

Rabby shook his head. "'Tis for Lochgarry."

Another man spun on his heel. "Here." He took the letter, nodded to the colonel, and turned away again.

McGillivray raised an impatient brow.

"Sir," Rabby began again. "The bog—"

The man's sharp look cut him off. "I ken it, son. We will have to compensate. It's too late now. Just do yer best for Scotland, and trust that God knows what he's about, aye?" He slapped Rabby on the shoulder, then stepped around him and was gone.

Rabby opened his mouth but no argument came out. How could he debate with the man? Who could question God?

But still, he had to try, so he started after the colonel who was high-stepping over the terrain in his hurry to return to the Clan Chattan at the other end of the line.

"Sir! I beg ye," Rabby called out, unconcerned with how weak he might appear.

A shout rose up and all eyes turned to a man mounted on a white horse. Guarded on both sides, the bonnie prince moved forward, smiling down at Jacobites as he came, as if he believed the day would hand him another victory over the Hanoverians. But Rabby knew better.

Someone grabbed Rabby's arm and pulled him out of the way and the prince's horse stopped where he'd been standing.

Hope jumped in his breast. The prince could stop the battle! And if he could, Robert MacDonald and thousands of others would live! He could spare them all!

He summoned his courage and stepped forward, but the hand on his arm pulled him back again.

"Easy, mon. Ye'll not be allowed to bend the prince's ear now, will ye?"

Rabby turned to argue but found himself staring into the face of his beloved father, Robert James MacDonald, distiller of Dalcross. His father stared back with a twinkle in his eye and a laugh waiting to burst forth.

Da! He wanted to fall on the man's neck and tell him all of what he'd endured on the moor since that horrible day. He wanted to warn the man what would soon happen here and leave the burden of changing history to someone older and wiser than he.

But most of all, he wanted to assure his father that, even though he appeared to be a man grown, he was still young Rabby MacDonald, his own son—a son so hindered by his own guilt he would still be afraid, three hundred years hence, to see what God would do with him.

"Come, son," his father said cheerfully. "Let's find a bite of something to quiet that belly of yers, and we'll find a good view for the wee stramash, aye?"

"Aye," Rabby whispered, his heart so full he could barely find a voice at all. Though Robert couldn't know who Rabby truly was, he'd called him son, and the sound of it nearly brought him to his knees. But falling to the ground wouldn't be as simple as it had been before he'd been given a tall, hulking body.

He followed his da through the rows of Highlanders toward the front lines. They stopped next to a man who sat resting on the ground nearly hidden from view by the others towering over him.

He looked up at Robert expectantly. "Did you speak to him, Rabby?"

Rabby jumped at his own name. It had been so long he'd forgotten that many called his father the same.

"I spoke to the captain," his da answered. "The captain was moved enough to speak to Lochgarry. He'll not hear it. Too late, says he. This lad tried to plead our case to McGillivray himself!" He pointed a thumb at Rabby. "But they are resigned. I'm afraid our fate is sealed, my friend."

Rabby peered closely at the second man climbing to his feet. Murdo. A swarthy man who had lived five cottages down the road in Dalcross. He'd had two wee boys and a very young wife that day last summer when he'd left with Rabby's father to join the fighting.

When Robert returned home a few days before the battle, he'd been alone, and Rabby had assumed Murdo had been killed in one skirmish or another. There had never been time to ask—never been time for much at all. Rabby had awakened to find his father had come in the night and was already preparing to leave again.

That was the moment it had all gone wrong. They'd argued. In silence, he'd helped his father pack what rations he could carry. The man had dawdled a bit to appease him, but soon he was bidding Rabby look after his mother and walking down the lane once more.

His mother…

His mother had been left to look after herself. Under the pretense of chasing down Dauphin, Rabby had run off to follow his father, his obedient hound running at his side.

In his dreams, some nights, he'd been awakened by the sound of his mother calling him. *"Rabby! To me, my lad. To me!"*

Even at that moment, he could hear her, and he turned and looked about just to be certain she wasn't calling from the edge of the field.

"What's yer name?" Murdo poked his fat finger into Rabby's targe.

"Rabby MacDonald," he said, still so distracted by his mother's voice that he'd almost forgotten his father was standing next to him.

"I'm blessed with the same name," said his da. The smile in his eyes held a strange glint that made Rabby wonder if the man might recognize something in him. "That makes at least three of us on the field this day." He pointed toward a rise behind them, to the west.

Rabby's heart nearly stopped as he realized what the man meant. Though he dreaded what he would see, he turned...and spied his smaller self standing where his father had bid him stay, his hand wrapped in Dauphin's thick black fur.

His father dug in his satchel, pulled out a small bit of a bannock, and handed it to Rabby. "Eat this, laddie. I'm sorry there is not more, but I gave the rest to my wee boy who stands there with his dog." He waved to the boy. The boy waved back with a sad smile.

"Dinna mind the lad. He's a bit sore in the backside. Had to give him what for, ye see. He ran away from home to follow me here. Disobeyed. I had no choice, ye ken."

Rabby looked into his father's eyes and struggled to keep his own dry. "I'm certain young Rabby kens it as well, sir."

His father fished a handkerchief from his pocket and wiped at his nose. "Aye. I believe he might at that. He's a right clever lad, my Rabby."

Again, that twinkle in his eye led Rabby to believe the man knew, somehow, that his son was standing in both places—beside the dog and before him at that moment, choking down the last bit of bannock—a bannock his own mother might have made.

How lucky he'd been. Had the others among Culloden's 79 been so blessed to see their families again? To taste again their own mother's cooking?

Surely not.

There was a sudden scrambling in the ranks behind them and Rabby realized that he would not have much time with his father. The clouds over the sun had tricked him. It was not so close to midday after all.

The Battle of Culloden Moor was about to begin in earnest! Again!

CHAPTER FIVE

Damn Cameron anyway!

After all those stories, the details of the real battle had been lost to Rabby long ago. Oh, the folks inside the Great Visitor's Center probably had it aright, but since few of the ghosts ventured through those doors, Rabby had avoided them as well, and whatever truths lay beyond were lost to him.

Too many mortals emerged from the building with tears on their cheeks. Rabby would have been foolish to go poking about. Or at least, he thought it would have been foolish to borrow trouble. But at that moment, standing close to the front lines waiting for the battle to commence, he wished he would have been a bit braver in his spirit form. If he'd paid strict attention, he might know of some way to save his father!

Hadn't that been the one thing, in all the world, he'd wished for? A chance to send his father home alive—the one thing that would make amends to his mother for running away and never returning?

It had been his fault, all of it. If Dauphin hadn't been told to stay at Rabby's side on the rise, the animal might have been free to protect the elder Rabby. But now he realized, thanks to the magic of Wickham, he was able to stand at his father's side and defend the man himself!

Seventy-eight warriors had taught him their best moves. He could manage this!

The first belch of bagpipes, with their discordant cries, caught him by surprise and curdled the blood in his newly enlarged body. He took his sword from the scabbard and stepped back between his father's line and the one behind, to wield the thing about and test the muscles that held up his manly form.

His new body seemed to know its purpose well, for the sword sang through the air and sliced where he willed the blade to slice. He ducked and sprang forward. Dodged to the left, then the right. He spun about in different directions and never lost his footing.

Aye. The body would serve him well. The grown version of Rabby MacDonald, the younger, was a fit and agile man.

But could one man make a difference?

Murdo laughed. "A dandy fighter, to be sure. But would ye mind saving some of that fight for an actual enemy? Or do ye just dance?"

"To me, Rabby," his father said, just as if he were calling to him from across the yard or a field of barley.

To me. Rabby, my lad. To me!

The scurl of pipes came from across the way—a reminder that Scots fought on the other side as well. A mean reminder that soured his belly and made his chest groan with hatred for all those who would fight against an English-free Scotland.

The deep murmur of voices around him said he wasn't alone in his sentiment. And that murmur grew into a rumble, and then a roar. The sense of being part of something great and powerful was much more impressive from inside the ranks than it had been when he'd stood upon the rise that day.

His chest swelled further with the knowledge that he shared that experience with his father. And in that moment, he understood what had driven the man to leave his family for a time in order to be part of that great rebellion. It was no wonder he was in a hurry to join his comrades again, to not miss the fight. And how magnificent it might have been to have strode up the lane to his home and deliver that victory to his family.

But there would be no victory.

Rabby glanced about at the faces of those beside and behind him. Stoic, determined. Resolved, and yet…resigned. Wickham had been right. History would not be changed that day. There was no sense raising a hue and cry to stop the butchery before it began—these men saw it coming. They knew the bog lay ahead. They knew there would be no victory.

And yet, they remained. His father remained. One look in the man's eyes and Rabby knew there was no use urging the man to flee while he could. A mix of foolish and honorable were all the men of that company that day.

When Rabby thought the tension could not stretch any further, the first shots were fired from the Jacobite artillery, such as it was. It was soon answered by the impressive guns of the Redcoats. One heartbeat, then another, and still the order to charge did not come.

A dozen more. Still nothing.

Rabby's legs shook from the effort it took to restrain himself, poised as he was to run. But still, the order did not come.

Boom after boom, after boom sounded from the far side, and a great cloud of smoke rose from the far right, almost obscuring the end of the red line. Screams and cries rose from farther down. But where Rabby stood, the enemy was farther off, out of range from all but the biggest guns.

Those guns didn't wait, of course. And still he and his father, along with the rest of Charles Stuart's Army held their ground and waited for the order to charge.

More screams to the right. More cannons boomed, and boomed again. Rifles fired. Men collapsed like birds picked off a tree by so many meanly thrown rocks.

It wasn't long before Rabby understood just why Culloden's ghosts were so angry with their bonnie prince. Why didn't he give the order? Had it been his plan to have them all line up to be shot? Had he never intended to do anything more than help the English Government murder the rebels?

It was almost easier to let his thoughts run wild than to listen to the horror unfold before him. The whistle of cannon balls, the cries of the wounded, and worse yet, the silence of the dead.

Finally, there was movement at the right end. Just as Cameron often told it, the right line broke ranks, fed up with waiting and watching their brothers die for naught, they charged forward, screaming their war cries and making the blood of their ancestors boil with pride in the very ground beneath their feet. So many of them fell by musket fire, but still they charged, and the lines behind them.

Surely the order to charge would come now!

But it didn't.

The middle line broke ranks next. And finally, finally, the men around him surged forward. But the way was quite different for those at the left. The bog was saturated. Sure footing was not to be had, and the pace slowed to little better than a crawl. Seeing their difficulty, the Hanoverians advanced and opened fire. Men died and remained upright, stuck so surely in the deep mud that only grew wetter with the addition of so much blood.

Murdo fell to his knees, then onto his face in the mud, but never struggled to rise for a breath. By the time Rabby reached him, the man was still as a rock. But he couldn't waste worry for a dead man, he had a living father to protect.

His own boots caught and dragged, but he pulled them free, refusing to allow his father to move forward without him. For long minutes they fought with the bog, and Rabby realized that even if they managed to find firm ground soon, all their energy would be spent. They'd be lucky if they could raise a sword, let alone find the momentum for a Highland Charge.

He had to get his father out of there. Surely, at this point, his father would find no dishonor in turning back.

No sooner had he thought the words than a wave of Redcoats charged toward the bog...

CHAPTER SIX

Time slowed even as he watched his certain death—his second death—loom closer. A few clansmen had gotten through the mud and were finally free to engage the Redcoats. At least those men had a chance, and they were buying the rest valuable time.

His heart dared not hope for much of it.

"Hurry, da," he said without thinking. But he realized the man had stopped moving altogether. A quick look at his face proved his father hadn't been wounded, like he'd feared, but his left boot was well and goodly fixed in the mud.

"Leave me," the man whispered.

"Never," Rabby replied and moved around behind his da to pull his shoulders back, hoping a new angle would help free the foot. But the boot wouldn't budge.

He glanced at the Redcoats. Still engaged, but the clansmen were falling. He remembered Cameron's account of the Butcher teaching his soldiers a way to beat the Highland Charge with nothing more than their bayonets. And it seemed as if Cameron hadn't been exaggerating.

Rabby couldn't free his father and fight at the same time. He needed help.

He ceased pulling on the man and turned to the west. It wouldn't be long now. The boy still stood on the rise with the dog at his side, but in a moment, he would be dead and the black beast with him.

It had already happened—long ago, or in a few moments, it would make no difference. But his father might be saved! The boy hadn't suffered, wouldn't suffer, and on the morrow, when he rose to haunt the battlefield, he would not be alone.

I was never alone.

He threw his head back and pled to the heavens. "Miss Soncerae! Mister Wickham! Hear me, I beg ye! Send Dauphin!" He ignored the enemy long enough to summon the dog. "To me, Dauphin. To me!"

Instantly, the black blur left the boy's side and shot straight down to the field and across the bog. And while he came, Rabby exchanged a look with his smaller self.

Again, that sad smile.

Rabby raised his hand and gestured for his younger self to go, to flee. "Go!" he cried, even though he knew the lad wouldn't truly be able to hear him, not like the dog had. "Go!" He waved again.

But the boy shook his head, shrugged a shoulder as if to say, "We both know how this has to end."

Oh, aye. He did. But standing by while a child was cut down? What man, or boy in man's clothing, could do that?

Wickham had warned him. One cannot change history. Had he been referring to his father's history? Or his own? His attempt to warn the colonel that the battle could not be won had made no impact. One or two voices, obviously, could not change the minds of so many leaders. But surely he could change one outcome. Else, why had he been brought back to that battle?

Could he save Robert MacDonald? Or was he supposed to save himself? Would Dauphin be enough to save the man while Rabby went back to save the lad? Could he take that chance?

CHAPTER SEVEN

Time was running out. The Redcoats were now entering the bog. Apparently, the twenty-four shots they'd been allotted had been spent and they intended to use their bayonets to good measure. With his da stuck as he was, all they could do was wait for the butchers to get close.

He couldn't think of the lad on the rise anymore. There would be no leaving his father. Wee Rabby had died soon after the Government's left flank had advanced, and with them, their large guns. Any moment now, a cannon ball would sail far over the heads of the Jacobites struggling in the bog and catch the younger him in the shoulder, killing him and the dog while they still listened to the whistle of it coming their way.

He could spare not even a glance behind him now. He would not risk the temptation of turning and running back to whisk the boy out of the way and send him running for home. He would not leave his father even if the man were doomed.

If only Soni had given him more guidance. If only Wickham could have said more than simply, *Do what ye must.*

Dauphin reached him then but continued past him until he stood before Rabby's father, facing the enemy, forcing the first

Redcoat to back beyond the point where his sword could reach the man still struggling to free his foot from the muck.

All growl and snappy jaws, Dauphin defended Robert as if the dog, too, had waited 269 years to redeem himself. He might have held off the whole of Cumberland's army alone, he was that vicious.

Rabby took advantage of the distraction and hurried to help his father try again. He pulled his father's skean dhu from his sock and bent to cut the laces, to pull the foot free at least, but the mud gave up the boot with a wet kiss and the man tumbled backward onto his arse.

A redcoat advanced with his weapon gripped tight, his bayonet aimed at Robert's heart. Had Rabby not been there to protect him, his father would have been cut down.

Was this how the man had died so long ago? Probably.

"But not today!" He pressed forward and knocked the man back with his targe. Then took a precious second to change hands, his targe into his right hand, and his broadsword into his left. The next Redcoat, trained to stab to his right, to take advantage of the usual vulnerability, found the targe blocking his way. The tip of his bayonet struck and embedded itself into the wood.

While Rabby swung his blade to cut down the first man, still intent on killing his father, he kept the second one busy trying to dislodge his weapon. Before the first Englishman sank into the mud for an eternal rest, Rabby swung his left arm out behind, rose it above his head, then came down over the top of his targe to smite the second man in the heart.

While he stood at the ready for the next wave of Redcoats, his father scrambled out of the black mud, got to his feet, and poised his weapons. But no new threat came from the smoky fog beyond.

A cannonball whistled high overhead and they both turned with horror to see it explode on the rise, just where the boy had been standing.

After a heart-wrenching denial, Rabby the elder struck out for the rise, but Rabby grabbed his arm and held him back.

"Trust me," he told his da. "The boy is already dead and gone. But ye must flee. Now. Rabby cannot go home to his mother now, but ye still can. This cause is lost. It was lost before it began. Now go!"

Anguish, mixed with something softer, twisted the man's tear-stained face. "But my boy..."

Rabby shook his head. "I will tend to him. Ye must trust me. God will comfort him in yer stead. Now go, so I may be comforted as well."

The man stepped forward and clapped Rabby on the sides of his arms. "Ye made me proud, Rabby. Ye're a mighty warrior, son."

Rabby swallowed the lump in his throat and pushed the man away. With tears flooding his face, his da turned and ran to the far right, and while he ran, his head turned, over and over, toward that spot all too familiar to Rabby.

The spot where he'd fallen so long ago.

Yet again, his father was walking away and leaving him behind. But it was different then. Rabby wasn't watching him storm onto a battlefield never to return, he was headed for safety and home, a chance to defend himself instead of being cut down while trapped in the bloody mud.

And somewhere near Rabby's middle, his world righted itself.

MacDonalds continued to be cut down, unable to charge, unable to retreat easily. A skirl of pipes lent false hope and false courage to those trying to make their way through the bog, hoping for a chance to fight the enemy hidden behind the smoke.

The familiar feel of coarse black hair slipped between his hand and the targe and he absently stroked the dog before looking down. "You should go home, Dauphin. Go with da. Protect him. Live as you should have, aye?"

The dog blinked at him.

He stretched an arm to point where his father had disappeared in the distance. "Go with him, Dauphin. Go."

The dog blinked, licked his fingers, then stepped away. But he didn't go where he'd been told. He took a few steps to the east, toward the enemy, then looked back.

Rabby smiled. "Ye want yer own revenge, do ye?"

The dog barked.

"Away with ye, then. And good luck."

The dog blinked at him once more, then took off like he'd been shot from a gun himself. The black blur disappeared into a thinning wall of smoke.

A musket ball whizzed past Rabby's ear, a reminder that he, too, was still in mortal form. So he picked his way carefully around spots where moss was softening from the flood of blood.

The dullness that clung to the moor long after winter ended had been replaced by a colorful carpet of various plaids still wrapped around the bodies of the slain. The bright red splashes of blood would turn to brown soon enough, then disappear under the pink of summer heather and the thick green growth of new grass.

English shouts at his back made him spin to face the fight, but the bog that had been the curse of the clansmen now cursed the enemy. Both parties forgot each other for the moment in the struggle to free themselves. None of them seemed to notice Rabby's retreat, so he turned away again, intent on reaching the wee version of himself.

He flung his mind back through his memories and tried to recollect if he'd suffered. Had the feel of Dauphin at his side given him comfort? He couldn't recall much before he'd risen the next morning, but it worried him to think he'd taken away that bit of comfort by calling the dog forward.

Brave, obedient Dauphin. He'd come to him as he always had. No matter if he'd been confused by the two different incarnations of himself. He'd been told to stay with Rabby, so, strictly speaking, he hadn't disobeyed by leaving one to be at the side of the other. Clever, clever beast.

And clever Soni...

A black line began where the hot cannonball had scorched the earth, but now that he was upon the spot, Rabby could see no sign of his fallen self. No bit of blood. No shred of plaid.

He spun round and round, making certain he was standing in the right place. And yes, there was the stone that was almost square. There was the bit of softness, an indentation in the ground that nearly matched the shape of his body and made a comfortable enough bed for him for nearly three hundred years. Next to it, a half-moon of thick grasses that Dauphin had preferred when they found their rest.

This is the place. But where am I?

CHAPTER EIGHT

He turned to face the battlefield once more, expecting the Redcoats to push through at any moment and find him, to kill him again. But still, none looked his way, and a familiar feeling came over him—a feeling of being…unseen.

A strong hand gripped his shoulder and he started, then relaxed when he recognized Wickham still dressed in jeans and a gray t-shirt. Rabby pointed to the empty spot that seemed to raise up to meet him. "Where is…the lad?" He knew no better way to ask.

The man shrugged. " *You* are the lad."

Rabby picked up one boot and then the other. Smaller now. As were his arms. The sword and targe lay on the ground beside him. They both appeared to be so much heavier than they'd felt a moment before. Hadn't he swung that broadsword over his head like an able-bodied man only moments ago?

Fraser would have been proud of him.

"We're all of us proud of ye, Rabby. As is yer father, if ye'll remember."

Rabby couldn't help grinning. "Aye. He was that."

"And there are others, of course." Wickham pointed at the melee, and just then, a soldier in bright green plaid turned to give him a wide grin and a tip of a cap.

Kennedy.

"Yes. Always been watching out for you, it seems."

Rabby nodded, but kept his lips closed for fear of loosing secrets. Kennedy sank back into another familiar resting place.

"Seems as though ye've proven yerself well and good, son," Wickham said, drawing his attention again. "Soni will be waiting to award yer boon."

"My boon?" He was distracted by the sight of Culloden changing before him. Gone were the billows of smoke and with them, the bodies of the fallen. The skirl of the pipes was just a memory ringing in his ears. And to his left... To his left, there was no sign of his father or anyone else fleeing to safety.

"Aye, yer boon, lad. No doubt ye're anxious to go give Bonnie Prince Charlie what for. After all, it wasn't an hour ago he failed to give the order to charge."

Rabby considered. Aye, he understood the frustration with the prince like he'd never understood before. But he was back to feeling like a lad of ten years, still wishing for the things lads his age wished for.

"Would Miss Soni mind much, do ye think, if I didn't care to see the prince?"

Wickham smiled and shook his head. "Then what would ye like, for yer boon?"

"I did have something else in mind, before I was made into a man grown. Now it seems a childish thing to ask for—especially since I've been given the best gift of all."

"And what's that?"

"The chance to..." Tears had begun mobbing together in his throat and he had to swallow them down in order to go on. "I saved m' da. In battle. I doona suppose ye saw it."

"I did indeed." The man slapped him on the back and nearly sent him tumbling, but it made his chest expand to think Wickham considered him hearty enough to handle such a blow. "And Dauphin was exceptionally brave as well, don't you think?"

His hand reached for the dog out of habit, but when he felt nothing but air, he tucked his thumb in his belt. While they'd been talking, it seemed the pair of them had moved from the far west point of the battlefield back to the path that ran before the memorial cairn. Soni waited for them.

Rabby ran forward and wrapped his arms around her, happy he was still substantial enough to do so. "I saved m' da," he told her, even though he suspected she already knew. Perhaps, somewhere, there had been a camera of sorts. After all, if Wickham could take him back in time, there was no reason he couldn't have taken a camera along.

"Yes. I heard. And I couldn't be more proud of ye, young Rabby." She patted the sides of his shoulders. "So? What is it to be?"

"No boon for me, Miss Soni. And I thank ye."

She was taken aback. "No?"

"No." He was simply too embarrassed to ask.

She nodded, frowned, then searched the pockets of her great black robes. She grinned when she found something. "Well, then, you might at least take these off my hands. I'm afraid they'll melt if someone doesn't eat them straight away."

She produced two great handfuls of sweets and chocolate bars, just like the ones he'd seen on advertisements for decades! A trip to the sweets shop was the very thing he'd been wishing for!

He pulled his hands away and tucked them behind him, embarrassed. "Ye kenned it all along, did ye not? Ye've been teasing me all the while?"

Her smile never wavered. "Aye. I've kenned all along, and I could hardly wait to give them to ye. A lucky thing ye're still able to taste." She held them out and waited until he took the treats. He tucked all but one into his satchel, then opened his first ever piece of chocolate.

It was strangely smooth with crispy bits of sweetness hidden within.

Heaven, just as he'd imagined it would be.

Soni pointed to the wrapper. "That's my favorite."

"And mine," he said before tucking in on another piece.

Soni laughed and exchanged a look with Wickham. "Take yer time, Rabby. We'll wait until ye've enjoyed them all."

The next bar was not so easy to swallow, remembering what would come next. He'd performed his brave deed, so now he would be moving on to God's judgment. And if God would judge him more strictly than his own mother would, he feared he would not fare well.

Soni gave him a sideways glance. "What troubles ye, Rabby? What nonsense have you been worrying over? Did Fraser not tell ye there is nothing to fear?"

He forced himself to open the third package, knowing his time might be coming to an end and not wishing anything to go to waste. He popped a few of the small, bright candies into his mouth before answering. The sweetness nearly made him forget the question.

"My mum will not have forgiven me for running away and following my da to the battlefield." He ate a few more. "And if she can't have forgiven me, I doubt God the Father will be much pleased with me either."

Soni chuckled, then laughed. "I knew it had to be something like that. And though I can't pretend to know the mind of God, I can tell you that yer mother has indeed forgiven ye, Rabby. And if she can, surely God can too." She gestured behind him and he turned to see what appeared to be a large mirror with the sun reflecting in it. But that seemed unlikely, what with the clouds gathering to prepare for the afternoon's showers.

Out of the bright light stepped a dark figure. None other than Dauphin himself looking brushed and well-fed. A dapper dog to be sure. He took a few steps in Rabby's direction, his tail wagging with such might that it shook his whole body from side to side. But then he stopped, barked once, then stepped back to the light. There he stopped and waited.

A hand reached down to pet the animal. It belonged to his father. Though the man stayed inside the bright doorway, his image was clear, as was the image of Rabby's mother standing beside him.

Those tears were back in his throat, but he had no hope of being rid of them, so he simply forced his voice through.

"Dauphin wants me to come, I reckon." He glanced up at Soni.

She mussed his hair, then pulled him close and gave him a kiss on the forehead. "I reckon they all do."

He smiled tentatively at his mother. She grinned back and opened her arms.

He nodded her way. "Bodes well for my forgiveness, aye?"

Soni nodded and smiled sadly.

"And if God needs a little persuading…" He patted his half-full satchel and gave Soni a wink.

The young witch gasped, then laughed herself silly while Rabby stepped toward the lighted doorway. His smile faltered when he finally looked into his mother's eyes. Seeing her sweet and unconditional forgiveness was his undoing. If only he'd known! If only he'd trusted…

He fairly howled as he greeted against his mother's breast, and when he paused for breath, he heard the unmistakable sniffle of a certain witch not too far behind. But he was far too busy to console Miss Soncerae, enfolded as he was in the welcoming embrace of his parents...

And one very happy dog.

THE END

MACBETH

CHAPTER ONE

The witch was back.

Just as she had the night of Summer Solstice, Soncerae arrived on the moor draped in a long black robe. The waxing moon hung near the horizon watching for the lass's return—like a child lying low, hoping for a glimpse of Santa Claus.

She strode with purpose toward the memorial cairn, empty-handed this time, but as she passed the first of the clan markers the ring of green light burst into view as if her shoes had scuffed the hard path and the spark from it had caught. Like a Hoola Hoop from the 1970's, a foot thick and a foot high, it rotated around her without touching, wobbling slightly in its orbit.

Though Macbeth watched closely, he could see no trace of faces in the light as he'd seen that first night. He wondered if he might have imagined it. After all, odd things entered one's mind on festival evenings.

When she reached the cairn, she walked a wide circle around the spot where she'd built her strange white pyre not a sennight before, keeping her eyes on the center. And when she'd finished her circuit, she raised both hands elegantly into the air and the pyre resumed burning just as if she'd brought her odd pile of wood and built the thing again!

A fine magician's trick it was. And Macbeth suspected their wee witch might have done it solely to excite him and his fellows. For he'd been quite impressed himself, and he was not easily moved.

Speaking of his fellows, there was no need to summon the remainder of Culloden's 79 ghosts who moved apart from the rest of the spirits wandering the battlefield. All but a few stragglers gathered to her willingly now, eager to see who she would choose next to send on their quest. Now that Rabby had gone, there would be none among them who could refuse the challenge and not be thought a coward.

If Rabby MacDonald had been courageous enough to do the witch's bidding, Macbeth expected the rest of them to step forward smartly and take whatever lay in store for him.

Macpherson, Number 33, showed no surprise when Soni bid him to come forward. Though the night was silent but for the snap and pop of her grand white fire settling in, Macbeth was unable to hear a word of what she said to the man. He moved closer, intent on eavesdropping, but the Highlander disappeared in the span between one beat of Macbeth's heart and the next.

No one was surprised when the MacGregors stirred up a ruckus yet again, but the wee witch held her ground and had them well in hand.

A fine, clever lass she was, able to hold so many with her will alone. Macbeth only wished he'd known such a lass in his day...

He took another step forward, looking for a clearer view of the excitement. Soni's gaze snapped up to meet his. She's misinterpreted his movement. But after a nod of her approval, how could he tell her he'd not meant to volunteer?

"Macbeth, my friend. Your timing is perfect."

He forced a smile and ignored the murmurs of surprise spreading behind him. He was known well among the 79 for his sullen disposition and reluctance to participate in futile activities. But his fellows were not nearly as surprised as he was himself.

Nine spirits and one dog had already left the field and not returned, so the wee witch's machinations might not be so futile as he'd expected them to be. He simply hadn't expected to be *next.*

He moved quietly forward and separated himself from the throng of sixty-nine others who were more curious than cautious now. He gave the dear lassie a courtly bow, but couldn't stop his mouth as he straightened.

"The lad is well?"

Soni smiled widely and spoke to the gathering at large. "Rabby is very fine indeed. As is the dog, Dauphin. I will break the rules just this once and tell ye what Rabby himself would wish ye to hear—that he was canny and courageous and was able to save..." She troubled her lip with her teeth for a few seconds, then continued. "He was able to save a man's life. And he reaped the finest of rewards."

Macbeth found himself grinning and ceased. He was pleased for the lad, sure. But there was no sense making a fool of himself over it.

"At yer command, lass," he said.

Soni nodded, dug into her pocket, and stepped close. With only the green ring between them, she held something out. "You'll need these, Seoc."

Seoc. His given name. He'd nearly forgotten it thousands of times. It was a gift to hear it again.

He lifted an open hand over the green hoop and a tendril snaked out like a serpent's tongue while she dropped her gifts into his waiting hand. Unnerved, he snatched it back and couldn't help retreating a step. But instead of the lads laughing at him, they muttered concern.

Macbeth understood, of course. Soon, it would be their turns to step close to the fire, and they, too, might have need to reach over the capricious green light. His fellows were watching, learning, assessing something that might well turn out to be an enemy, even though, by all rights, they shared the same goal as the green ring—protect the well-being and safety of one precious, sixteen-year-old lassie.

A lass who seemed to be the only person on God's green earth who could see and hear them, who truly cared for them.

He opened his hand and found a credit card and a five dollar bill in American currency. He tucked them into his sporran and buckled it.

"And when I've accomplished my brave deed," he said quietly, "I'll have no need to face Charles Stuart. Exacting a pound of his flesh or bleeding him won't bring back the lives he threw away. I want peace is all. I want away from the place, from the senselessness. I want to have done with all of it. And high time, too."

Soni rolled her eyes and sighed. "Aye, Seoc Macbeth. I ken what ye most desire. And ye'll have it if ye do what is asked of ye." She leaned a bit closer and whispered. He barely heard it himself, but he understood the jest. *"All hail, Macbeth that shalt be* mortal *hereafter…"*

CHAPTER TWO

Seoc opened his mouth to argue with her, for the hundredth time, over the difference in Shakespeare's play and the truth about his ancestor that was, historically, one of Scotland's finest monarchs. But the lass disappeared before his eyes along with her bright fire and green Hoola Hoop. Blackness surrounded him as if he'd been placed in a deep dark pit. But after only a breath or two, colors returned, bright and sharp, and bathed him in light all about.

When his eyes were able to discern details again, he was standing in a queue inside a well-lit establishment. The two men before him were easily a head shorter than he and stood before a long counter waiting for service. He turned to see what threats might come from behind and found a woman ogling his kilt with wide eyes. It took a long moment to realize that no one had noticed how he'd arrived, though they were surprised by the way he was dressed. Thankfully, his kilt and sleeves were clean of the blood and mud of the moor.

The lass behind him couldn't seem to drag her attention from his knees.

Behind him. In line. Waiting her turn.

Embarrassed to be found in such a position, he stepped aside and bid her to go before him. Reluctantly, she stepped forward, but her gaze darted back to his kilt every few seconds.

The man who had been immediately in front of Seoc turned. After a long moment, he, too, realized his rudeness and asked the woman to go head of him. Seoc gave him an approving nod and the man smiled and turned red all the way to his bare pate before offering the tiniest nod in return.

The man at the head of the line was sadly oblivious to the fact that a woman stood behind him, and even though Seoc cleared his throat twice, the man never turned, but eventually moved down to the end of the counter. The woman blushed and finally faced forward, since it was now her turn to order.

"What would you like tonight?" The lass behind the counter smiled cheerfully, then her brow puckered when she found herself ignored. The other woman was clearly still distracted, so the younger lass repeated her question.

The woman pointed her thumb over her shoulder at Seoc. The younger lass tilted her head so she could get a look at him, then the pair of them laughed together. The woman then pointed at the board hung high on the wall and murmured something.

"Spell your name, please," the younger one requested, then penned the letters on a cup in her hand.

He was in a coffee house! He should have known it from the fragrance hanging like an invisible but heavy cloud blocking out most of the subtle tastes in the air.

A dainty bell dinged behind him. Two young women walked through the large glass door and stepped behind him before they, too, took a moment to appreciate his plaid. Again, he stood aside and insisted they go before him. After all, he was in no hurry. No danger seemed imminent unless someone was on the verge of burning themselves with the steaming stuff in their cups, and he could hardly be expected to anticipate which of the dozen or so patrons were about to do such a thing.

He was pleased when the balding man, now at the head of the line noticed the lasses and stepped aside for them as well, but his smile was more of a grimace then.

Seoc gave him a hearty slap on the shoulder. "Take heart, mon."

The lass behind the counter noticed what had transpired and laughed outright. "If you guys keep at it," she said, "you'll never get your coffee."

She finished her business with the two young women and waved the chivalrous fellow forward with a frantic wave. "Hurry, before someone else comes in!" Then she laughed again. As before, she asked the man to spell his name, told him the cost, then instructed him where to insert his card.

The fellow dug into his pants pocket, pulled out some one dollar bills, then stuffed them into a large container marked *tips* before moving to a small table to wait.

Seoc stepped closer to her counter.

"What would you like tonight?"

He took one last look at the door to make sure no women were entering, then faced her. He was pleased she'd taken the time to meet his gaze. However, his tongue seemed to lose its purpose for a moment while he appreciated how her cheeks curved when she smiled. Hundreds of years ago, a smile like that might have seemed quite encouraging—had she not bestowed that very smile on every customer she'd served before him.

The sobering thought helped his tongue to work again. "What would you suggest?"

She was taken aback by the question. "I don't know. What do you usually drink?"

Usually? A tricky question, that. The last things he'd used to cool his throat and quench his thirst he'd scooped into his hand from little better than a trickling burn. Before that, a wineskin.

"Tea...with milk. Though I'd like to taste this American coffee you have." He'd added the bit about milk so she wouldn't think him poor if he'd had no milk for his tea, even though he didn't fancy it that way in the first place.

She cocked her head and narrowed her eyes for a few seconds, straightened, and grinned again. "I'll take a stab at it," she said, "and if you don't like it, I'll make you something else."

He didn't care for the term she used. After all, he'd been finished off by a bayonet to the chest the last time he'd been living, and the word *stab* brought the moment, and the sensation back to mind. He resisted the urge to rub at the site of his wound and gave the lass consideration for not knowing. In reply to her offer, he nodded.

"That will be five twenty-five." She tapped on the small black box. "Just slide your card in there. Unless you have cash."

He unbuckled his sporran while he felt dozens of eyes upon him and pulled out the two items Soni had gifted him with only moments before. The fiver was obviously not enough—which he couldn't take the time to comprehend—so he slid his card in the little slot as he'd been instructed. The machine beeped rudely at him.

"Here." She took his card, turned it round, and inserted it again. A more pleasant beep signaled a nod from the lass, and she returned the card.

He took another step to the left and added the fiver to the tips.

"Wait." She poised her pen over a new cup. "Spell your name for me, please."

Name. Name. Cannae forget it now! And the spelling, ye dolt!

"S. E. O—"

The lass glanced sharply at him.

"C." He nodded to let her know he was finished.

She lowered her chin and gave him a dubious look. "S. E. O. C?"

"Aye."

"How do you pronounce it?"

"Seoc. Like Shock, but more of a z than an s." He demonstrated.

"Like Jock?" She shook her head. "They'll slaughter it. How about your last name?"

He frowned from side to side, wishing fewer people were within hearing. His last name always drew more notice than he wished, especially from a non-Scot.

He leaned close and lowered his voice. "Macbeth." Only after he'd said it aloud and noted the surprise on her features did he realize he could have used any of a hundred other names and still known when his coffee was ready for him.

He closed his eyes and waited for her pithy comment. The lass had been quick-witted thus far. Surely she would have something clever to say.

Perhaps, "I am, in coffee, stepped in so far..."

"Thank you," she said, suddenly straight-faced. "If you want to take a seat, it will just take a minute or two." After a quick glance at the empty doorway behind him, she took the cup to the small kitchen area and forgot him.

Probably doesn't know her Shakespeare.

After he'd made certain that no females would be left without a seat, he lowered himself onto a metal chair and tucked his sporran between his legs like a gentleman.

The chair was cold. And what's more, he could feel it!

He kept his face a smooth, emotionless mask, but inside he was jumping about like a wee child let outside to play. Of course Soni had told Culloden's 79 she'd be giving them life again so they might perform their daring do. She'd even teased him with a quote from the Bard's play, telling him he would be mortal. But he'd supposed she would simply cast some spell that would give him substance for the duration of the quest, not life in truth!

He was a learned man. Barring some miracle like unto the Frankenstein tale, he couldn't fathom any way a body could be reanimated. But Soni hadn't had bodies to work with. They'd been spirits only!

Admittedly, he'd been educated in an era little more advanced than medieval times. But he'd studied what he could on the telly. He'd learned much more after death than he'd ever learned in life. But still, his respect for otherworldly things held strong for obvious reasons.

He was a ghost himself—something that couldn't be explained by science. And he'd respected the fact that Soni was a witch and she was able to see them and talk to them. None of which could be explained by physics.

So truly, he shouldn't have been so surprised that Soni was able to give him this gift—the gift of feeling the chill of metal beneath his...well. And yet, he was.

A server called out two names and the young women stepped forward, collected their beverages, and gave him a fleeting glance before stepping out into the dying light of the gloaming. Much earlier in the day than Scotland, then. Six hours at least, for he'd left the moor long after midnight.

The small slip of paper the lass had given him read *The Press Gang, Portland, Oregon.*

Oregon. The west coast of The States, then. Far, far from Culloden's boundaries. He gave himself a moment to consider whether or not he might miss his ghostly home. Although he'd been eager to quit the place, he'd anticipated regret for leaving it. It had become a part of him just as permanently as he'd become a part of it, so he expected something akin to homesickness to affect him, at least until he was settled elsewhere. But no.

Perhaps Soni's magic extended further than the ability to anticipate the cost of a cuppa.

"Phillip."

The bald man stood and collected his prize, then gave a nod to Seoc as he passed. His expression seemed quite cheerful compared to earlier, and Seoc wondered if the man was that delighted to have his hot drink in hand, or if he was pleased with himself for remembering his manners.

"Mac," said a quiet voice. The lass with the too-charming smile stood at the end of the counter holding a cup out to him.

He reached for the drink and inclined his head to acknowledge what she'd done to avoid embarrassing him.

"Take your time. It's hot," she said. "And if you don't like it, let me know. I'll keep trying until I find something you love." She gave him a bright wink and started to turn, but his fingers had overlapped hers and she had to wait until he released her else the hot coffee might have spilled.

With a smile like that, and words like *love* tripping so easily off her tongue, he was tempted to hold her captive just a moment longer.

It was a temptation he found himself unable to resist.

She laughed. Eyes turned their way. He had no choice but to release her. And when she hurried back to serve a new customer, he knew she was relieved for the excuse.

Poor lass. It must have been a frightening thing to have a stranger take such a liberty. And when he imagined other men doing the same, his stomach lurched.

Surely the lass would be wise not to work in such a place where she would be forced to speak with strange and untrustworthy men all day. And due to the nature of her product, some of those men might not be pleasant while waiting for their addictions to be satisfied.

He glanced about the tables to judge for himself what sort of man might visit the place on a regular basis. It only made him crosser when he found nothing objectionable in the current lot. His frown grew weighty but he couldn't seem to help himself. So he bent his head to hide his features within the drape of his hair and returned to his small table. As any canny soldier would do, he turned his back to the wall and waited for the next round of customers to fill the seats.

It shouldn't take much time to find the justification the lass would need to locate other employment. And perhaps, if he pointed out that justification to her, her life well might be saved in the doing.

If nothing better came along, it might be the good deed he'd been sent to do. For it would take no small portion of bravery on his part to give the lass such bold advice. And he'd take heed—ensure she wasn't holding a scalding cup of coffee in her hands when he broached the subject.

CHAPTER THREE

Cat was pretty proud of herself for keeping her cool. The trick was to look the guy in the eyes and keep her attention away from those knees. And how cute was he for letting all the female customers go ahead of him?

Cute? Are you crazy? You hate Scots, remember?

She took a deep breath and tried to concentrate on the customer in front of her. "Decaff. Of course. It's late." She nodded and asked the guy to spell his name.

Jack. Easy. Thank goodness.

When she saw how shaky the letters were, she chucked the cup and started over.

It had been enough time. She should check on the Scottish dude. He'd had plenty of time to taste his coffee and decide.

She handed Jack's order off to Spencer and walked to the end of the counter.

Don't get close. Eyes off the knees.

She'd given her grandpa a hard time for the way he went on and on about Scotland. He'd told her if she ever went to Scotland she'd probably fall in love a dozen times over and never come back to the states again. She'd doubted. She'd blamed it all on Hollywood.

But at the moment, she wondered if the old man knew something about Scotsmen she didn't.

Of course her grandfather had never been to Scotland. He'd inherited a little Scottish blood from his grandmother, but that was it. There really was nothing to his obsession, and she'd pitied him for not having something better to give his loyalty to.

In his attempts to pull off the whole Scottish package, he'd taken up smoking a pipe. *If he'd just found a football team to root for...*

With long dark hair and sharp blue eyes, her Scottish customer would be mouthwatering no matter what he was wearing. But he was downright heart-stopping in a kilt that looked more like ruffled bedcovers than the pleated things bagpipers wore.

Lucky for her, she was able to keep her reactions hidden better than that other woman had. But she still had to speak to him again! Would she stutter? Would she drool? Would she trip and fall at his feet like every other woman in Portland was probably gearing up to do and they didn't even know it yet?

What she needed was a reason not to like him. A second later, she remembered she already had one. The obsession with Scotland was why her grandfather was on his last lung, and it helped wash away any magic love potion the guy might be carrying in his pouch.

"Hey," she said, hoping she wouldn't have to walk over to his table to get his attention. But that wasn't necessary—his gaze nailed her to the spot. "Um... What do you think? Will it do?" She nodded at his cup.

"Aye, lass. Whatever ye've added to the coffee is perfection itself."

The whole cafe fell silent at the trip of his tongue. He probably had a speech coach. Was probably some weirdo from Spokane or something, had to move on to the next city where no one knew his story. But she didn't care about his story, or his brogue, or his plaid...or those knees.

"Great," she snapped and turned away. "It's kind of slow, Spence, and there's only a half hour before—"

"Go." Her manager gave her a wink. "But if you want me to walk you, you'll have to wait."

She was already halfway to the break room. "No need." She clocked out on the computer, hung her still-clean apron on a hook, then got her stuff and went back out front. Four customers bumped around each other to get in the door. She turned to look at Spencer.

"Go." He pointed to the door and plastered a smile on his face for the new crowd.

She didn't need to thank him. He knew how important it was for her to get home and he'd only chew her out for dawdling. One day, when it was all over, she'd have to give in and go out with him. She owed him at least that much.

She swung the door open and glanced to the side, out of curiosity, not interest. But the guy in the kilt was gone.

Not that she cared.

A cold raindrop splashed against the back of her hand. It was as good as a kiss. The skies above Portland loved her, knew how much she loved the rain, and seemed to give her a shot of cheer every time she needed it.

The Great Northwest. No better place in the world.

The sun hadn't been down for long, so walking home alone didn't bother her. Surely the creeps wouldn't be out for hours yet.

And if it rained any harder, they would be hiding in their holes all night. Besides, the street lights reflected off wet cars and made her route home seem brighter than usual. A cheery place. No creeps allowed.

She ignored the hood on the back of her vest and let herself get wet. It was more like a summer rain anyway with no cool breeze to hide from. Just a casual shower of tiny droplets washing away tiny droplets of worry. Or maybe not so tiny.

She took a deep breath of fresh air and wished the stirred-up dust could replace the smell of coffee in her nose. When she got home, she would open all the windows and smell the rain on the screens—

The hairs on the back of her head tingled. She was being followed.

She moved her bag over in front of her body to let her stalker know she wasn't going to just give up her stuff without a fight. She also slowed just a little to prove she wasn't afraid. Nearly everything she'd ever been taught in self-defense classes rubbed her the wrong way. She wasn't about to let someone mess with her life. She'd worked too hard for everything. And she sure as hell didn't have time to go get a new driver's license and replace her credit cards.

Give up her purse?

Not a chance.

And if someone wanted a piece of *her*, they weren't going to get the piece they wanted.

She fished in her pocket and slipped her fingers into her brass knuckles. With her left hand, she plucked the taser out of her purse. A car passed and made that whispering, splashing noise that meant the road was wet, but not yet soaked. Then another car. When they passed the alley where Cat was walking, the noise echoed into the darkness and died. Next to the buildings, the sound bounced and seemed louder.

Then there were no cars at all. Nothing but the sound of footsteps behind her. At least two sets. And she could hear them whispering. Another alley was coming up. If she was going to be attacked, it would be there.

She gripped the taser, lifted it clear of her pocket, but held it in front of her. Then she imagined turning and shocking the spit out of some couple out on a date. What if she was wrong? What if the hairs on the back of her neck stood up just because of the rain, or because she had wondered about the guy dressed in a kilt who was out there in her city...somewhere.

She was at the alley. One, two, three...now six steps, seven—cleared it. Still no mugging.

Another car passed. The wheels hissed against the wet asphalt. The sound died along the alley, then picked up again. Everything normal.

The hairs on the back of her neck changed their mind and lay down again. Her ears strained for the sound of footsteps, but they were gone. People walked on the other side of the road headed back toward the coffee shop. They paid no attention to her side of the street.

Nothing interesting then—no gang of thugs preparing to jump her.

Her phone rang once, twice. In order to answer it, she'd have to let go of the knuckles or the taser.

Not a chance.

It rang twice more, then stopped. Her pocket stopped glowing.

The steps were back. The hairs all over her body came alive and apologized for not listening to her before.

Shoot someone, they screamed.

Her heart raced, but she wasn't going to let her adrenaline make her decisions. Whoever it was certainly hadn't gotten the message, that she wasn't going to go down without a fight. So she took a deep breath and she spun around to face her pursuers.

But there were no punks behind her. No couple out for a stroll in the rain. Just a large Scotsman pausing in mid-step, startled to be caught in the act of stalking.

Alone with him, on the street, he seemed a good foot taller than he had in the coffee shop. A menacing psych patient following her home on the dark city streets.

She pulled the trigger.

CHAPTER FOUR

Some tasers are more powerful than others.

Cat had purchased something with teeth to it. In the wintertime, it started getting dark at five, but she'd been home before then. Now that she was also taking late shifts, to cover the cost of the nurse visits, she knew she'd need protection. And a taser was just the ticket to keep her from worrying herself to death.

However, just because Catherine Dabelko had a little backbone didn't mean she was capable of true cruelty. So she'd taken a class and learned how to use her weapon. She'd even allowed herself to be tasered so she wouldn't go around hitting every suspicious character she met. She *knew* how much it hurt. And she'd given herself a good three seconds to decide whether or not the tall, hot stranger deserved a taste of the concrete and a jolt that would shake the marrow of his bones.

He'd crossed the line.

And deep down, she believed that she hadn't made her decision based on the fact that she blamed the Scottish nation as a whole for her grandfather's lung cancer. At least, not consciously.

He didn't shake like any taser victim she'd ever watched before. It looked like he was doing a pretty good job fighting it, jerking only occasionally instead of just convulsing as Spencer had done when he'd insisted she practice on him. Of course her boss had been trying to earn a little pity so she would start going out with him.

He'd been so wrong.

She was careful to release the trigger after just a few seconds. Fifty thousand volts could convey a pretty clear message in no time, despite how intelligent the receiver was.

The guy rolled onto his back and slapped his arm against the sidewalk, making a noise that was somewhere between an angry growl and a sharp, short war cry. Then he lay still, gritted his teeth, and blew out his breath like he was trying to blow up a balloon. His broad chest rose and fell like bellows feeding a fire.

Yeah. She knew what that burn felt like. Her fingers tingled in sympathy, remembering the sting of electricity hitting a dead end in her fingertips and just...sizzling.

She retraced her steps until she was standing two feet from his shoulder. "I'm sorry I had to do that."

His left arm shot out and his hand caught painfully around her ankle and held her. She yipped, fearing some leftovers of electricity might enter her body through the connection, but she couldn't struggle without landing on her butt. She wasn't really afraid of *him*, for some reason, but she still held onto the brass knuckles.

"Let go of me, please." She figured a guy with gentlemanly manners in a coffee shop would react to a polite request—unless he was out of his mind in pain.

"One of us is a fool, lass." He released her ankle and rolled away from her.

She suspected he meant her, but wasn't going to ask.

She looked around the street, but no one seemed too concerned about the guy on the ground. It was dark, and most faces had phones pressed against them. Cat turned to find they weren't as alone as she'd thought.

A very curious woman came closer. Cat was disgusted when she realized the chick wasn't as concerned for the big man's safety as she was for how high up his kilt was going to ride. So Cat moved around to stand between the two, blocking the rude woman's view. It didn't seem to discourage her until Cat finally put her hands on her hips and gave an exasperated grunt. Only then did the woman show the least bit of embarrassment and walk away.

When Cat turned back to see how he was recovering, the Scot was gone. Like, *gone!* Not ducking into the alley, not turning the corner in the distance. She hadn't had her back to him for more than a few seconds. He couldn't have gotten far.

The hairs on the back of her head were screaming at her again. She turned in circle after circle, but saw no one. So she decided the best way to get that screaming to stop was to grab up the leads of her taser and run for home. It didn't matter what it looked like. She was done trying to prove to the creeps on the street that she was willing to fight.

You can't fight what you can't see.

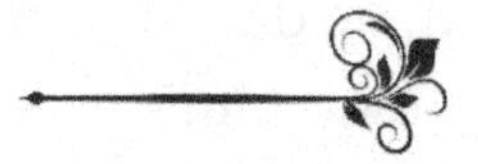

Seoc was pleased when he heard the slap of the lass's running feet. He'd ducked across the street and behind a parked car while the young woman had been distracted, and now that she was gone, he was able to breathe freely and recover.

And to think, he was savoring his reclaimed sensations only a short while ago...

Auch, but he wasna proud of calling her a fool, but he'd had no control over his tongue at that moment, nor control of much else. But he'd been lucid enough to know that she'd decommissioned the one man on the street determined to protect her.

She clearly felt threatened by him—which proved her opinion of him—when she'd pulled the trigger on her taser. She obviously thought him a thug, no better than the three men he'd dispatched a block away who had been bent on harassing her.

Perhaps he should have been less discreet when knocking their heads together. Then she would have known his gallantry. She'd have felt no need to wield her weapon, let alone use it on her savior.

It had happened so quickly, and yet he remembered all of it, despite the electricity still humming through his body…

A misstep. He'd forgotten for an unfortunate moment that he, no longer a ghost, could not simply follow someone about without them knowing. A few centuries of habit were to blame. And he'd been so surprised by her sudden turn, he'd had no time to form the words that might ease her mind.

A full second of surprise on both their parts.

Another second of consideration on hers.

He'd been certain she would give him the time to explain, but then, in that third second, he'd read something else in her eyes—a conscious decision to shoot him! An innocent man—or fairly innocent in any case. Of course he was guilty of following on her heels, but nothing so egregious as to earn him the bite of her weapon.

A she-devil to be sure. A she-devil that hid behind a come-hither smile.

And the devil was getting away!

Seoc jumped to his feet and started after her, hoping the slap of her shoes on the wet pavement would lead the way. He also hoped the small act of discouraging the trio of ne'er-do-wells wouldn't count for his heroic deed, for he wished to enjoy his mortality a wee bit longer—at least long enough to replace that electrified memory with something more pleasant.

And long enough to put a certain mean-spirited lass in her place.

Seoc stood and made for the road, intending to cross and go after the wench, but he paused for just a moment to consider.

Was there a chance wee Soncerae intended for him to remain at the coffee shop? Was he missing the opportunity to prove himself? Or, had he already done so when he'd frightened away the three young rabble-rousers who had been following the lass?

It was a light detail, to be sure. They'd given up the fight so quickly he doubted they would have truly caused the lass harm. But who was he to judge? He'd seen a fair number of pocket-pickers and their ilk on the grounds of Culloden who had appeared harmless. And some who caught his attention simply because they looked like trouble—with unkempt hair and clothes, and a bit thin on the bone—had turned out to be the nonbelligerent chaps who'd wanted nothing more than to enjoy the peace Culloden had to offer.

So, no. He could not say the trio were harmless at all. But since the wee witch had not yet come to collect him, he supposed the deed that awaited him would be a greater challenge. However, with no weapons to hand, he doubted it would be a bloody battle he'd be facing.

But where was this test to be played out?

He glanced back toward the tea shop. It was still close enough he could almost taste the dark, robust coffee in the air. It would be a simple thing to return and wait for trouble to find him. And to soothe his pride, he could see if another coffee confection might help erase the memory of convulsing on the walkway while the mean lass looked on.

His chest tightened at the memory. Pride, surely, beat on his breast from the inside, demanding to be let loose.

Before he made the conscious decision, his feet carried him across the street and to the left, following after the lass.

He could only hope that trouble could find him wherever he happened to go.

CHAPTER FIVE

It was a full two blocks later when he finally caught sight of her again. Her pale, sleeveless jacket fairly glowed at the far end of the path and he wondered if it was a trick of the light, or if locating her was what God—or a certain witch—intended. But even if he hadn't suspected the lass of being involved in his personal quest, he was heartened by the sight of her. And considering the grudge he now held against her, that was mysterious indeed.

Some heaviness in his chest lightened—and not just his chest, but his entire body felt a bit lighter, as if he could fly to her side if necessary.

A story came to mind, a scene from a Superman movie where the fellow discovered he had the power to fly and practiced at it until he mastered the skill. And while Seoc hurried along on the half-deserted street, he put a bit of spring in his step just to see what might happen. Unfortunately, however, it only served to make his gait clumsy, so he stopped.

The amused giggle of a young witch echoed in his head.

He growled. "Go away, Soni. If ye've no more direction to offer, dinna be listening in on my very thoughts, aye?"

Though he strained to hear, there was no further giggling and he chided himself for entertaining such foolish thoughts. Witch or no, how could the lass listen inside his head?

Until a week ago, Soncerae had simply been his young friend, the visitor to the battlefield who enjoyed some strange connection with Macbeth and his 78 fellow warriors—those who had risen from the dead after the battle and found themselves together, and at the same time, apart from the other spirits who wandered there.

Was it true, then? That they'd all lingered all these years from a common thirst for vengeance, wanting their chance to be heard, to berate Bonnie Prince Charlie for taking such little care with their lives?

It made no sense. It certainly wasn't what had kept him tethered to the moor.

His steps slowed while his thoughts wandered back to the battlefield. His lean, powerful body was tiring with the new exertion. If he'd still been a ghost, he would simply allow his mind to clear itself. And in the doing, he'd find his rest for a bit. Quiet and unthinking, he would lie on his back near the well of souls and let time get away from him.

But he couldn't do that anymore.

He picked up his pace and was soon only half a block behind the lass, which is where he remained, disinclined to catch her attention again, and wise enough not to come within reach of her wee but vicious weapon.

No. He would never again be able to allow time to slip away. He was allotted precious little of it to perform his heroics. After that, only God knew what was in store for him.

Well, God...and perhaps a young sixteen-year-old Scottish lass.

Seoc knew the moment the lass touched foot upon home ground. Her shoulders relaxed. Her hands came out of her pockets, and she began looking at the faces around her, waving and smiling, calling out a greeting here and there. He only hoped she wouldn't take the time to look behind her. After all, she was still clipping along at a goodly pace, intent on getting somewhere as quickly as possible. A husband, perhaps?

The thought drew his attention away from his feet and he nearly tripped over the unseen leash of a small dog. The animal yipped and the owner turned just as Seoc was backing away.

"Pardon," he said and quickly moved around the beasty before the man at the other end of the tether took issue.

So many people in current times took special care of their animals and yet treated each other with such distain. He would never understand it. He'd spent nearly three hundred years on the moors with Dauphin, Rabby's beast, and he never would have thought to treat one of his fellows poorly in favor of the dog. But times were different now. Perhaps loneliness ran in direct proportions with the growth in population. Private space seemed to be much more important than the people one chose to share their space with.

But there seemed to always be room for a dog, or a pair of cats.

The lass neared the end of the block and her path veered toward a large apartment building on the far side of the street. Seoc's instincts told him to slow and wait. He ducked into a wide doorway for good measure and peeked around the edge.

She strode purposefully for the door, then paused and looked behind her before turning her attention to a keypad. Careful to shield her motions from onlookers, she entered a code, pulled the wide glass door open, then disappeared inside. He imagined her making her way to the elevator, taking time to arrive at another floor, unlocking another door, then turning on a light. He watched closely for a new window to light up.

There. Top floor. Front west corner.

On the fire escape, a dark figure scrambled about, then pulled open the window and ducked inside!

Seoc took off in an all-out Highland charge. He paid no mind to the people who stepped out of his way or to the looks that followed him. He only knew he was needed. This was the reason why he'd been sent to Portland, dropped in a coffee shop, and lured away by the mean lass wrapped in a cheerful package. He was meant to save her from the intruder who waited for her return!

He considered the front door for only a moment, but he didn't know the code and there didn't seem to be much traffic coming in and out of the place. Chances of catching the door open were slim, and he had no time to dally. So he headed for the fire escape.

He was lucky to be as tall as he was, for the end of the ladder was within reach of his most energetic leap from the large rubbish bin. An inch shorter, he would have failed.

His arms strained as he pulled his body up the ladder until his feet could find purchase. As each story became harder to climb, he thanked God the building was not taller. For when he stood before the lass again and accepted her apology and her eternal gratitude, he would prefer not to be winded.

CHAPTER SIX

Cat hurried through the door and dropped her stuff on the mirrored table. She didn't worry about waking her grandpa because he always stayed up for a while after the nurse left. He looked forward to hearing the rundown of her day. And since she was home early, she could give him that rundown, fix him a bite to eat, then get an extra half hour of sleep.

She was way too young to crave sleep the way she did. People her age were staying up all night earning degrees or trying to keep their new businesses alive. She looked forward to the day she could be that kind of workaholic, or a sleep-deprived mother, instead of a sleep-deprived workaholic keeping someone else's business alive.

That day would come, she knew. But when it did, it would mean her grandpa was gone, and she was in no hurry for that.

The cloud of rubbing alcohol and chemicals filled the living room and made her glad for the coffee smell still lingering on her clothes. She would have liked to burn a fragrant candle, but an open flame was forbidden around the oxygen tanks.

Her only option was to cook a little celery and onion in the oven, or a sliced apple with a little cinnamon sprinkled on it. But tonight she didn't want to take the time. Since she'd be home in the morning, she would open all the windows and make the old man forget he was sick at all.

A whole two days off! Imagine the naps I can take!

She stepped up to the mobile privacy screens and cleared her throat. "Grandpa? I'm home."

She always waited for an invitation. He had so little privacy anymore, she made sure he at least had it whenever possible.

He cleared his throat with real effort, then coughed a few times. "Sweet Catherine, you're early!" She heard bedclothes rustling. "Come in, come in."

The privacy screens weren't nearly as effective as hanging curtains would have been, but they were cheap to rent and they did a good enough job creating a bedroom out of half the living room space. And he was able to keep to himself or be sociable at the drop of a hat, depending on his mood.

Fortunately for her, Alonzo Dabelko had a knack for staying positive, even though his lung cancer hadn't responded to treatment and he was living on borrowed time.

She plastered the brightest smile of the day on her face and stepped around the screen. "Hello, Grandpa."

She stepped forward to hug him, but he waved her back and started coughing. She plucked tissues out of the box on his hospital tray and held them out to him. He hated to be watched when he coughed, so she turned her back to him and pretended she didn't notice. In reality, she listened to every little wheeze and grimaced at the sound of such a rough throat.

She pulled the blue curtains closed on the front windows. They were tall and wide and allowed in a generous amount of sunlight in the morning, and if she stood close and looked to the east, she had a great shot of Mt. Hood. In the late afternoon, the windows invited a wonderful cool breeze to slip through if she opened all three of them by a few inches. There was a trick to it.

"That nurse forgot to open the windows again," she said, after the coughs grew further apart. "But I promise to do it in the morning. Unless you need some fresh air now?" She looked over her shoulder and he shook his head at her before starting up again. She straightened the pillows on the couch while she waited for him to settle down.

A strange clanging sounded from outside. She held still and listened.

Metal. Against the building. Someone was on the fire escape and wasn't being quiet about it.

Out of habit, she rushed to the entry table and dug her phone out of her purse, ready to call the police if there was trouble. They'd lived there four months without anything more alarming than a bike being stolen from the hallway, but that kind of luck couldn't last in a big city. She was sure.

Her grandpa gasped, then stilled. She hurried to the screen and shoved it out of the way, worried the man was choking.

He was fine. His attention was on the side window where some dark form moved on the landing of the fire escape. The window flew open and a pair of large, bare, very manly legs stretched down to the floor. A drape of plaid cloth barely covered the guy's unmentionables, but she didn't dare turn her back. After all, this streaker was only a few feet away from her grandpa's bed!

Her fingers found 911. The call connected. Rang once.

"911. Please state your emergency."

"Um..." She was distracted by the fact that the plaid cloth looked familiar, and her heart dropped when she realized what was still left to come through the window. She started backing away.

"Your emergency?"

"Uh, a streaker... I mean, a stalker. A *man* just came in through my fire escape. I'm pretty sure he followed me home from work."

The stalker in question paused while straightening his kilt and lifted his head just enough to skewer her with a bright blue eye and a raised black brow. Chills rushed up and down her spine and exploded into each other like a liquid form of the three stooges. She nearly dropped the phone.

"We'll send a squad car right away. Did you say he's nude*? Can you lock yourself in another room? Or can you get out the door?"*

"I can't leave. My grandpa is an invalid."

"Ho, ho!" The invalid in question sat up in bed, clapping and waving the big Scot closer. "Come in, laddie. Come in!" He turned and called to Cat. "Sweet Catherine! Did you arrange this?"

"Ma'am? What's he doing now?"

"He's... He's shaking hands with my grandpa."

"Your intruder is shaking hands? Ma'am, are you sure this is an emergency?"

She shook herself to get a grip. "Yes. Please send the police. I have an intruder in my house. Apartment 404." She gave the address.

"Aye. Ye have an intruder," the Scot said. "I saw him crawl through yon window when ye turned on yer lights." He frowned at the old man for a second. "Or perhaps...it was another window... It was hard to tell, ye ken, from across the street."

He faced her again, his eyes narrowed like they had when she'd tased him. Only then, he'd still been incapacitated and lying on the ground. Now he was there, in her house, probably remembering every little volt.

"I think you'd better hurry," she said quietly into the phone.

"Why? What is he doing now?"

"Remembering that I shot him with my taser."

"When? Just now?"

"No. About fifteen minutes ago, on the street."

"Officers are on their way. Stay with me if you can."

For about five minutes, Cat and the dispatcher listened to each other breathe. The Scot started answering her grandpa's questions, but from where she stood, halfway into the kitchen, she couldn't hear the details, just the tone. Her grandpa was like a kid coming face to face with his idol, which really ticked her off because the old man didn't know who he was talking to!

"Ma'am? Officers will be there in a couple of minutes. Is your taser live?"

"Nope."

"And where is the intruder?"

"Just standing there." And he was, glancing back and forth between her and her grandpa while the old man rattled off questions faster than his hoarse voice could handle.

"Well, if you don't have a weapon to defend yourself, you might want to apologize."

"Apologize!?"

"I accept." The guy grinned at her, winked, and sat down on the corner of the bed to give all his attention to her grandpa.

"Ma'am? The officers are at the door. Can you ring them in?"

"Yep." She sidled to the entrance and pushed the buzzer, then left the door ajar before stepping to the edge of the living room again. Both men ignored her and kept chatting like old school chums. She focused on her breathing while she waited for the cavalry.

She realized she was holding her phone in front of her like a gun, but she couldn't seem to stop, even when she heard the ding of the elevator from the hallway. She was seriously frozen in place, watching the Scot's mouth move, watching her grandpa laugh and smile at words she couldn't make out. Scottish small talk, probably.

I hate Scots! At least she tried really hard to hate them the whole time she stared at the poster boy for all things plaid.

"Ma'am?"

She turned toward the officer standing behind her right shoulder. He was trying not to smile.

"Ma'am? You can put your phone down now." He tapped her raised arm and the touch seemed to unfreeze her.

"Thanks." She put on a brave smile. "I'm sorry to bother you guys, but this guy followed me home from work, climbed in through the window, and now he's like, casting a spell on my grandpa...or something."

A bigger cop stepped up behind the first. They exchanged glances but kept straight faces. She had to give them credit.

The second cop glanced around nervously. "Someone got shot with a taser?"

The Scot raised his hand.

"And who shot you, sir?"

That raised hand folded and pointed at her.

The cops stepped away from her a little and the first one gave her phone a worried look. "And where is that weapon now, ma'am?"

She pointed at her purse lying open and unthreatening on the table. "It's yellow. Look," she pointed at the Scot, "*he's* an intruder. I didn't hurt him. I shot him out on the street, not in here."

The smaller cop glanced at the window. "On the street?"

She didn't know why that mattered. "Yes. He was stalking me, following me home. I was sure I was in danger—"

"Aye, the lass was in danger, officers." Adonis was frowning again. "Three lads followed her out of the tea shop—er, coffee house—and had nefarious plans for her, I have no doubt—"

She grunted. "You were the only one following me—"

"Aye. I followed to see ye safely home is all. I frightened the three away, but I worried there might be others."

"Look—"

The bigger cop held up a hand to interrupt her. "These *three lads*. Was one of them blond? Curly hair?"

"Aye. With a large slash of red paint on his jack."

"Jack?"

The Scot nodded. "A light coat, if ye will."

The first cop smiled and nodded. "He means jacket."

The Scot rewarded Sherlock Holmes with a smile. The man was still blushing when he faced her. "Three guys flagged us down half an hour ago to tell us that some creature roughed them up in an alley. We were pretty sure they were high. Maybe they weren't." All four men laughed in stereo.

What was this? The Twilight Testosterone Zone?

She put her hands on her hips. "So, are you going to arrest him?"

The first cop acted like she was the one that wasn't making sense. "He said he was protecting you. And the three thugs have pretty much verified it. What more do you want?"

She gasped—three times—waiting for someone else to come to their senses. But none of them did.

"I want him out of my home. And maybe those thugs want to press charges."

"Charges? I doubt it. Not if they'd been following you in the first place. But hang on." Little Sherlock looked at the Scot. "You wanna press charges against *her*, for shooting *you*?"

Those bright blue eyes sparkled. His lips curled. She could tell the second he'd made his decision. Not only was she *not* going to get her extra half hour of sleep, she wasn't going to be able to sleep *in her own bed* that night. She was actually going to be arrested!

Then something in those eyes changed.

"The lass has already apologized. As a gentleman, I must forgive her." He inclined his head like he'd just won a joust or something in her honor.

What a joke!

The bigger cop gave her a look that said she should be counting her blessings and kissing her intruder's hem. The truth smacked her in the face—if she stomped her feet and insisted on pressing charges against her stalker, he could change his mind and press charges against her.

And he could probably produce that witness too, the chick who had tried to look up his kilt while he was lying on the ground. Cat was pretty sure the woman would be able to remember every detail.

CHAPTER SEVEN

In an act of pure treason, Alonzo Dabelko turned on his granddaughter.

He claimed the Scot was a friend of his whom he'd invited into the house. An upstairs neighbor who had agreed to give his granddaughter a bit of a thrill. He knew how much she liked men in kilts.

Ha ha ha.

Since she wouldn't call her grandpa a liar in front of the rest, she'd simply excused herself and went to her room, locked the door and got in the shower. If the cops weren't going to arrest the guy, she wasn't going to waste any more of her sleeping time. She had a routine. If she didn't keep to it, she wouldn't be able to sleep. And no one was going to keep her from her daily dose of shut-eye.

And if Grandpa wanted to fraternize with the enemy, he was on his own—at least for a little while. He wanted to go ahead and trust a stranger who had followed her home from work? He could just fend for himself for a while. Maybe he'd realize the guy was nuts before the cops got around to leaving.

While she washed the smells of coffee and vanilla from her face, she prayed that the little party in her living room was breaking up. Her chest tightened, but she took some deep cleansing breaths to wash away the anger. The cops couldn't be blamed, of course, for not being more alarmed. They'd probably expected to find a standoff, not a perp having a friendly visit with a sick old man. And of course they couldn't really take her side of things when they'd learned that she had in fact attacked the perp.

The tightening returned in a heartbeat.

Of course they *could* have taken her side. They *should* have taken her side. She's a young, single woman in the city and they were supposed to be protecting her. It was her home that had been invaded. It didn't matter how charismatic that invader was!

She hurried through her routine, dried off, and slipped on a t-shirt and sweats, hoping to catch those cops before they were gone. She would give them a piece of her mind, and the Scot too, if she moved quickly enough. She wasn't the type to hold grudges. She wasn't even the type to tell someone off. But she was pretty sure she wouldn't be able to sleep a wink when she felt so mistreated.

Catherine Dabelko might be a kind, positive person, but she was no doormat.

In her hurry, she grabbed for the bedroom door and the leg of a chair caught her baby toe and nearly ripped it off her foot. She gasped in a deep breath and it came out in the form of a long string of every curse word she'd ever heard in her life, and a couple originals. Unfortunately, she'd been opening the door when she'd said them.

While the pain in her toe subsided to a howling throb, she stared into the faces of four startled men. The cops looked at her with a combination of disgust and disappointment. Her grandfather was downright embarrassed. But the Scot looked pleased as punch. She'd just given the other men another reason to side with the guy. If he and she were at war, this would be the point where her own troops would turn coats and sneak to the other side.

Led by her own grandfather.

She glared at the smaller cop. "I nearly ripped my toe off, okay?"

He looked doubtful, so she reached back, grabbed the chair, and slid it into the living room. It caught the edge of the rug and toppled over. His hand moved to his holster.

She rolled her eyes. "I wasn't throwing it *at you.*"

The guy was still unimpressed. He exchanged a look with his partner that said whatever she got now, she deserved, then he headed for the door. The bigger one said goodnight to the Scot and her grandpa, then followed. He stopped with his hand on the door and addressed her. "We're going to let you and your grandpa work this out. Since he lives here too, you should let him have some say in who gets to visit. He's a sick man. Try to remember that."

When the door closed, her mouth was still hanging open. And though she'd never in her life thrown anything in a fit of temper, she was tempted to throw the stupid chair at the door. The way her luck was going, however, there was a good chance they'd come back and arrest her—for being rude to her grandpa's guest!

She turned and glared at that guest and was not surprised to find him still smiling.

"You may have them fooled, but the three of us know the truth." She spared a glance at her grandpa and he had the decency to look guilty. To the Scot she said simply, "Get out."

"Now Catherine," her grandpa said in a rare stern tone, "I won't allow you to be rude to the man. He clearly came to your rescue tonight, and we owe him some gratitude."

He leaned back against the raised bed and panted like chastising her had taken all his strength. But he could have been acting, like he often did if he wasn't getting his way. She just couldn't be sure.

"And Seoc." The old man lifted his hand half-heartedly, then dropped it to the bed again. "My friend. Trust me. Catherine has never acted like this before. I don't know what's gotten into her. Maybe she's just...excited."

"Grandpa!"

He wasn't too exhausted to flinch at her tone but quickly went back to playing the part of a dying man.

The Scot bought it all—hook, line and sinker—and hurried to her grandpa's side. He touched the old man's forehead. "Can ye fetch me a cloth and a bowl of cool water, lass?" He glanced up at her. "Sweating," he said. "Could be a number of reasons."

Sweating?

She went to the linen closet and got a washcloth, trying not to feel too defensive. The word *fetch* didn't sit well with her, but it was probably a Scottish thing. Bring, fetch, same thing. She got some water in a small ice cream bucket and took them both to the bed and nudged the Scot out of the way.

"I can do this," she said, trying not to sound like a witch. She wet the cloth, wrung it out, and patted her grandpa's forehead. "How are you feeling?" She still suspected he was acting.

His lips moved a little, but then stopped. After a few deep breaths, he was asleep.

She turned off the lamp next to the headboard and pressed the button that lowered the head of the bed. She couldn't lower it too much or he would start coughing, but she was able to make him a little more comfortable.

A couple of weeks before, he'd been able to lie nearly flat. Soon, she wouldn't be able to lay him back at all. What would she do then? Make him sleep on his stomach?

She smoothed the covers and touched his hand for a long minute. All part of the ritual. Ritual was all that kept her going these days.

Suddenly self-conscious, she turned and found that the Scot had given her some privacy. He sat at the table in the kitchen staring at his fingers like they were new to him. He looked up when she flipped on the light above his head.

"I am sorry, lass."

"For?"

"For yer fairly immanent loss." He nodded toward the living room.

She sighed and shuffled over to the stove to turn on the kettle. It was going to take a little herbal tea to get to sleep this time. The stressful day ritual.

"I'm going to have tea. Would you like some, before you *go*?" The slight stress she'd added to the word *go* had sounded pretty rude, but she was too tired to care. Besides, the Scot brought out the worst in her. Not her fault at all.

"I can go now if ye prefer it, lass."

She shook her head. "That's all right. We'll call it apology tea."

He inclined his head.

"And you can tell me what the hell you're really doing, following me home and climbing through my window."

He bit his lip for a second, then nodded.

The rest of the ritual went on in silence. She opened up her tea box and let him choose what he wanted. Chamomile for her. Since he was obviously Scottish down to his boots, she figured he was probably used to having a snack with his tea, so she pulled out a tin of chocolate chip cookies she'd made two nights ago when she hadn't been able to sleep. She took off the lid and set it on the table and nodded for him to take one.

"They've got walnuts," she warned. "My grandpa likes anything that crunches."

He took a bite. "Divine, truly. I thank ye." Then the rest of the large cookie disappeared in two bites. She pushed the tin toward him and watched him down two more.

It had been a long time since anyone had complimented her cooking and she tried to hide her blush behind her cup. But then again, sitting so close and staring at his handsome face might have been the real reason she felt flushed. It was a little unnerving to be facing any stranger without a nice, high counter between them, let alone Adonis.

She finally forced herself to set her cup down. "You want to tell me what's going on?"

He pushed the tin away from him and took up his tea. "Not dangerous, that is for certain."

"Except to thugs?"

He nodded. "Not dangerous to you nor Alonzo."

His use of her grandfather's first name didn't bother her as much as she thought it might. It was kind of nice having someone else think of him as a person and not a patient. Usually, people called him Mr. Dabelko when speaking about him, even if he was still in the room.

"Okay. So let's pretend I believe you. Why are you here?"

He frowned and took so much time deciding what to say, she knew it wouldn't be the truth.

"Don't worry about it. I don't need to know." She took up her cup again and drank the rest in spite of the temperature. "He'll be waking up in a few hours, so I need to sleep while he sleeps."

The Scot got the hint and stood. He carried his cup to the sink before walking back to the living room. She pointed to the door and raised her eyebrows.

He shook his head and all that lovely hair with it. "I'll just go the way I came, aye? Instead of fumbling through the building trying to find my way out of it." He unlocked the window, then turned to look at her again. "I've no doubt ye've been a fine nurse to yer grandfather," he whispered. "But I believe ye should prepare yerself. He's not much time left."

She hurried around the bed and stood close to keep her grandpa from overhearing any more than he already might have. "He doesn't need to hear anything negative, do you understand? Especially from a stranger that doesn't know anything about him. You're not a doctor—"

"Aye, lass. I am." His hand rose up and cupped the side of her face. The lamplight from the far corner reflected in his eyes, and they were filled with such sincere regret it nearly shattered her.

"Get out." It was a little more than a breath, but their faces were so close he had no trouble hearing her.

He nodded but didn't move, like there was something more he intended to say, but she didn't want to hear it. She tried to pull his hand away from her face. Only, when she laid her fingers on his wrist, they just kind of...stuck there. It was so warm and firm and strong, she could almost imagine borrowing some strength from it.

The silly thought passed and after a slight tug from her, his hand fell away. He lifted the window and disappeared in one smooth, drawn out movement. The tail end of his plaid was the last to disappear through the opening before the window lowered again.

She moved closer to the bed and watched her grandfather sleep peacefully on with the clear forks of a cannula stuck up his nose. He hadn't heard a word, thank goodness. His hand was still warm and soft. He was no worse than he had been the day before. No need to turn up his O's—his oxygen. Everything was fine.

She ignored the warmth that lingered on her face in the shape of a man's hand...

A doctor? Please. Doctors didn't run around in costumes and break into apartments to visit patients that weren't theirs. He was just crazy!

She reached for the latch to lock it, but paused. Just one more glimpse of him wouldn't hurt anything, and she could rest easier knowing that he had really gone. So she lifted the sash and stuck her head out.

The rain had stopped, but the smell of wet streets and damp bricks swirled around her head along with the remnants of smoke. Poindexter, from the apartment below, had been smoking something on the fire escape again. Maybe that was who the Scot had seen and tried to rescue her from. Maybe he hadn't been making up that part either.

Though she searched the shadows, there was no trace of him. She would have expected it to take him more time to reach the ground. But it wasn't the first time he'd disappeared on her. After she'd tased him, he'd gotten up off that sidewalk and disappeared awfully quickly.

She turned her head and looked up toward the roof, but there was no movement on the small metal ladder that led from her own landing to the top of the building. Besides, you'd have to be a ghost to get up the rusty old thing and not make a noise.

A ghost? She laughed to herself. Only moments ago, she'd had a firm grip on one of his wrists and he definitely was not a ghost. Some self-appointed superhero was more likely. But either way, he was gone, and good riddance. Her grandfather's health was holding its own, and as long as she kept the coffee flowing and the home health nurse paid, Alonzo Dabelko wasn't going anywhere.

CHAPTER EIGHT

When he heard the window open, Seoc peeked over the top of the ladder and was pleased to see the lass was at least curious about him. It had taken a trick or two to get the lass's attention and he'd begun to think his appeal might have been omitted from his new body. But perhaps she'd only been pretending her indifference.

Her bonny head turned to look up the ladder and he quickly backed away and held his breath while he waited to see if he'd been caught.

A canny lass, to be sure.

A stubborn lass as well. She clearly had no intention of letting her grandfather leave this world without fighting God or Lucifer for him. But in the end—in the very near end—she would lose that fight.

While the lass had been in her room, he'd asked the old man some pointed questions. And after the policemen had realized he was a doctor, they stood back and gave them some privacy.

It was clear the man's body was shutting down, something he didn't want to tell his granddaughter. And when she'd told Seoc to get out just a moment ago, he'd realized why the fellow had wanted to keep his secrets. The lass would likely try her hand at resuscitation on the spot!

It had been Alonzo out on the landing, enjoying a precious private moment and a pull on his pipe. And in his current state, it was a wonder he was able to make it back into bed before his granddaughter found him. She'd come home early, it seemed.

Luckily for Seoc, the old man held Scotland near and dear even though he'd never stepped foot there. So the sight of a Scotsman in full regalia had given him a shot of adrenaline to see him through the evening. He'd pressed Seoc for details he wasn't willing to share, but after he'd confessed to the old man that he did not have a place to lay his head for the night, Alonzo had pointed to a key hanging beside the window on a wee nail.

An enclosed shelter awaited him on the roof, a potting shed of sorts where his granddaughter puttered around when she had the time.

Seoc waited for the lass to close the window once more before he dared move about. It took a few moments for his eyes to adjust to the starlight, but he easily found his shelter. The lock turned, the door opened, and the smell of rich earth welcomed him into the darkness.

A damp night, to be sure, but he left the doors wide and stretched out on the long chair. Rich earth, rain, and a wet chill in the air. He couldn't have felt more at home.

He took a deep breath and bid welcome to a mortal night's rest, but the lass's face sprung to mind. So many expressions to choose from. The welcoming smile at the coffee shop. The split second when she'd decided to shoot him. The drop of her jaw when he sat on the bed, and when the officers would not share her concern.

And as much as he'd wanted to make her admit that there was a meanness inside her—something that didn't smile at the world unconditionally—he now wanted something else more.

He wanted to wipe away the terror he'd seen in her eyes when he'd warned that her grandfather was not long for this world. He'd seen that same terror a hundred times when he was alive, and hundreds more at the Battle of Culloden, when the wounded realized they were going to be murdered where they lay.

No matter what he did, or how he begged, he was unable to save more than a few of his fellow Scots that day. But maybe, if the minx downstairs would allow him to get close again, he could save her some of the heartache that now stalked her...like a Redcoat wielding a bayonet.

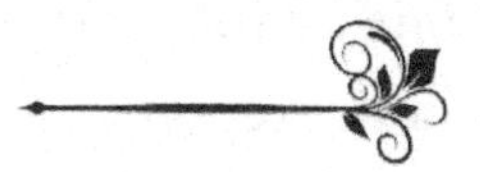

In spite of the fact that Grandpa's face had twisted when she'd mentioned food, Cat was cooking him the most tempting breakfast she could.

"If this bacon doesn't make him hungry," she murmured, "nothing will."

"What's that?" he hollered.

"I said," she hollered back, "that I wasn't going to call you a liar in front of the police, but next time you tell stories about a neighbor from upstairs, you need to remember that we're on the top floor."

Grandpa laughed, then coughed, then laughed again. "I was wondering when you'd catch that."

She plated up a large mound of scrambled eggs, added buttered toast and a pile of bacon. A mug of coffee was already cooling and she scooped that up too and headed for the other room, chuckling as she came around the corner. "I'm just glad you didn't offer him the key to my shed—" She stopped and stared at the empty nail beside the window. "You didn't!"

"What?" Her grandpa looked at the nail and frowned. "I certainly did not. I don't know where you've lost it this time." He pointed to the plate. "Is that all for me?"

She watched him for signs of guilt, but didn't see anything obvious. The way he was eyeing his breakfast made her a little suspicious, of course, since he'd made such a face when she told him she'd be cooking it.

"Yes. It's all for you."

He was a little too excited and it broke her heart, knowing he was pretending just for her. But she wasn't above taking advantage of his overacting. Every bite he took made him stronger, so as long as he was eating, she didn't care why.

Or at least, she would pretend not to care as long as he kept eating. But as soon as he stopped, she was headed to the roof.

She glanced at the nail again, then at the window. No way the guy could have shimmied up that ladder without making a racket.

Her grandpa tried to distract her by moaning over the breakfast. "This is just what I needed. I thought you were going to make me eat mush again."

She'd made him eat mush the first week they'd been in the apartment. Trying to be clever with their money, she'd made a detailed meal plan that would save hundreds on their food bill. But cracked wheat mush had been a bad idea. And the oatmeal.

He'd forced it down the first four days because she'd sold him on the idea of eating a traditional Scottish breakfast. But then he'd googled *Traditional Scottish Brea*kfast and called her on the carpet.

The breakfast in the photos he'd found included sausage, eggs, ham, mushrooms, tomatoes of all things, and baked beans. Photo after photo had been the same, only some of them had some black stuff they'd learned was either Haggis or Blood Sausage, and she certainly wasn't about to cook him those.

After the debate, she'd realized the cheapest option was to run down to the corner and get him a Sausage McMuffin most mornings.

Grandpa took a small bite of bacon and smiled. Then he turned green so fast she lunged for the empty ice cream bucket from the night before. He was able to keep down what he'd already eaten, but he insisted she take his plate away.

She came back with a cup of tea. He shook his head and closed his eyes, so she set the tea on his tray and turned to open the window.

"What are you doing?" He was wide awake again.

"Going up to see if I left that key in the shed, or in the lock."

"Wha...what if my breakfast comes back up again?" She almost felt bad. He sounded so weak. But she stayed tough.

"You've got your bucket. I'll be right back."

The door buzzer interrupted. A climb up to the roof would have to wait, even though she wanted to get away from the thick, greasy smell of bacon that hung in the air like a cloud waiting for gravity to bring it down.

She went to the door and pushed the intercom. "Yes?"

"Hello?"

"May I help you?"

"Aye, lass. Ye can. This is Seoc Macbeth, from last eve. I'd appreciate the chance to apologize if ye will allow me to come up."

She stepped to the end of the entry to exchange a look with her grandpa, whom she could see clearly with the portable screens moved out of the way. She half expected him to be jumping out of bed to come push the buzzer himself, but instead, his eyes were closed again. He'd dosed off. She couldn't tell if it was a trick of the light coming through the big windows, but his color was wrong.

She hurried back to the intercom and pushed the speaker, while at the same time pushing the buzzer to release the door to the building.

"Yes. Please come. Apartment 404. And hurry!"

CHAPTER NINE

Cat already had the pulse/oximeter on her grandpa's finger and was replacing the cannula with an oxygen mask when a very different looking Scotsman rushed into the room. His hair was tied at the back of his neck and he wore jeans and a baby blue t-shirt that was at least one size too small. It had a white logo on it, but she didn't dare stare long enough to read what it said.

"He usually doesn't need much oxygen in the mornings," she explained in a quiet voice. "But he looks a little gray to me. And he's usually not sleepy until about ten."

The Scot came around the bed and she made room for him to get a close look. He picked up a pale, soft hand and looked closely at the nails. The oximeter beeped.

She peeked around his arm to read it. "Seventy-nine." She adjusted the oxygen gage. "I should have tested him first thing."

The Scot frowned at her. "Dinna look back, lass. Regrets are futile."

She nodded. "Should we wake him up and make him take some deep breaths?"

He shook his head. "Maybe allow him to rest a wee while, aye? Let the machine do the work for a piece?"

She read the oximeter again. “Ninety-two. It’s recovering.” Only then did she start to shake with relief, or maybe from holding her breath too much, but either way, she was careful to hide her hands with her long sleeves.

With the Scot’s help, they placed the screens along the side of the bed, closed the curtains, and moved quietly into the kitchen. By that time, she was feeling normal again.

“I have to admit,” she said, “I’m glad you came when you did. I usually don’t freak out like that. I just...”

“Ye doona get enough sleep? Mm?” He stooped a little to make her look at him, then winked.

They’d ended up standing face to face in the narrow gap between the table and the cupboards. She smiled, but had to look away fast. The baby-blue of the t-shirt brought out the blue in his eyes and she was determined not to get lost in them. They were like two bright little puddles that she was careful to walk around or she’d ruin her shoes...or her life.

She’d always been careful to tell herself and everyone else that she would worry about making her own life later. She would date later. Have a family...later. Choose a real career...later. And no matter how long she held things off to take care of the grandpa, she knew she would never regret a day of keeping him close.

Besides, it wasn’t as if someone that looked like that would ever be interested in a simple barista with no time to waste at the gym, let alone go shopping for trendy clothes.

In a rather smooth move, she put some distance between them by turning her back and stepping to the stove. “Have you had breakfast?” When he didn’t answer right away, she faced him again. He was fidgeting with his hands.

With most of his hair tied back, she could see his face clearly. She couldn’t imagine what he was embarrassed about.

Finally, he spoke. “I admit I was up and at ‘em early this morn. I found a pastry shop and thought it would be a shame not to sample some of their confections while they were warm. And though I had intended to bring a box of them to share with ye and Alonzo… I am ashamed to say they did not survive the journey."

She laughed. "Don't tell me. Voodoo Donuts?"

"Aye," he grinned. "They say the magic is in the hole, but I believe they are wrong."

They laughed together then, but quietly.

She lifted an empty plate and shrugged. "If you ate the whole box, I don't suppose you'd like bacon and eggs then."

He craned his neck to look at the stove like a starving teenager. She rolled her eyes and told him to sit down at the table.

"Ah. Before I do that, I must make a confession, lass. Perhaps ye'll wish to recant the invitation."

She leaned back against the oven door and folded her arms. He'd sounded pretty nervous, which made her nervous too. But the only thing that might really upset her was if he started talking about Grandpa going downhill. If he did, she figured she could use the spatula to get him back out the door before he said too much.

He dug two fingers into his jeans pocket, pulled something out, and set it on the table. It was the key to her potting shed on the roof. She would have recognized the little jute loop anywhere.

"I took advantage," he said, then stood at attention and waited.

"I don't think you took the key on your own." She glanced at the living room. "You couldn't have known what it unlocked unless someone told you."

His brow furrowed like he worried she wasn't taking him seriously. "I accept all responsibility."

"Oh, sit down, would you?" She turned her back to him again, dished up a plateful, and set it on the table in front of him. "Some protein to go along with your donuts."

He pulled out a chair and sat, apparently willing to forgive himself. She fixed another plate and two cups of coffee. He popped back to his feet when she joined him.

Manners. There in her own kitchen.

"So, are you homeless?"

He took a napkin from the pile on the table and wiped his mouth. She tried really hard not to watch, but failed.

"Only for a pair of days," he finally said. "I'm…fresh from the boat, ye might say."

"From Scotland?"

"Aye. And I've no ken how long my…plastic will last—"

"So you don't want to pay for an expensive hotel?"

"Just so."

She relaxed a little. Pinching pennies she could understand, but a doctor pinching pennies? Then again, maybe they didn't pay British doctors like those in the U.S.

"So, what kind of doctor are you?"

He took a long sip of coffee and wiped those chiseled lips again. "Battlefield."

Wow. The guy was just one surprise after another.

"Afghanistan?"

He finished off his last bite of toast and wiped his mouth again. She would have stopped grilling him while he ate, but he was already done. He pushed his plate back, gathered his mug between his hands, and leaned forward. The sleeves of his t-shirt would have groaned if they were capable of making noise.

"I served wherever my fellow soldiers fought." He watched her face closely, then shrugged. "But I haven't doctored anyone for quite a while now."

That explained why he might have to pinch pennies.

"Well, I'm sorry you had to sleep on a lounge chair."

"The chair and the fresh air was grand, lass. It was generous of yer grandfather to offer it, aye? But it pained my conscience to do it behind yer back, and I would ask yer forgiveness."

"Forgiven."

He insisted on helping clean up. For the next twenty minutes they danced around each other while they washed pans and tried not to clang them together. Every once in a while, one of them would make a misstep and they'd bump into each other, or clink the coffee cups, and they tried not to giggle. When it was all finished and the dish towel hung on the back of a chair to dry, she was almost sad it was over.

They faced each other in front of the sink. There was no reason for him to stay, no excuse to ask him to. But he wasn't exactly running for the door.

"I'd like to thank ye for the breakfast, lass."

"You're welcome. And my name is Catherine."

He shook his head. "Nay, Catherine. I'd like to thank ye properly." He took two tiny, slow steps closer, swaying as he came. His hand rose to the side of her face just as it had the night before, and she realized he was going to kiss her.

He's a stranger. Don't let him do it!

The angel on her other shoulder urged her to wrap her arms around his neck and make it last until he ran for the door. She settled for something in between.

He lowered his head toward her, glancing back and forth from her lips to her eyes, giving her plenty of time to protest, giving her plenty of time to burn the moment into her memory. Finally, when he touched his lips to hers, she was relieved. In the back of her mind, she was expecting him to come to his senses and turn away at the last second.

But he didn't.

Much to the disappointment of both angels on her shoulders, she didn't push him away or hold him hostage. His hands rested lightly on her waist for a second or two, then he broke the kiss and stepped back. It was then she wished she would have taken the advice of angel number two...because it was going to be a very long time before anyone would get close enough to kiss her again.

"You're welcome," she said, then ducked her head, embarrassed. Avoiding his gaze, she turned and headed for the bedroom. "I'll be out in a minute."

Terrified of what sound might come out of her mouth next, she closed the door behind her, hurried over to the bed, and buried her face in a pillow. Her outburst was a cross between a scream and a laugh. It was just too insane to believe that a guy like him would look twice at her, let alone everything that had happened since she'd seen him at the coffee shop.

Was there a catch? Was there something she didn't understand?

Maybe she'd been so busy with her current responsibilities that some fairy godmother had been forced to bring Prince Charming to her.

Now, wouldn't that be nice?

But there was no room in her life for Prince Charming—at least not for a while. And it sounded like the guy wasn't going to be in Portland for long anyway.

She sighed and rolled over onto her back, then got to her feet.

I guess he was just meant to be a one morning stand.

After a quick check in the mirror to make sure she wasn't blushing anymore, she walked out into the living room with absolutely no idea what she would say next. But it didn't really matter.

He was gone.

CHAPTER TEN

Seoc could have kicked himself all the way back to the coffee house. And mentally, he tried.

He was a fool. He'd allowed a lass to ruin everything!

Why hadn't he made his excuses and gone on his way as soon as he realized the old man was terminal? Why? Had the Battle of Culloden taught him nothing?!

There had been a mistake made, of course, and young Rabby had made it. The morning after the battle, he'd met Seoc rising from his grave and pronounced he was the 76th ghost to join what soon became Culloden's 79. What the others hadn't understood was that he was never meant to be counted in their number. It should have been Culloden's 78.

The blame lay on his own shoulders, of course. He never corrected the boy even after he'd gotten his bearings and realized he was, indeed, a ghost. It didn't take long, however, for Seoc to understand that his reasons for holding tight to the in-between was not the same as his comrades'.

The others felt cheated, he knew. They were angry to have been taken from the physical world before they'd had their fair share of it. And they longed to be revenged, or at least to have their tragedies heard, and rightly so.

But for Seoc Macbeth, it was different. It wasn't the physical world he clung to, but the next life he fended off. On the far side of that shimmering veil that appeared from time to time to beckon him onward... stood a good sized army...waiting for him.

For two hundred sixty-nine years, he'd ignored that beckoning. He'd been content to bide out eternity on the moors. After all, there was no substance to time as it passed. No regrets for time squandered, no desperate search for the meaning of his existence. And when he felt a twinge of loneliness, there were humans to examine, tellies to watch, or 78 other ghosties who gathered from time to time to play at war.

Although, he did share one thing in common with the others—his attachment to a certain wee lassie who turned out to be a witch. He'd watched her grow, watched her interact with Number 79 and others. And all along, he'd suspected she had not come in vain.

On the night of the Summer Solstice, when she'd put forth her challenge, it had all become clear to him. She was to be their savior, but she'd meant to doctor their souls first. The carrot she'd dangled before them, the chance to exact their revenge on Prince Charles Stuart himself, had been the perfect bait for the rest.

Obviously, the offer hadn't interested Seoc, and he'd wondered, when Soni got down to the last of them, how she might compel *him* to leave the moor. She'd been so confident. Had she known he was not like the rest?

Of course she had. She'd told him, there at the end, that she knew the desires of his heart.

Surprisingly, it hadn't been until Rabby was sent away that Seoc truly considered leaving Culloden. The lad couldn't have been harboring revenge in his heart, for he'd been too young for that deep a passion.

Nay. In a child that young, it had to have been a fear for the next life that had tethered him to the moor. And in Seoc's case, it wasn't a fear, but a knowledge of what awaited him...

This patch of common ground between him and Rabby is what made him ask himself if he might be ready to face that wee army after all. It had been a long while since the shimmering veil had come to beckon him. And the new door Soni opened between one world and the next might well and truly close for good.

Content as he was to stay at Culloden for eternity, there was enough curiosity left in him to give it a go. Surely, what that army had in mind for him wouldn't last forever either.

He was eager to face it and have done—if a certain witch would simply give him his task and remove him from Portland, Oregon before he did any more damage to the living. The night before, he'd slipped back into his old ways, thinking he could make a difference for the lass. But he couldn't remove that terror from her eyes or her heart unless he lied about her grandfather's condition. And then, when the old man died anyway, her heartbreak would be trebled.

Better to leave her and her grandfather be.

CHAPTER ELEVEN

The scent of coffee grew stronger the closer he got to the building to which Soncerae had delivered him. But with it came the memory of a certain kiss.

Damn that smile.

He lifted his forearm to his mouth, intending to wipe away the memory, but he couldn't make himself do it. Had he so many such memories that he could afford to wipe this one away?

Nay.

He dropped his arm and left the tingling alone.

The line for coffee was out the door, much like the line for Voodoo Donuts had been just before dawn. His mood turned more sour when he stopped to wonder how many of the men in that line had come to patronize not the coffee house, but the sweet lass who worked there. Those fellows would be sorely disappointed.

Feeling smug, he pardoned his way past the line and into the building. The coffee he'd just enjoyed had been far superior than could be anything on the menu, what with a kiss for a sweetener. But he wasn't there for coffee. He had come to clear his head and perform his task. Better to complete his quest and go before someone's heart was injured—not just the lass's, but his own.

A fine kettle of fish.

He bit his lip to curb his ire. It would be blasphemy to question what God had intended by putting him in cupid's path only *after* he'd been dead for so long. Ungrateful of him to wonder why some charming woman hadn't stumbled across his path while he'd been a mortal young man. And it would be downright sinful of him to pursue sweet Catherine's affections while in his reanimated state. What good would it serve to woo her only to leave her in another day's time?

No. He had a duty to perform. He had a reward to collect. And he had an eternity to worry over the lass. Or not.

"Soncerae," he bellowed to the ceiling, hoping she could hear him. It was no concern of his what the coffee patrons thought of his antics. He only needed a bit of direction so he would know just where he was meant to go.

A gust of wind blew past the souls holding the door open in order to keep their place in line. It swirled around Seoc and nudged his duffle bag against his knees. In its wake, a single, fuzzy blossom from a tree twirled around his head. He half expected it to land on the floor and turn into his beloved wee witch.

"Soni?" he whispered.

The blossom twirled again, then bobbed for the open doorway, unnoticed by those who simply watched to see what the foreigner would do next. And Seoc was a fool if he allowed it to leave without him.

Outside, it took a moment to locate the fluff again. It danced around the top of a tree while it waited for him to catch up. He nodded to it, and thankfully, the teasing bit moved on. North again. Back the way he'd come. At least he hadn't been too far amiss when he'd followed the trio of thugs the night before.

Had it been so recently? Less than a day since he'd met the lass over a gleaming silver counter? Only a day since she'd taken such consideration not to shout his family name and embarrass him?

Half a day since he'd chatted with Alonzo and learned how near the man was to his last breath? And now that he knew Catherine better, he'd understood that her grandfather only fought death with such passion because he worried about leaving the lass.

But what could Seoc do for the sorry pair? Nothing at all. He could neither heal the grandfather, nor ease the burden of the granddaughter. So, rather than flounder in futility, his precious last day would be better spent searching for a truly heroic act that would signal Soni to collect him.

The blasted bit of fuzz continued north.

Folks on the street stopped and followed his gaze, but none seemed to see the will o' the wisp but him. Was it only his imagination then?

He slowed and stopped, stretched his head from side to side, and looked about him. A flurry of bicycles passed, the riders all wearing numbers on their backs. No one in need of help. No one glancing his way.

Finally, he looked up again. The fuzzy blossom hovered just overhead, barely out of his reach. It bobbed, as if it would speak to him, then headed along the footpath again. It did not wait for him to catch up this time, nor did it dance about with the air stirring along the street. The little blossom seemed to mean business.

So like Soncerae.

Seoc passed intersection after intersection. His wee guide made nary a turn from the path he'd followed the night before. After a while, he knew with a certainty where it was taking him, so he wondered why Soni bothered to continue.

He nearly stepped out in front of a moving car he was so intent on retracing his steps. The driver hit her brakes but did not honk at him. She was simply content that he wasn't harmed and waved for him to cross the street with her blessing.

He worried she was too shaken to continue on...until she whistled at him.

The blossom waited for him near the door of Catherine's apartment building, just as he'd expected. When he was half a dozen steps away, the fuzz became a large dark blur that spun and twisted into the figure of a man. His form was still undefined when he locked gazes with Seoc.

"Macbeth."

"Aye."

The man grinned. "You are, in *coffee,* stepped in so far that, should you wade no more, returning were as tedious as go o'er."

The twisted lines of Macbeth, the play.

"You mock me."

The man rolled his eyes. "You understand full well what I mean."

"And who are you? I summoned Soncerae."

"I am Wickham. Soni, my niece, prepares for the long night ahead of her. So I've come in her stead."

Seoc folded his arms defiantly. "She wouldn't have mocked me. She would have told me where my quest lay."

The fellow pointed up, his finger angled slightly toward the front west corner of the building. "You are, in coffee—"

"Cease yer nonsense. What ye meant to tell me is that I've gone too far to turn back now."

"You kissed her."

He lowered his head and narrowed his eyes, feeling much like an offended bull. "You watch me?"

"No. I see it on yer mind at this very moment." Wickham stopped smiling. "Go to her. Help her. Prepare her for the long night ahead of her."

For the long night ahead of her...

From the mouth of a Muir. Alonzo wouldn't last the night, then. No matter what, the old man would find his immortal rest, and the lass would learn to deal with her loss. Seoc wouldn't be mortal long enough to see her through it. Funerals took days now.

He shrugged. "I cannot help her. And false hope is the cruelest offering." He ignored the twist in his gut when he said it.

"Who else but you?" Wickham's brow puckered dramatically, then cleared as if inspiration had struck him. "Never mind, Macbeth. I'm certain that Spencer chap can offer a shoulder—"

"Go on with ye!"

The man laughed. "I'll come for ye by morning." He turned his head and the whole of him was suddenly naught more than a swirling black fog that spun itself into nothing.

CHAPTER TWELVE

A stooped old woman hobbled toward the glass and pushed the door open an inch, then two. Seoc grabbed the handle and pulled the thing wide, then offered the woman a hand down the steps, all the while holding fast to the door. After a smile and a wave, the woman toddled down the sidewalk and he slipped inside the building.

He found the stairs, unwilling to ride in the elevator again. The scenes from the movies he'd watched combined with his last experience, after he'd left the lass, ensured that he would never trust the box to spit him out again if he risked stepping inside.

The doors hadn't opened when he'd needed them to, and closed far too quickly. It lurched from floor to floor as if a demon possessed it and teased him. He was a nervous, quivering lad again before someone had stepped inside with him and got the box to open on the main floor. It had taken a full five minutes to calm his stomach.

Seoc trudged up the stairs with heavy feet. Even the knowledge that he was returning to see sweet Catherine again wasn't enough to make him hurry. It was Culloden all over again. Only this time, he knew just how futile his efforts would be.

Alonzo was such a brave gentleman. If there was aught Seoc could do to ease his passing, he would do it.

He reached the fourth floor well out of breath. By the time he found Catherine's door again, he had regained his composure, but then nearly lost it again when she answered his knock.

She'd been greetin'.

"Lass, what is it?" He pushed his way into the apartment and continued into the living room. Beneath the blankets at the end of the bed, Alonzo's feet lay perfectly still. Seoc looked back at Catherine to silently ask if the old man yet lived.

She frowned and shushed him. "He's still sleeping." She waved him toward the kitchen, but then reconsidered and drew him down a hallway toward the rear. They passed her bedroom door, which she quickly pulled closed, then she led him into the water closet and shut them both inside.

He ignored the surroundings and took hold of her shoulders. "Ye've been weeping. Did ye not see my note?"

"Note?"

He huffed out a breath. "Aye. I left a note on the table, that I'd be back in the morning if I could."

She shrugged. "It's not morning."

Her lower lip stuck out slightly, but it was sufficient to attract his attention. He tried to fix his gaze on her eyes instead.

"Auch, aye. The...appointment I had for today has been postponed until tomorrow, in the morning." It was mostly true. "So I came back to help watch over Alonzo, if ye'll accept my aid."

She searched his eyes for a moment. Whatever she saw there brought her generous smile back. He'd nearly forgotten what an impact it had, like a well-swung targe to the chest. He caught his breath and held it, savoring the moment.

If only they weren't standing in a water closet, it might have been even more memorable. But he wouldn't have her looking back at a kiss from a Scotsman with a roll of toilet paper poking into his thigh.

"I'll just wait in the hallway, shall I?"

She didn't protest as he made his escape. And from the other side of the door, he heard the delicate roar of the lass blowing her nose. When she emerged, that smile was still in place, and he ignored the twinge of guilt in his gut. It was little comfort, that if he fell for the lass, or she for him, he could lay the blame at the feet of that Wickham fellow.

They leaned back against opposite walls and tucked their hands behind their backs. A bare two feet separated them.

"So." She bit her bottom lip. Her right shoulder rose and fell. The sweatshirt she wore shrugged with her and promised to be soft to the touch. It was best his hands were trapped behind him.

"So," he echoed. "Tell me, do ye always smile so? That is, when ye're not weeping?"

She rolled her eyes. "I don't cry much. So I guess, when it all builds up, it comes out in a rush. Just emotional buildup in my body. That's all. I'm good now. I was just tired, I think."

He nodded like he understood when in truth he understood little. No matter why someone weeps, he was fair to certain all tears come from the heart. But he wasn't about to point out the simplicity of his theory. It was clear the lass was still not prepared to speak about her grandfather dying, even if her *body* was already mourning his loss.

"And now you are not so tired?"

"Nope. I'm fine." She smiled a little harder. Not quite as genuine as before.

She rocked nervously against the wall at her back for a moment while he took in the sight of her. Her jeans were frayed, whether by intent or not, he could not say. Her sweatshirt showed its wear in the stretched-out holes created for her thumbs. Her hair was simply cut, long and sable. No fancy bleaching or coloring of her tresses, no elaborate designs on her fingernails, and he realized the lass would have little time to pamper herself with all her responsibilities, especially if she hardly had enough time to sleep.

A generous lass...who was staring at his chest.

Her head gave a subtle shake and her eyes dropped to the floor. Then her attention caught on the duffle bag he'd dropped at the end of the hall.

"Is your kilt in there?" she asked.

"Aye."

"Ah," she said, but he didn't miss the slight wrinkle of her nose.

"Ye doona care for kilts today," he teased, letting her know he was fully aware of how much she'd appreciated his traditional garments the day before.

She rolled her eyes. "Grandpa was teasing about that. I don't like men in kilts. Not at all." She grimaced when she realized the insult. "And it's not kilts, really. It's Scotland I don't like."

His surprise could not be hidden.

"Look. Grandpa's a little obsessed about what little Scottish blood he has. And he started smoking a pipe because it was a Scottish thing to do—"

"And ye believe it is this pipe-smoking that invited his lung cancer."

She sighed. "Yes. I'm sorry. I can't help it."

"No worries, lass. I assure ye, Scotland and its inhabitants wouldn't begrudge yer bias."

Her smile was real again. "Thank you."

Immediately, he remembered the way he'd thanked her for breakfast, just around the corner in the kitchen, and the memory drew his attention to her lips. She caught her breath, but didn't move.

He wondered if it was part of his duty to distract the lass, to lure her thoughts to something other than her grandfather's condition.

He pushed off the wall and took a step. Her attention fell back to his chest again and he had to resist the urge to flex his muscles for her. When her gaze lifted again, it only made it so far as his lips, and it was the last bit of encouragement he needed.

"As soon as you two are done dancing in the hallway, I'd like to go down to the waterfront." Alonzo stood at the end of the wall pretending he wasn't hanging onto it for dear life.

The moment was lost.

"I'll get your chair," Catherine chirped and ran into her bedroom.

Seoc hurried around behind Alonzo to give him a little support until his wheeled chariot arrived. The man didn't seem the least repentant for the interruption.

Soec murmured, "Ye have poor timing, *Grandpa.*"

The old man chuckled. "Do you think? Here I was thinking I was a little late to the party."

CHAPTER THIRTEEN

"He hasn't felt up to coming down here for a few weeks," Catherine whispered while her grandfather exchanged greetings with the old woman returning to the building as they were leaving it. The lass's tone implied she was heartened by the new development. She believed she had a reprieve, but Seoc knew better.

This trip to the waterfront was a last hurrah.

The morning of the battle, Seoc had realized that without some miracle, it was likely he would not live through the day. So many details combined to doom the Highlanders that every man on that field should have recognized them. And while he'd stood there waiting for the Jacobite leaders to make their decisions, he'd thought of a dozen things he wished he could do with what time was left to him.

He would have jumped in a loch and enjoyed the cold kiss of Scotland in springtime flowing over his body and prickling his limbs. He would have indulged in warm scones and sweet honey and paid no heed to the mess as the heat-thinned honey poured over his fingers.

He would have hit his knees and bit a mouthful of grass just to make the taste of Scotland a sure and everlasting part of him. And he would have run to the lass he loved and made her part of him as well.

But there had been no such lass. It had only been a dream for a future never reached, a dream that had been lodged in his head for centuries. And if the dream continued to haunt him in the afterlife, at least there would now be a face and a name to it.

Catherine. In another life, she would have been his, he was sure of it. He'd have kept at her until she relented and promised to share her sweetest smile only with him.

He took a deep breath of city air and shook the pointless thoughts from his head. He had the remainder of the day to spend with her, and that was all. He would not squander it on futile wishes. He had a city to explore.

First, they boarded a transit train named MAX. There was a special area for wheelchairs and with few others in the car with them, there were, blessedly, few witnesses to his indignity.

He had seen all manner of travel on the telly. And he himself had travelled a quarter of the distance around the world in a heartbeat or two. But speeding so quickly from inside the train was like the disturbing episode in the elevator, only sideways. Though he expected the tracks to be clear, he couldn't keep from grasping onto the hand rails and holding on for dear life, sure they would crash into something unforeseen and suffer horribly for it.

Catherine laughed at him. Even Alonzo was able to raise a chuckle or two, so Seoc gave them both a merry wink and pretended his antics had been for their amusement. However, the wobble in his walk, when they'd disembarked, was real indeed.

Their first stop was the Portland Saturday Market. White tents were set up and filled with all manner of food and colorful trinkets. There was a bridge nearby he would have liked to inspect more closely, but there was no time. Alonzo pointed, and there they would go.

A clever and gifted fellow by the name of Estefan stretched bread dough and fried it in a dangerous caldron of hot oil. When it had transformed into a veritable pillow, toasted and brown, he presented it on a paper plate and plopped a helping of honey butter in the center.

Alonzo declared he would have one and Catherine was only too happy to oblige. She purchased one for Seoc and another for herself as well.

"I suppose, since ye knew of my new affinity for Voodoo Donuts, it was an easy guess I would like this. What is it?"

"A scone."

He choked on his next bite. "I'll tell ye, lass. We've scones in Scotland, but they're a tenth the size and four times the weight of these heavenly clouds."

She grimaced.

He realized his mistake. She was against all things Scottish. It was a wonder she allowed him near at all, doctor or no.

"Where next?"

Alonzo pointed to the river. "Chess," he said.

Catherine groaned. "That's pretty far, Grandpa."

The old man chuckled. "Don't worry. I'm up for it." He leaned back in his wheeled chair, closed his eyes, and looked as if he was preparing to take a nap.

"No worries," Seoc assured her. "I'll push him. Where do we go?"

It was a long walk and Catherine wished she would have refused to go. Despite her grandpa's energy, his color still looked off. But Doctor Macbeth didn't seem to think it was anything to worry about, so she went along with the plan. If the patient had a serious coughing attack halfway between the two bridges, though, they'd be in trouble. Sometimes the oxygen wasn't enough to settle him down again, and if he passed out, she would prefer he was at home.

He'd forbidden her to call an ambulance for him ever again, to just let him go. But the next time he passed out, she didn't know if she could do what she'd been told.

By the time they got to the Salmon Street Fountain, she was pooped, and she didn't think it had much to do with the exercise. If her grandpa suddenly decided he wanted to rent a bike and take off, she couldn't stop him. She was done.

There were three tables set up under the trees. She had the Scot park her grandpa at one of them while she went to the bike rental guy to get the chess pieces. The old gentlemen Grandpa usually played with weren't around, so she was going to have to play him herself.

She hated chess. It seemed like a Scottish game.

When she returned with the board and pieces, the blue t-shirt was sitting opposite the wheelchair. Her heart jumped with hope. "Do you play?"

Seoc winked at her and waved her close. "I've told yer grandfather I'm a bit green at it. He assures me he hasn't played in ages, and he doesn't remember all the moves." He leaned closer to her and whispered even louder. "I don't believe him for a moment."

"Smart man." She grinned at both men then pulled the thin blanket from the gym bag she always hung behind the wheelchair. "While you two duke it out, I'm going to shut my eyes." She spread the blanket on the springy, soft grass and stretched out on her stomach.

Grandpa had a babysitter, and that babysitter was a doctor. What could a nap hurt?

CHAPTER FOURTEEN

Cat never dreamed.

A lot of people say that, but what they really mean is that they don't remember their dreams. In Cat's case, though, she really didn't dream. When she wasn't jumping up to hit the alarm button in the morning, she would hold very still when she awoke and try to remember the last thought she'd had. But it was always the same, always the last thing she'd been thinking about the night before. Nothing ever happened in between. Not even when she started sleeping lighter—ready to jump out of bed if an alarm sounded next to her grandpa's bed, or if he rang the dinner bell she left on his tray for times when he needed help, or just needed company, in the middle of the night.

She just wasn't wired for dreams. Or maybe she'd programmed her brain that way. Career, later. Fall in love...later. Dream big...later.

But this time, when she pressed her face against the soft cotton of the quilt and her conscious mind clicked off, she did dream.

She was lying on a blanket in the middle of a wide field in Scotland. The grass was soft. It was tempting to just keep sleeping even though a heavy ground fog kept covering her up. She wasn't suffocating or anything. Just...getting lost beneath it.

To her left, King Macbeth—or at least the actor who played him in a recent movie—sat in a wire chair and played chess with her grandfather, who was also sitting in a flimsy wire chair. Grandpa's color looked better in spite of the creepy atmosphere.

"Catherine has it wrong," the old man said. "I picked up my first cigarette when I was in the Service. I just never told her that."

"I see." It wasn't King Macbeth sitting across from him anymore. It was just Seoc.

"So, tell me about the battle." Her grandfather moved a chess piece and tapped the top of a square clock sitting next to the board.

Seoc shook his head sadly. "It was doomed from the start. Over in forty minutes. But that was when the next horror began. Everyone I'd patched back together, every man who could be saved, was cut down, run through. We'd already beat the Hanoverians in every battle, so when they finally won something, the Duke of Cumberland, either from battle fever or the evil in his soul, ordered that no quarter was to be given. No wounded were spared. I begged and pleaded for them. I tried to stand in the way and talk sense into the English soldiers. But they soon tired of my harping and slayed me as well."

"You were there?" Her grandpa's voice shook with awe, but he moved another piece, tapped on the clock, and waited.

"I was." Seoc said it with a straight face.

"In 1746? The Battle of Culloden? You were there? And you died?"

"I was, my friend. And I did."

"Then why are you here?"

Seoc made a chess move and tapped the clock. "What would you say, Alonzo Dabelko, if I told you I am the Angel of Death, here to take you home?"

Cat tried to scream, tried to sit up so they could see her above the swirling mist, and stop saying such things. But something held her down.

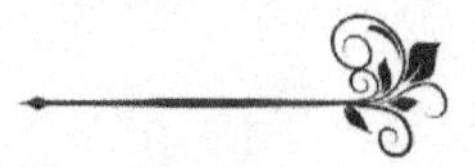

Seoc heard a muffled squeak and looked over. Catherine was still asleep, but faced downward on the blanket and rocking from side to side. A nightmare, sure.

He slipped off his chair and knelt beside her, then carefully rolled her onto her back. "Wake up, lass. Wake up." He shook her shoulder and patted her face. "Wake now, Catherine."

Her eyes flew wide and she recoiled, then she jumped to her feet. "You!"

"Ye were having a nightmare, lass. Forgive me for manhandling ye—"

"What does Culloden mean?"

His stomach lurched. He thought the lass had slept too deeply to overhear any of his conversation with her grandfather. "Culloden?"

"Yes. What is it?"

"It's the name of a moor in Scotland. Why do ye ask?"

She stepped closer, laid her hands to either side of his head, and leaned over him. "Tell me you're not the Angel of Death."

The Angel of Death? What could have possibly made her say such a thing? He knew that nightmares could feel very real for a good while after he woke, but he usually knew them for dreams before he was ever out of bed. The lass hadn't had time to recover, that was all.

He opened his mouth to speak, but was distracted by how fearfully she watched his lips, waiting for his answer.

There was her terror. Could he lessen it by denying it? Or by confronting it?

He pressed a hand against one of hers, then turned his head and kissed her palm before answering. "What would ye say, lass, if I told you...I am?"

CHAPTER FIFTEEN

For a long, drawn out moment, Cat stared into the blue eyes of Death, and all she could think was, *shouldn't they be black?*

Her hand tingled where he'd kissed her and it returned her to reality. She'd been having a nightmare, that was all. And the Scot was just teasing her for asking him such a stupid question. But still, he shouldn't be saying that kind of thing with her grandpa sitting five feet away! And she'd warned him to keep his negative thoughts to himself.

If she'd brought her taser along, she would have been tempted to use it on him again, and she told him.

He bit his lip, but said nothing. His expression was unreadable when she shooed him off the blanket and started packing up. Thankfully, her grandpa didn't complain when she announced they were going home.

"I need to start some soup," she explained while she rolled up the blanket and tucked it into the bag. "You always like my soup." That was her way of telling him he was going to eat some whether he wanted to or not.

He'd only taken a bite of his scone, then played with it until he had a chance to slip it to the Scot, who sneaked it into the trash along with his own empty plate. If he was a doctor, he would know that it was important for the old man to keep his strength up.

Did that mean he wasn't a doctor?

She fought to keep her face from revealing her thoughts while she waited for him to return the chess game to the bike guy. But seriously, what kind of doctor jokes around about being the Angel of Death?

Could his callousness have come from being on the battlefield.

Even so, he should have been more considerate. Hadn't he seen firsthand how fragile Grandpa was? That a negative thought the size of a feather could knock him down?

An unlucky flat tire on the wheelchair made it impossible for her to get her grandpa onto the train and into their apartment. Otherwise, she would have suggested to the Scot that their little outing was over and it was time for them to part ways. There was also the matter of the duffle bag he'd left behind.

At the time, she'd been glad he would have to return with them. Now, she almost regretted it. But, seriously, it was like Fate made sure she had to keep him around!

A little shiver ran up her spine.

Fate? Angel of Death?

She couldn't believe she was even entertaining such silly thoughts. The guy wasn't the Angel of Death. Fate was something for the movies. And when she really thought about it, she figured she'd just over-reacted to having her first dream/nightmare.

Her real-world worries were simple. Life and death. She and her grandpa were alive. That's all that mattered. Now all she had to do was keep the seeds of negative, Scottish ideas from planting themselves in Grandpa's brain.

Lots of people had survived stage four cancers. Some had healed themselves naturally. It was possible. With all that chemo and radiation behind him, maybe her grandpa's body was ready to bounce back, ready to fight.

No one could say for sure, least of all a doctor that didn't know anything about cancer.

What did he treat on the battlefield, anyway? Wounds, that's what.

If he really was a doctor.

They sat uncomfortably close on the train, but since her grandfather's wheels were locked in place and a good five feet away from them, she decided to take advantage.

She leaned toward the Scot and whispered. "Which are you? A doctor? Or Death? Huh?" She gave him a dirty look. "It's not like you can be both, right?"

His lips made a little grimace and he said nothing. She could tell he regretted something, but what? That Angel of Death comment? Or telling her he was a doctor? Her heart tripped. Was it the kiss he regretted?

She turned her head away and watched her grandfather. He was dozing. A frown kept twisting his forehead—like he was having a nightmare.

"Grandpa!"

He started awake, looked over, and forced a smile. The look he gave the Scot was something altogether different. It was like…relief that the guy was still there.

Well, that was just great. Now she couldn't just toss his bag into the hallway and close the door on him when he went out to *fetch* it.

She leaned sideways, but didn't look directly at the man whose baby-blue t-shirt no longer made her think about kissing him. "Look. I don't want you talking to him, do you hear? After we get to the apartment, I'd appreciate it if you'd make some excuse and go. I don't want him thinking I've kicked out his new best friend. Okay?"

His large muscled arm stretched forward and his warm hand rested on her knee. He gave her a gentle, but firm squeeze. "Nay, lass." He kept his voice low too, like he didn't want the old man to hear them arguing.

She would have to think fast if she was going to be able to ditch the guy and get her grandpa into the building by herself. Maybe she should walk to the back of the train, call the cops, and have them meet them at the train stop.

A glance out the window proved it was too late. The short ride was over. The enemy was stuck to her like glue. She'd have to wait for the right moment to make a move. If she just dialed 911, they wouldn't have any idea where she was, and the guy would probably take her phone away before she had a chance to speak.

So much was promised in that gentle squeeze.

The train stopped. She stood up and faced him. "Why are you doing this?"

"I have come to help ye, lass. And I will help ye all I can. But I can do nothing if ye send me away. I'll be forced to tell Alonzo the truth."

She touched her lips without thinking. The Scot noticed the movement and smiled.

"Not that," he said. "I'll tell him who I really am. And ye doona wish him to hear it."

"Still going with the Angel of Death story? Are you kidding me?"

She still didn't know who he was. But she knew what his crazy talk could do to someone fighting for his life. And he knew it too.

She sighed. "So, you're blackmailing me?"

"So it seems." At least he didn't sound cheerful about it, so maybe she could still convince him to go away and leave them alone. He had seemed so reasonable, so genuinely kind, before. She couldn't imagine what had changed.

Once again, she watched his arms strain to get the wheelchair moving, but he was careful not to jiggle the delicate passenger any more than he had to. They were still a block from home when her grandpa started whistling a tune that matched up perfectly with the rhythmic squeak of the traitorous wheel. A mild breeze ran its fingers through the trees overhead that lined both sides of the street, and she took a little snapshot in her head—as long as she could edit out the large man forcing himself into the picture.

A moment to remember. A moment when her grandfather felt happy enough to whistle, and had the strength to do it.

You see, she wanted to say. *He's improving. You were wrong.*

The whistling faltered, weakened, then stopped.

The Scot picked up the tune and whistled loud and clear. She glanced at her grandpa, expecting him to look a little disappointed. But the man was beaming, as pleased as if he were able to whistle so well himself.

A rare emotion hit her chest like a medicine ball and she realized why, all day long, every positive thought she'd clung to had been chased out of town.

She was jealous.

Since the second he'd climbed through their window, all Seoc Macbeth had to do, in order to win her grandpa's heart, was to wear a kilt and roll his r's every now and then.

The fact that she understood what she was feeling and why she was feeling it didn't stop her chest from burning or her thoughts from turning mean.

"I wouldn't think a Scot would know that song," she snarled.

The man stopped whistling. "All soldiers ken the tune, lass." And to prove it, he started whistling it from the start while his eyes laughed at her.

"Someday I'm going to murder the *buuu*gler," sang her grandpa. "Someday they're going to find him dead. And then I'll get that other pup...the guy who wakes the bugler up..." The last bit was sung by both men in unison, like a couple of drunks stumbling home from a long night, and it galled her like nothing before.

The rest of the song was an irritating whistle, far too loud and cheerful. By the time they reached the front door, she had her fingers in her ears. With a warning glance, she told both men to pipe down before she used one hand to enter the code. The Scot tried to get her goat by humming then, but she just smiled that fake customer service smile she had honed for years. And she went on smiling when it was obvious he didn't care for it.

Poor baby.

On the elevator, he turned to her, scowling. "Do ye always smile like that?"

She smiled harder. "Yes. I do. Being happy is a choice, right? So I choose happy."

"Ye don't ever have sad days—that is, when it isn't just your body ridding itself of unwanted emotion?"

She stopped smiling, but only for a few seconds. "Sad is a choice too, right? Bad days, sad days. It's all a question of attitude. I get sad, I just choose not to stay that way."

He snorted.

She snorted back.

And the elevator fell quiet.

CHAPTER SIXTEEN

Once they were all inside the apartment again, Alonzo asked Seoc to park his wheeled chair near the bathroom.

"Don't lock the door," the lass warned him.

The old man winced. "Then promise you won't come looking for me if I happen to take my time."

"I promise," she said. "I'm going to start the soup."

Seoc made a silent offer of aid, but Alonzo shook his head and hobbled inside alone.

The evening was upon them. In Seoc's mind, the clock began ticking in earnest.

"Seoc!" the man hollered from behind the door.

He hurried to it, but his hand paused a few inches from the handle. "Aye?" He would not go inside unbidden. Not after Alonzo had warned the lass to leave him be.

"You'll stay, won't you?" came the worried voice.

"Aye, my friend. I'm going nowhere." He waited a few seconds to see if the old man had more to say, but there was only silence.

At the end of the hallway, he scooped up his duffle bag, took it into the living room, and pushed it into a corner and out of the way. There was room to walk around the bed without tripping on it, and it couldn't be seen cluttering up the place.

He sat on the couch and tested its cushions.

"What are you doing?" Catherine stood near the end of the kitchen table with a large wooden spoon in her grasp.

"If ye must know, I'm testing the couch."

"What for?"

"Yer grandfather has asked me to stay."

"Of course he has." She turned and stomped back into the kitchen.

He opened the curtains and cracked the windows a few inches to counter the humidity gathering on the glass. The soup smelled divine and he resisted the temptation to tell her she cooked it in vain, that her grandfather would be wanting none of it. For anything that kept the lass busy, for the rest of the night, would be a blessing.

Twenty minutes passed and Alonzo had still not emerged. Hopefully, he was simply enjoying a bit of peace and quiet without Catherine hovering over him.

It was high time for a truce. There was little daylight left and he didn't wish to waste any of it staring out the windows or studying a bloody wall. If he was to gawk at anything, he preferred it to be the lass in the kitchen.

He stepped up to the table and she said nothing. The sudden stiff posture told him she was aware of every move he made, but her silent treatment continued.

"I would offer to take out your garbage, lass, but I fear ye wouldna allow me back inside the apartment."

Her lips started to curve, but she stopped them. "Good thinking."

He took a step to the side of the table and something pressing demanded her attention at the opposite counter. Since she would need to return to the stove at some point, he moved closer to it.

A timer rang and she reluctantly stepped closer to him. "Excuse me." She tried to go around him but he blocked her path.

"Let's no' fight, shall we?"

She rolled her eyes, feinted to her left, then scooted around to the right. When her hand stopped the ringing timer, she grinned like she'd won some race.

He so loved that grin.

She sobered quickly and opened the oven to lift out a pan of fresh rolls. He breathed in the smell of them and her eyes narrowed. "Surely Death doesn't need actual food." Then she waved the pan about, knowing the scent swirled around the room when she did so. "Too bad."

He bit his bottom lip to keep it from sticking out like a petulant lad. He'd tasted fine things in the past day and a half. If he never tasted another, he would not feel cheated.

He was almost sure of it.

She pulled out two dishes and ladled two heaping scoops into both.

"I think yer grandfather would prefer only the broth, lass," he said, then realized he should have gone on biting his lip.

"He needs to eat something," she argued. "And this is the most nutritious thing I can make for him." The bowl grew too hot and she quickly set it on the table.

He held up his hands and backed away, hoping she'd forget he'd said anything.

"Oh, no." She put her hands on her hips. "Let's hear it, Doctor. Whatever it is, I'll need to know it when you're gone."

The look in her eye reminded him of that moment when she'd deemed him worthy of tasing. And if not for that, he might have been able to control himself. But alas…

He swiftly closed the distance between them and took hold of her arms, ensuring she could not elude him again. Then he whispered, "Yer grandfather's body is done for, Catherine.

Nothing more can go in because nothing can come out, do ye ken? His digestive system has ceased functioning, among other things. He doesn't look well because he is a bit yellow. The toxins in his system have nowhere to go."

Horror rose behind her eyes as understanding dawned, and it made him physically ill to know that he was the one to put it there. But at least he hadn't given her false hope. Never that.

He wrapped his arms around her and held her tight as much to comfort her as to hide from that look on her face.

No hope. No way to run. The heartless bastards were advancing with their bayonets at the ready.

"Sometimes," he whispered, "sadness will come, lass, whether we choose it or no."

There was movement by the hallway and they turned in unison to see the old man leaning with one hand against the wall. In his other hand, he held the yellow taser the lass had plugged in to gather a charge. His finger was on the trigger and the dangerous end tipped carelessly to the side.

"Grandpa. You need to put that down. It's charged."

Seoc could tell by the way her fists bit into his skin that her casual tone belied true alarm. So he gently pushed her aside and took a step toward Alonzo.

"Would ye mind if I took a look? I've only seen the dangerous end of it m'self, aye?"

The dangerous end suddenly came to attention and pointed at Seoc's chest. The man was much more alert than he seemed.

"I want to know what you two have been fighting about all night," he said.

"Grandpa, please. At least sit down. The soup is ready and the rolls are hot."

Alonzo nodded, then moved to the end of the table and pulled out a chair. The thin clear oxygen hose was missing from his face.

His breaths were careful and constant, but shallow. In another few minutes, he might well lose consciousness.

"I'm not hungry, sweety," he said. "But you two go on." He panted a few times. "And while you eat, you can tell me what you've been fighting about."

She put her hands on her hips again. "I'm not going to sit at the table with a loaded—" She gasped when the weapon turned and pointed at the bearer's chest. "Grandpa, please!"

Seoc stayed calm. "Ye're scaring the lass."

The man chuckled. "I'm a little scared too. I'm...pretty sure this would finish me off, but what I want to know is how bad it would hurt."

Seoc shook his head but was careful not to make any threatening moves. "I'll tell ye the truth of it, Alonzo. Having been on the hot end of the stick, I don't know that I could find it in my heart to shoot it at the devil himself if he were standing right behind you." He lowered his head and his voice. "I canna imagine a meaner way to leave this world."

The old man was surprised. "Really?"

"Really."

"Bummer." He straightened his wrist and set the weapon on the table, but his finger was still on the trigger. "You were about to tell me about this fight..."

After a silent argument between himself and the lass, using nothing but their eyes, Seoc finally spoke. "Yer granddaughter is having difficulty accepting that ye're dying, sir."

Alonzo nodded. "I know. Dying is the D word, and the D word is not allowed. But he's right, Catherine. I'm dying, and I'm fading fast."

Seoc held out his hand and looked pointedly at the taser. The old man took his finger off the trigger and scooted it his way.

"The truth of the matter," he said, "is that ye will not last the night. And perhaps it is best that the pair of ye have the chance to say goodbye."

Catherine's head shook rapidly. "No," she said, "no. You can't know that."

Alonzo sighed. "It feels true."

The lass ran around to her grandfather's side and wrapped her arms around his neck and sobbed. Tears poured out of the old man's eyes as well, but he seemed relieved of the burden of putting on a strong show for the lass.

After a while, Catherine kissed his balding pate and fled to the water closet. And in her absence, the man sobbed as well. All Seoc could do was stand behind him and try to imbue him with a bit of his own strength through the hands he placed on the fellow's shoulders.

It was not much better than he'd been able to do on the moor that day. A bit of consolation for some. A bit of hope for others. But in the end, luck proved bad for them all.

Catherine rejoined them at the table and she and her grandfather linked hands. She frowned up at Seoc suddenly. "His own doctors couldn't predict how long he had left. They said weeks, maybe months. You say hours?"

He sighed and walked around to the far side of the table and sat. "I've witnessed hundreds of final hours, lass. I ken the signs—"

"I don't think so. Try again." She narrowed her eyes at him, assessing his honesty, recognizing that he was hiding something from them. The canny lass.

"Ye wish to ken the truth."

"I do."

He looked then to Alonzo. "And you?"

"I think the truth would be refreshing, son."

Seoc nodded, then suggested Catherine bring the old man some oxygen so he didn't think he was hallucinating. Finally, when they were all settled in and the food cleared away, Seoc gave them the truth.

He started with his name, where he'd been born, where he'd died, and the year. Catherine rolled her eyes but didn't interrupt. Alonzo was mesmerized.

Next, he told them about rising from his grave and haunting the battlefield for nearly three centuries. By the time he got to Soncerae's story, they were both entranced. Leary, but entranced.

"And I was sent to a coffee house in Portland, Oregon to fulfill my quest. The rest of it, you know."

"I don't get it," she said. "What heroic deed are you supposed to do here?"

He shrugged and shook his head. "Maybe I fulfilled the bargain when I chased that trio of lads away. Perhaps when I was on hand to push a defective wheelchair halfway across the city."

"Maybe it was helping an old man say the D word again." Alonzo winked at Catherine and gave her hand a hearty squeeze. "That doesn't explain how you know that I won't last the night."

"Ah, that." Seoc shifted uncomfortably in his seat. "Well, I wondered, after breakfast, if I might have been needed elsewhere, so I went back to the coffee shop. I demanded that Soni show me where I was to go, and she led me back here. Only it wasn't Soni, it was her uncle who came to verify my duty. If a Muir witch says something is to be, you can bet it is to be."

Catherine was suddenly wide-eyed and quiet.

"What is it, lass?"

She shook her head. "Your appointment. It's been moved—"

"To tomorrow, aye. The uncle said he will be collecting me in the morning."

The regret in her eyes was gratifying, truly. But the pain in his chest was not. The soreness spread just beneath the spot where he'd been mortally wounded, and he recognized it. Though it was much stronger than it had been the last day, he knew it for what it was—hopelessness.

Not *false* hope, but no hope at all.

And, if he wasn't mistaken, the lass was feeling it too. But all they could ever be to each other, now, was a memory.

CHAPTER SEVENTEEN

Grandpa insisted that, since Seoc could not be around for his funeral, they would hold a wake then and there. He forbade anymore tears and ordered the Scot to carry him to his bed where he would play the part of the deceased. He admitted that was the only assignment he felt up to.

As soon as Seoc lifted him out of the chair, Cat folded her arms on the table, pressed her face into them, and wept just as fast and hard as she could. Seoc cleared his throat and bellowed for her to turn on her computer and find some bagpipe music.

"Bagpiping has been placed on the bucket list," he said.

She was never going to survive this! And she wasn't sure, yet, if she was grateful, or furious that she'd been told the date she was going to be orphaned. And when she did decide which way she felt, both the Scot and her grandpa would be gone and there would be no one to thank or rail against. But at least she knew for sure she was going to feel cheated.

The first bagpiping she found on line was horrible. Even Seoc agreed. But eventually, they found a station that didn't sound like a drill going through her brain. The important thing was her grandpa loved it. And he tapped his toe in the air for a minute while Seoc danced her around the space next to his bed.

When the mood threatened to falter, she produced a card table and a deck of cards. She taught Seoc how to play Canasta while Grandpa dosed on and off beside them. The Scot was atrocious at remembering the rules, and when he cheated at counting his points, they laughed so hard that tears leaked out of his eyes.

He wiped at his face and stared at his wet fingers. "I don't know as I've ever laughed so hard I cried before."

"Really?" Though she couldn't name exactly when, she was sure she'd done it dozens of times.

"Of course, there was little to laugh over on the moor," he said. "And I canna remember laughing much in my life before Culloden. The first rising, in 1715, had come before I was born. Afterward, when I was old enough to mill around with my father, the only talk among men was of another rising. Rebellion was served with every supper. And rebellion was hardly a cheerful topic. Oh, there was hope of someday getting a Stuart back on the throne, but the subject hardly leant itself to cheerful fantasies for young lads.

"Even younger, with a small wooden sword, I'd been soberly fighting back the wraiths of English soldiers. A shout or two for imagined victories, and other than a bit of holiday cheer, there had been little to smile about. Survival. Struggle. Rebellion. Hardly visions of sugar plums, aye?"

"A poem," her grandpa said. His voice was weak, but she pretended not to notice.

"You have a poem in mind?" She took the improvised bucket list from him and tried to make out the writing, which she did. "Oh, no, grandpa. Not this one."

"It's a wake, isn't it?"

She sighed and begrudgingly walked to the end of his bed, where his gnarly finger pointed. There was just no getting out of it.

"Stop All the Clocks, by W.H. Auden," she said. If she recited it quickly, maybe she could get through it all without falling to pieces. It had been her grandma's favorite, and to Cat, it seemed like she'd known the words all her life.

She took a deep breath and dug in.

"Stop all the clocks, cut off the telephone,
Prevent the dog from barking with a juicy bone,
Silence the pianos and with muffled drum
Bring out the coffin, let the mourners come."

That was it. That was all she could do. Tears filled her throat and made it impossible for another word to get out. So she covered her mouth and shook her head, hoping the old man would take pity on her.

Seoc suddenly stood and faced the bed.

"Let aeroplanes circle moaning overhead
Scribbling on the sky the message He Is Dead,
Put crepe bows round the white necks of the public doves,
Let the traffic policemen wear black cotton gloves.

He was my North, my South, my East and West,
My working week and my Sunday rest,
My noon, my midnight, my talk, my song;
I thought that love would last for ever: I was wrong.

The stars are not wanted now: put out every one;
Pack up the moon and dismantle the sun;

Pour away the ocean and sweep up the wood.
For nothing now can ever come to any good."

With tears in his eyes, Grandpa started clapping. His soft hands barely made a noise and fell back to his sides.

Cat moved up next to him and started unwinding the tubing for the oxygen mask, but he waved for her to stop.

"I'm fine. No need." He was breathless. He was lying. But she wasn't about to argue.

It was late, but they left the curtains open so they could gaze at the stars. Seoc moved around the room and turned out the lamps so they could see them better. He left the small light on over the stove.

She showed him how to stand close to the window and look off to the east, to see if Mt. Hood was visible. He pressed himself against the glass beside her and did as he was told. His hand rested on her shoulder and gave her a lingering squeeze. Tears rolled from her eyes across her smashed cheek and expanded against the fogged-up window.

"Yes," Seoc said quietly. "I can see it fine."

Together, they stayed that way for a long minute before she was finally able to get a grip and turn around. Grandpa hadn't noticed. He was asleep. And without the oxygen mask on, he snored a little. The most reassuring sound in the world.

CHAPTER EIGHTEEN

Seoc led the lass to the couch, stretched out, and bid her to lie beside him. He was sure she would never consent to going to her own room.

The bubbler on the oxygen tank created a bit of white noise to go along with the snoring, for which he was grateful. At least, if the man stopped breathing, they wouldn't be left with deafening silence.

"I should hold his hand," she whispered.

"Nay, lass. He doesna want ye to. He said so while we played cards, aye? He needs ye to let go."

Her tears fell from her face and onto his arm. He never made a move to wipe them away. He felt privileged to have been available for the soaking. And to think, he'd walked away from them that morning...

He hoped he'd helped. He had tried to, but in the end, all he'd done was make her cry a day before she would have. The only one who seemed to be gaining anything from his attendance was him, for he was able to hold the lass in his arms for a wee while.

So much for brave deeds.

"Oh, ye think so?" Wickham stood just inside the living room. Lit from behind by the stove light, his clothing appeared to be black as the devil's. "Don't be so hard on yerself, young Macbeth. Ye've done a kind deed here, and kind is as good as brave, aye?"

Seoc held perfectly still, waiting to see if the man was visible to her as well. Anything was possible if the uncle could materialize in the lass's apartment without so much as a knock on the door.

"Seoc?" She said. "Am I dreaming again?"

He considered lying to her, but she'd realize the truth unless Soni's uncle decided to disappear.

The man snorted. "I'm going nowhere without ye, laddie."

Seoc nudged Catherine's legs off the couch so he could sit upright. She rose with him and wrapped her arms around his middle, and thus entwined, they stood.

"Please don't take him," she said sweetly. "I need him a little longer."

Wickham shook his head. "Sorry, lass. We must stand by the rules."

"And Soncerae? May I speak to her?" Seoc crossed his fingers and hoped like mad that his wee witch had the power to grant him a little more time. After all, it wasn't yet morning.

The devil flipped on the light and looked him straight in the eye. "It's morning in Scotland, aye? And besides, Soni can change nothing. Two days were paid for, and dearly. Two days have been spent. Mortality must end again, Seoc Macbeth. Bid the lass goodbye."

"*I* am Seoc Macbeth." The declaration from Alonzo was followed by a weak cough. "Come and tell me goodbye," he said after he caught his breath. "Give me a squeeze, Catherine, so I can go with this gentleman." He stepped around Seoc's open duffle bag and stood half-bent at the end of the bed. The thin, long nightshirt he slept in was covered with a sash of plaid. The rest of the material was wrapped a number of times around his waist in the poorest attempt at kilting Seoc had ever seen.

And it touched him more than he could have imagined. The old man was willing to take his place, no doubt so his granddaughter wouldn't be left alone. But Alonzo couldn't imagine what he was dealing with. Soni was indeed a witch, and likely her uncle was a male version of the same, but their powers obviously were limited. His brave gesture couldn't work.

"I thank ye, Alonzo. 'Tis a brave thing ye suggest—"

"He has but hours to live," Wickham pointed out. "A few hours given can hardly account for the full life ye might enjoy in exchange."

"Exchange?" The word inspired an idea and he set Catherine away from him to face Wickham alone. "I've done my duty."

"Ye have, but—"

"I have earned my reward."

"Ye have. But you cannot—"

"For my reward, I want you to heal this man." He pointed to Alonzo. "If Soni can turn 79 ghosts back into mortals, she can heal one man of cancer, surely."

Wickham took a menacing step forward. "Ye cannot name yer own reward. One was offered, in the beginning, and ye can choose to take it or not."

Seoc closed the distance between them and tried to make the dark one understand. "Granting this man his health would go far to make up for all those others… All those others, on the moor, to whom I gave false hope. It would make up for my cruelty, don't you see?"

Wickham offered a gentle smile and nodded. "Indeed, I do see. And I see this army you imagine waiting for ye in the next life."

"Ye do?"

"Aye." His smile broadened. "But Macbeth, they only wait to give ye praise and thanks for giving them hope—"

"False hope."

"Nay. The hope was real. And dashing that hope was done by others, aye? Better a man have a few moments of real hope and be disappointed, than to wait in terror for what was to come. If ye had to do it over again, would ye walk away and let them die of their wounds before the bayonets reached them?"

Seoc shook his head and admitted Wickham was right. And if he was right, that meant there was nothing left to dread.

Wickham gave Alonzo an almost kind nod. "I cannot heal ye, old man."

Alonzo nodded, but he showed no disappointment.

Seoc took Catherine into his arms. "Forgive me, lass, for loving and leaving ye. But try to dwell on the loving bit, aye?"

She nodded and forced a brave smile, every inch of her cheeks wet.

"Come," said Wickham. "We need to make our accounting."

"Accounting to whom?" Alonzo pushed away from the bed, forced his shoulders back, and inflated his chest carefully. "I say I'm Seoc Macbeth. Now, let's blow this taco stand."

Catherine moved in front of the old man and wrapped her arms around him. "You're so brave, Grandpa. You don't need to prove it. I know." She straightened. "But I don't think it's going to work." She turned back to Seoc and worried her lip with her teeth, obviously torn between which man she should kiss goodbye. So he made it easier. He went to her and pulled her into his arms.

"Know this, Catherine, that ye have been loved well and true by yer grandfather and myself. And though we love ye still, another will come along and recognize yer generous heart and love ye for it. Dinna chase that one away with yer mean taser, aye?"

She got up on her tiptoes and pulled his head down for a ferocious kiss. He wrapped his arms far around her and held tight, worried he stole her breath, but unable to let go just the same.

"A fine kiss, lass. I shall remember it for eternity." It felt as if his heart was being ripped from his chest as he stepped away from her.

"And I'll come find you. I don't know how, but..." She dissolved into tears again and lunged forward to sob against his chest.

"Have you no shame," Alonzo barked at Wickham. "Look what she means to him. Take me, damn you." He took another step toward the dark man but had to stop for a fit of coughing. Catherine turned toward her grandfather, but he held out his hand to stop her.

"Done," Wickham said, then rolled his eyes and disappeared completely. No swirl of black smoke. No fading. Just...gone.

And yet, her grandfather still stood in the center of the room, coughing.

Seoc suddenly understood. It wasn't the old man's body Wickham would be taking, but his spirit!

Seoc lunged just in time to catch the brave old man as he crumpled toward the floor. He wheezed and struggled for breath while Seoc carried him over to the bed, laid him down, and reached for the oxygen mask. Catherine was right behind him, fumbling with the oximeter. She dropped it on the ground, then dropped it again while she tried to fit it onto the old man's finger. Seoc was grateful she was thus distracted when Alonzo's spirit gave his body a final shake and freed itself.

He turned to Catherine and shook his head. She grasped the old hand and began greetin' in the usual fit of denial that came from losing someone beloved. He held her shoulders for a long moment, then moved over to the couch to give her time to realize her grandfather was truly gone, and that the shell that remained was no more than that.

When it took her a bit longer than expected, he went back to her side and led her away, grateful when her weeping eventually subsided and she was able to breathe normally again.

She shook her head against his chest. "I can't believe he took your place—and they let him!"

"I can hardly believe it myself. It means that this body of mine is permanent now."

"I'm so glad."

He had a thought that made him laugh. She insisted he explain why.

"It just occurred to me that if Alonzo took my place, then he might be meeting Bonnie Prince Charlie at this very moment. What would he do, do ye suppose?"

"Oh, I'll tell you exactly what he'd do." She grinned up at him. "He wouldn't knock out his teeth or anything like that."

"No?"

"No. But he'll definitely talk his ear off. Can you imagine? Without a cough to slow him down?"

Seoc grinned. "I hope there is no time limit to this meeting of theirs."

EPILOGUE

The lad left his seat again and started up the auditorium steps. Seoc could not chase after him what with his daughter, Soni, on his lap and the wee bairn in the crook of one arm. So he had to stop the boy with a stern whisper.

"Alonzo! Where do ye go?"

The lad danced a bit and glanced at the zipper on his pants. "To wash the bark off a tree, da."

Seoc shook his head. "Ye're mummy's about to come through the door, aye? Do ye suppose ye can hold it?"

The lad rolled his eyes and nodded his round wee head. Just then, the professor stepped onto the stage and beamed. "Ladies and Gentlemen, may I present…Dr. Macbeth."

Seoc caught his breath and fought back tears as sweet Catherine stepped onto the platform, her blue graduation gown draped with half a dozen tassels and ribbons. His chest burst with pride. He gathered Soni close and jumped to his feet. But since his arms were occupied, he could but whoop and cheer. And he did so…with the same enthusiasm with which he'd once greeted Bonnie Prince Charlie himself.

Unfortunately, his outburst left him with two greetin' lassies. He glanced at his son, pleased to see the lad cheering his mother as well. But sadly, Alonzo was jumping up and down in a wee puddle, self-made.

Reacting to the moment as his wife had taught him, he allowed his head to fall back and his eyes to close in a prayer of thanks for all the positives in his life.

Puddle and all.

THE END

Look for Volume III in The Ghosts of Culloden Moor Collections, in which you'll find the stories of DOUGAL, KENNEDY, AND GERARD.

Follow The Ghosts of Culloden Moor on their own Facebook page.

You'll find LL Muir on Facebook as well.

To sign up for the L.L. Muir newsletter, with new release alerts, visit www.llmuir.weebly.com.

Also by L.L. Muir

*The Ghosts of Culloden Moor

1. The Gathering
2. Lachlan
3. Jamie
4. Payton
5. Gareth (Diane Darcy)
6. Fraser
7. Rabby
8. Duncan (Jo Jones)
9. Aiden (Diane Darcy)
10. Macbeth
11. Adam (Cathie MacRae)
12. Dougal
13. Kennedy
14. Liam (Diane Darcy)
15. Gerard
16. Malcolm (Cathie MacRae)
18. Watson
19. Iain (Melissa Mayhue)
20. Connor
21. MacLeod (Cathie MacRae)
22. Murdoch (Diane Darcy)
23. Brodrick
24. The Bugler
25. Kenrick (Diane Darcy)
26. Patrick (Cathie MacRae)

27. Finlay
28. Hamish
29. Rory (Jo Jones)
30. MacBean (Diane Darcy)
31. Tristan (coming soon!)

*Scottish Time Travel Romance

Going Back for Romeo
Not Without Juliet
Collecting Isobelle
What About Wickham
The Curse of Clan Ross Series (bundle of the first 3)
Christmas Kiss
Kiss This

*Scottish Historical Romance

Kilt Trip: Part 1
Kilt Trip: Part 2
Kilt Trip: Part 3
Kilt Trip: Part 4
Kilt Trip: Part 5
Kilt Trip: Part 6
Kilt Trip Complete
Pirate Trip (in the works)

Under the Kissing Tree

*Regency Historical Romance

Blood for Ink
Bones for Bread
Body and Soul
Breath of Laughter (coming in 2017)
The Brothers Grimm (starting 2017)
Lord Fool to the Rescue

*Romantic Suspense
Gone Duck

*Young Adult Paranormal Romance
Somewhere Over the Freaking Rainbow

Freaking Off the Grid

*Middle Grade Children's Books
Where to Pee on a Pirate Ship

*Western Romance
under the pen name *Bella Bowen*

*BRIDE SCHOOL Series
Book One: GEN
Book Two: LIZZY
Book Three: MOLLY
Book Four: MARY
Book Five: NADIA (coming soon)

*The Infamous Mrs. Wiggs Series
PICKLESFORK

*American Mail-Order Brides Series
(50 books by various authors)
DARBY: Bride of Oregon

About the Author

L.L. Muir lives on the Utah side of the Rocky Mountains with her husband and family. She appreciates funny friends, a well-fed campfire, and rocking sleepy children.

If you like her books, be a sport and leave a review on the book's Amazon page. You can reach her personally through her website— www.llmuir.weebly.com, or on Facebook at L.L. Muir.

Thank you for playing!

Made in the USA
Las Vegas, NV
28 April 2024